New Beginnings

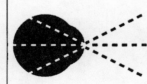

This Large Print Book carries the Seal of Approval of N.A.V.H.

New Beginnings

Sharon Lee Thomas

Thorndike Press • Waterville, Maine

Published in 2006 by arrangement with Tekno Books and Ed Gorman.

Thorndike Press® Large Print Clean Reads.

The tree indicium is a trademark of Thorndike Press.

The text of this Large Print edition is unabridged.
Other aspects of the book may vary from the original edition.

Set in 16 pt. Plantin by Al Chase.

Printed in the United States on permanent paper.

Library of Congress Cataloging-in-Publication Data

Thomas, Sharon Lee.
    New beginnings / by Sharon Lee Thomas.
      p. cm. — (Thorndike Press large print clean reads)
    ISBN 0-7862-8815-9 (lg. print : hc : alk. paper)
    1. Wagon trains — Fiction. 2. Women pioneers —
Fiction.   3. Overland journeys to the Pacific — Fiction.
4. Fatherless families — Fiction. 5. Large type books.
6. Diary fiction. I. Title. II. Series.
PS3620.H6425N49 2006
  813´.6—dc22   2006012300

Dedication

To my husband, Ron, for his love and encouragement, to Mike, Mark, and Kelly Thomas and to Marie and Don Coffland for their support, and lastly, to Erik, Zak, Jacob, Sadie and Gabie for being the great joy of my life.

Acknowledgements

Very special thanks to Elizabeth DeMatteo, Jena MacPherson, Liz Osbourne, Megan Chance and Melinda McRae for their guidance and expertise in making this book happen. I also appreciate the patient assistance of my editor, Alice Duncan, and the generous loan of period medical books from the University of Washington.

One

*   Papa is gone.*

I recorded the words as though chiseling them in stone. Papa was gone. It had all happened too fast — the wagon's dreadful hesitation before slipping back, Papa's futile attempt to stop it and the river's current lapping against his broken body — fingers of bright red trickling into clear waters. In one moment, all was changed. I slumped back against the tailgate, brushing my cheeks dry with the sleeve of my nightdress, its worn flannel soft against my skin, sharpening memories of my father's tender touch.

Then, a gust of wind slapped the canvas sharply against the wagon hoops overhead. I jerked upright, dropping my journal into the lamp-lit shadows. The noise must have startled Mother, too. Still sitting next to Papa, gripping his lifeless hand, her head shot up. She quickly recovered from her own thoughts and glanced over at me, frowning.

"Marjory."

Her voice cracked against the emptiness of our crowded wagon.

"The camp will be stirring soon. There is much to be done."

She leaned forward and placed Papa's hand on his chest. For a second she hesitated, her head bowed. Then Mother straightened. From habit, she fingered the braided coil atop her head. Wisps of curls, usually tightly confined, broke free as she tried to restore order.

Papa had always thought her a handsome woman. And she was. But now her dark hair looked more faded, her proud figure less rigid. Mother steadied herself as she got to her feet, and bent to gather the rags we'd used when Papa had begun to retch up blood.

"It'll be dawn soon. Hurry and dress, Marjory. There are things to see to before the train moves on."

Without looking at me, she crammed the rags into a pillow casing, almost as if our loss could be as easily bundled away. I wanted to stop her, to call out. Instead, I clamped my mouth shut, yanked my skirt over my nightdress and reached for my shoes.

I had desperately wanted to help with Papa during the night. Instead, I'd been sent off with orders to take Danny, Jamie and little Sarie over to the Meyerses' wagon and fetch Mrs. Meyers back with me.

Wanting to be there when Papa asked for me, I watched Mother and Mrs. Meyers struggle to keep him comfortable. He and I had always been close, but never more so than while we planned this trip. Mother's lack of enthusiasm contributed to the strain in our relationship this past year and, while Papa recovered, I knew I would have to work harder to avoid crossing her. For Papa.

As I tried to close out the awful rattle of Papa's breathing by closing my eyes, my decision became a promise — a promise I clung to in the exhausting stillness before morning. The bursts of wind outside died down and the fumes from the lamp seemed to suck the air from our wagon, as I willed my mind to endure the wait.

Some time later, the barrel I had settled against shifted, jarring me awake. The lamp had been turned low and Mrs. Meyers was gone. Mother sat next to Papa, smoothing his hair, and it looked as if his distress had eased. He almost looked comfortable.

Or so I had thought — until the slight restlessness of his hands fluttered to a stop.

As Mother bent her ear against Papa's

11

chest, I had held my breath, praying he only slept. Silently, she took his hand in hers and sank back against the sideboards, closing her eyes in her own private grief. I'd sat there frozen, looking at her, seeing nothing, feeling nothing but a pitiful tingling somewhere in my body, which was separate from my mind. That had been when I first realized the truth.

That was when the distance that spread between my mother and myself had finally hit me. We could not even share our pain.

I had recorded his death but nothing more. I couldn't. I was full of words, but had no one with whom to share them, and I felt Papa's loss all the more because of it. How I ached to talk to him, to tell him my thoughts, as I had always done before.

Perhaps such a need was in part why he'd been so pleased, that first night on the trail, when he had presented the wrapped journal to me. "As a substitute friend," he'd said, knowing how busy the trail would keep us — knowing, too, how much I would miss our leisure confidences. "Record everything, Marjory. Share our journey in this. It'll become a handy friend for you, remembering all, but arguing nothing."

"We haven't much time, Marjory."

Mother's words broke into my thoughts,

interrupting memories to which I clung. I gripped the buttonhook between my fingers and fastened my shoes. Papa could never have known then, I thought, how much I would need the friend he'd given me, wrapped in brown paper.

"You best empty the pan beside Papa first," Mother said, when she noticed I'd finished with my shoes.

With too many thoughts, too many feelings to sort through, I tried to focus on attending to Mother. I watched her clear away the clutter. Papa's rifle swayed gently from a hoop overhead as she made her way forward, and I remembered how often he used to swing around from the driver's box to join us in the wagon, only to bump his head against the heavy butt of the gun. It became a game that gave the boys a happy opportunity for making sport of Papa, which prompted his response of engaging in a serious tickle attack.

There had been a time when Mother would have joined in the fun. But her sense of humor had long since faded. I especially noticed its absence on occasions when celebrations were left to Papa and me. Papa did, too.

When our wagon train finally pulled out of Independence, past the springs and beyond tents of greedy profiteers hawking their wares, he had shouted out and hugged me from the pure joy of being on our way. Farming the land. Working with his hands. A new life once we reached the Oregon. But he hadn't even made it halfway.

"Marjory. The pan."

Again, Mother's voice sliced through my thoughts, sharp, effective. I hauled myself to my feet and maneuvered past the trunk to get the basin. Taking an opportunity to whisper goodbye, I knelt beside Papa. His eyes were not quite closed, and for an instant I almost expected him to meet my glance with a teasing wink.

But he didn't. Instead, an awful slit of sightless vacancy stared back, ignoring my tears.

I seized the pan, left him and slipped outside. The icy blue stars had already lost their brilliance to the relentless dawning of a new day. Yet I wanted the peace of night's solitude. I needed time. Time to dam the raging emotions coursing through my veins. Anger and love, hate and guilt, all mixed together. And I needed time to examine the terrible regret that began to fester within my loneliness.

I should have talked to Papa. I should have insisted. Now it was too late. Now, all I could do was empty the last of his life's blood onto the roots of nearby scrub.

For a memorial, I chose the healthiest bush that I could find in the semi-dark. Because we hadn't made it to water, I dared not use what little we had to rinse the pan, so with a strange sense of intimacy, I wiped the tin with a clump of dirt, tipping the reddened earth out beneath the scraggly bush. I stood looking at the stain-darkened earth under the spindly branches.

I wish it could be a tree, Papa.

A moment later, I noticed faint streaks of color low in the sky as the sun neared the horizon. I took a long, deep breath and returned to the wagon.

Mother sat on her knees before the open trunk, folding the blankets away. When she shut the lid, I saw traces of tears on her cheeks.

"Mother? Are you all right?"

She shoved back a strand of hair, whisking the moisture from her cheek. "Of course, I am. Now, you better roll up your bedding, Marjory. The camp will be readying to leave soon."

I didn't know what to think anymore. It was hard to guess Mother's feelings. Yet I knew she had loved Papa, even though she seemed a different person this past year. I wanted to believe there was a reason for her sharpness, or even that I judged her unfairly. After all, she was alone now — alone and getting on. She had to be near forty. And, now that I was almost sixteen, I alone was left of an age to help her.

Impulsively, I moved forward, but she had already turned to another chore. She gathered clothes together for my brothers and sister before speaking.

"You were gone quite a time, Marjory. You must understand our new situation."

"I do, Mother."

"We're alone," she continued as if I hadn't spoken. "Without your father's leadership or his protection. We must be as little trouble on the train as possible. It's hard, I know, but . . ."

She sighed, as if the effort to explain took too much of her energy. Handing me the clothes, she gave up trying.

"Just go, Marjory." Her voice grew harsh. "Take these to the Meyerses and tell the men we're ready. They'll know what to do."

As she turned, she stumbled over one of Papa's boots. She scooped them up and added, "Here. Take these, too. Mr. Meyers might as well get some use of them. They are much too big for us."

I stood rooted, looking at her. I had not

misjudged. There would be no remembrances for Papa, no words of comfort, just orders and instructions. She was who she was.

"There's nothing more we can do for your father, Marjory," she continued as I hesitated. "He's gone and we must move on. Now go, girl. And hurry." She turned to remove Papa's clothes from their pegs.

"Yes, Mother," I said, aware of the chilling obedience in my voice. Memories of Mother's gentleness were from childhood, I reminded myself. She wasn't that person anymore.

As I turned to step down, she sighed and quietly added, "He'd expect courage, Marjory. That's what will get you by."

But her conciliatory words, her tone, fell short of my willingness to hear. All I could think was that she'd never understood Papa. And I knew now that she would never understand me.

The relentless digging beyond our wagon drowned out sounds of horses and oxen being backed into their harnesses. I scarcely heard the noisy activity of camp that marked our inevitable return to the trail. It was only the sudden silence, the absence of shovels breaking through the hard, dry prairie that caught my attention. The waiting had ended.

They came for Papa. Mrs. Meyers returned with Jamie and Sarie. Mother followed the men as they took Papa from the wagon and carried him some thirty feet ahead, before setting their burden alongside a shallow trench. I hurried to take little Jamie's hand. At four years of age, he was shy and fell back from the mourners who followed Mother to the burial site. Danny waited near the grave for her, then took his position. Though he was only eight, he stood straight and silent, a little behind Mother, much like Papa might have done. Only the questioning pain in Danny's eyes betrayed his reaction to the men lowering our father, wrapped in a meager blanket, into that shallow, dusty pit.

Mother stood at the foot of the shabby gravesite, holding little Sarie. Sensing our sorrow, even at nine months of age, she clung to Mother, who remained rigid while carefully overseeing Papa's interment. My hand tightened around Jamie's. Poor Papa.

Captain Marshall, the wagon master of our train, spoke over Papa. "Keep watch, O Lord, over this husband, father and fellow traveler. His spirit is now with you, as his dust blends with that of the prairie about us.

We must take comfort in knowing that now this man is truly home. Amen."

I stiffened as the Captain bent to sprinkle a handful of dust over Papa. Next Mother moved forward and did the same. Then Danny. I knew I would have to follow. But how could I? This lifeless, drab roll of blankets couldn't be all that was left. Papa could never become a part of the miserable dust that swirled in aimless circles about our feet. Never!

Still, I bent down, my dry hands picking up cool sand. I poured a little into Jamie's tiny hand and took him along as I forced myself forward. My arm rose, my fingers opened and loose earth fell into the breeze.

Jamie threw his dirt down and whirled around, running for our wagon. Heavily laden shovels began returning the dirt from where it came.

I closed my eyes. Soon, too soon, the sound of shuffling shoes faded away — all headed back. Back to the trail. Mother nodded, and I knew she intended to remain until the grave was filled and that I was to take the children back to the wagon. I felt conscious of a tight hardening that began growing from deep inside. Why couldn't she understand? I needed to stay with Papa, too.

She walked over to me and dropped Sarie into my arms. Chubby arms, deeply creased by baby fat, clung to me, while brown curls burrowed against my neck as Sarie reacted to the grief surrounding her. Her need for reassurance tugged my thoughts away from myself. Her soft, hot little sobs melted the awful anger that had threatened to strangle me. Grateful for the release, I held her tight as we returned to our wagon.

The Captain had asked a neighbor's oldest son to drive our wagon for the day. Mr. Wilkins nodded at my approach, then climbed up and took Papa's seat. I waited alongside our wagon for our leave-taking, wanting to walk, needing to walk, but as the Captain rode past us down the line, he motioned for me to get in.

"You can walk a little later on, Miss."

So I climbed in, with Sarie clinging to my neck, and leaned back against the tailgate, waiting for Mother. Through the front flap, I watched her climb up to the box and sit beside Mr. Wilkins. He took up the reins, just as Papa used to do. I looked away.

When our horses finally took up the trail, I looked back at the team of oxen following us. They veered off the path toward the lonely gravesite ahead. The other wagons took up the same course. It took me a minute to realize what they were about. I turned away and shut my eyes. It was too horrible to watch. It had to be done, but oh, how I hated it.

Papa, Papa. Mama was right. This is a wretched trip.

Two

July 29, 1847 — a.m.
Dear Friend,
Only our fragile tracks — etched into the desolation that surrounds Papa — can be seen as we take our leave. There is nothing here, no tree or rock to mark his final resting place. I cannot watch as the wagons behind turn off the trail, but I will record it all — every painful image. It is burned into my brain — the awful sight of team after team heading for that narrow mound of dirt, trampling across the freshly broken earth, dragging their burdens of heavy wagons — compressing, crushing, obliterating all trace of my father's resting place.

I accept the Captain's orders, for I couldn't stand the thought of scavenger Indians finding Papa. Or worse, the wolves.

Tears change nothing, or so Mother says. But it is hard. I have to remember that Papa will not be hidden from God — he is not alone. In truth, however, I confess, my faith and courage are sometimes wickedly shallow.

After waking long before dawn and with the shock of Papa's funeral, the children immediately burrowed into their blankets. Even Danny slept once we returned to the trail. I, too, must have napped for several hours after putting my journal away, because my head jerked when the wheel hit a bump, and I came to myself with a sharp start. I wondered how long I had slept.

Then I heard familiar sounds of wagons slowing — the echoing *ho* passing down the line, the team's protesting harness, wood and metal grinding to a halt after tedious hours of motion — all routine sounds signaling our nooning stop. Mother glanced back to see that I was awake and ready. By the set of her chin, I knew our grieving time was spent.

My mind sorted through the noon chores as I sat up. I had no time to brush out my hair, even though the ever-churning dust did its best to turn my reddish blonde twist into an ashy gray nest of tangles.

Already the sun heated the stale air beneath our canvas. I hurriedly tied my apron, careful to conceal the tear Mother had earlier told me to mend. I had no taste for more lectures. Her insistence that we maintain all possible niceties, even while traveling, seemed fruitless. For myself, sweltering under the heat and dust of the trail reduced good grooming to the basics. Not so for Mother. During this past year, I had found it best not to argue with her.

I had to admit, however, Mother's judgments were not always unreasonable or ill conceived. Her selection of clothes for our journey proved wise enough. My dark wool not only shed heat, but wrinkles, too, obviously holding up better than the cottons I had favored. But admitting as much to her fell on deaf ears. She had no time, even for apologies.

After reining the team into a suitable camping spot, the driver handed Mother down from the box. He was tall and swung her down with ease.

Mr. Wilkins adjusted the harnesses and then nodded in her direction. "Back after dinner, Ma'am."

He touched the brim of his hat and walked toward the wagons ahead, his stride long and easy. His hint of formality seemed pleasant, yet not too familiar. Somehow, his attitude eased my anxieties.

Mother came around to untie the box of cooking utensils from the backboard.

"Bring leftover drippings and bread, Marjory. We'll have a quick but hot meal today. Danny, wake Sarie. Jamie, too, if he's sleeping."

I returned my attention to the wagon, dug out the tin of drippings and gave it to Danny. After scooting my tow-headed four-year-old brother out of the wagon, I went back for Sarie. A thick, brown mop of curls peeked above the quilt. She resisted my efforts to wake her and, blowing a soft breath into the baby's ear, I smoothed damp tangles away from her brow.

"Get up, sleepyhead. Time to eat."

A glimpse of blue fluttered, then steadied as two large eyes fastened on me.

"That's a girl, Sarie. Let's get you dry and ready for dinner."

Jamie and Sarie drank their broth and chomped on their hard bread, but Danny, Mother and I barely ate. Danny soon gave up and wandered off among the wagons.

Within minutes, Mr. and Mrs. Meyers brought him back to ask if he could go with them. They were a Godly couple, older than my parents, but younger than Grandfather. Even before Papa's accident, the Meyerses had shown an unusual fondness for children, offering to amuse one or the other of our youngest during times of cranky boredom.

"Mr. Meyers wants to take me to see the Devil's water, Mama. Should I go?" Danny asked, hesitantly.

It saddened me to hear the anxious uncertainty in his voice. Normally his avid curiosity kept him buoyant and self-assured.

"It's just up hill, yonder," Mrs. Meyers said. "It's called the Devil's Gate. A huge, deep gap with the water down below, rushing something fierce. Supposed to be a real sight to see." She hesitated. "Thought it wouldn't hurt none to take the boy's mind off things a bit. Of course, it's for you to say."

"That's very kind," said Mother. "Especially after the help you've already given."

"No more'n the Good Book says. Nothing to fret over, and we won't be gone long."

While the river worked itself through the narrow gorge far below us, our wagons were forced to go around, leaving us beyond reach of water until our evening stop. Most families didn't have time to take the short hike to view the spectacle during our stopover. I was glad the Meyerses made the effort to take Danny. But I wondered at Mother's indifference to his unnatural hesitancy.

While I brought water to the horses, I couldn't help resenting her lack of concern.

26

Surely if I wanted to talk to Mother about Papa, the want must be worse for Danny. Even though he hadn't asked questions or demanded reassurance, a year ago she would have anticipated his pain. Now, she didn't seem even to notice.

Yet, as I watched, she shoved a nearby box over for Sarie to grasp while practicing her standing skills. And without a wasted movement, Mother covered the fire trench with dirt. Then she pulled the children's bedding from the wagon and shook out the eternal sand, fluffing the feathers with fresh air. A thousand times before, I'd seen her do the same things.

As I gave the last horse his pail of water, Mother swooped Sarie up and returned her to the blanket, then stopped to inspect a strange bug that had caught Jamie's attention before continuing with her work. It was the first time I had paid attention to Mother's routine, and I had to appreciate the many details she attended to so effortlessly. In some ways, I admitted, she seemed much the same as always, and yet more and more, I felt I hardly knew her.

"Marjory!"

"Yes?" I answered, dreading any further discord between us.

"Marjory. Come and mind the children,"

she ordered. "I think the Captain is heading this way to talk with me."

The Captain, an elderly man who must be nearing fifty, walked with purpose toward our wagon. His rumpled appearance was somehow diminished by his decisive manner. His speech lacked polish, and his manners, if not always polite, were direct. The man who followed alongside acted as scout for our train. They met Mother at the front of the wagon, where she took a seat on an overturned bucket and folded her hands, waiting. The Captain rested one foot on a spoke and bent down to talk to her.

Frantically, I dug out a biscuit and gave it to the children so that I could eavesdrop. I leaned against the back wheel, busily drying a pan. Keeping my head down, I could just catch sight of them from the corner of my eye.

". . . all have their own hands full, Ma'am. You can see, only makes sense. Seems best for you, too."

"Yes, I can see your argument. We don't want to be trouble. You're perfectly right, I guess. We have no one there."

Mother's voice trailed off in thought. A hard lump formed in the pit of my stomach. I glanced up in their direction. What seemed best for us?

"Good," he said. "Always seen you ta be a sensible woman. Young Wilkins can still help out fer the time bein'. He'll teach you ta drive and what not."

The leathery old man removed his hat with one hand, and with the other, swiped the inside band free of sweat with a kerchief, then mopped his forehead and resettled the brim to slant forward, shading his eyes.

"Anyways, he'll do what he kin fer you. Any rough trail an he'll do the drivin'."

"We hate to take a man from his own duties."

"You let us worry 'bout that, Ma'am," said the scout, speaking up for the first time.

He was somewhat younger than the Captain, small, weather-beaten in appearance and a little on the grubby side. I heard him spit, and remembered his tobacco-juice-stained beard and how his deadly aim gained him fame as being a *sure-spitter*. Supposedly, the term also referred to his reliability.

"True 'nuff," continued the Captain. "Wilkins's pa's got two big wagons of store goods they's haulin' to the Oregon. And with the youn'est son helpin' out, the oldest is free to drive fer ya."

I resented strangers taking on Papa's responsibilities so soon. But there was no time for niceties on the trail, and if it meant we could go on . . .

"We're grateful for his help," Mother said.

"Nothing to be done but make the best of it all way 'round. Now then, 'tis all settled? You'll stay over at the fort, where you kin return with the first escort goin' East?"

East? What was he talking about? I waited for Mother's response. The hesitation was unbearable. She couldn't be considering . . .

"Yes," she said. "I suppose it's for the best. We'll turn back at Fort Bridger."

Turn back. I could not believe it. Mother hadn't even discussed the possibility, and now she was letting strangers decide our future. How could she allow them to dismiss Papa's plans? He'd set his heart on the Oregon, on the challenge of being a part of new beginnings, new opportunities. The anger I'd swallowed earlier returned. To go back would mean Papa had died for nothing. We were almost halfway there, and I was sure the hardest part was over. Nothing could ever be worse than Papa's accident. Somehow, when the time was right, I had to make her understand.

We must go on.

When we returned to the trail, Mother

and I had our first lesson in driving the team. Mr. Wilkins began with Mother as I sat behind the box with Sarie. I noticed how he paced his instructions when he saw how uncomfortable handling the horses made her. After glancing at her clenched grip on the reins, he slipped a blade of grass into his mouth, chewing the end of it while he talked in an easy manner. He drew her attention away from the team with an idle comment about two children playing ahead of us. I couldn't hear from where I sat, but I saw his gesture toward the boys who had devised a dangerous game of hitching rides on passing wagons. Nothing could have diverted Mother's attention more effectively.

Earlier, I had noticed Mr. Wilkins's deep, soothing voice. I found his manner most calming during hectic stops when we no longer had the luxury of depending on Papa. I had to admit that our driver had a way about him. Even the team seemed less excitable under his handling. Getting them to step into their traces used to try not only Papa's patience but the horses' as well. That chore had gone easier and even faster this morning. Of course, Mr. Wilkins was a younger man who, unlike Papa, probably had prior experience with animals.

After an hour of teaching Mother, it was

my turn to drive. I had sat on the box with Papa lots of times, but now it seemed higher and scarier. I settled myself above the broad backs of Papa's best team of four prized horses, determined not to give way to the brute strength they possessed.

"This is very different from when Papa did the driving," I said after awhile.

Mr. Wilkins smiled. "It'll get easier. You will have more control, if you get the feel of your animals." He nodded toward the team. "Concentrate on the power at your command. You can sense a lot through that leather that's wound between your fingers."

He was right. By the first hour, I felt an electrifying tension through the reins resting across the powerful flanks of the team as each ribbon linking us together responded to the lumbering progress below me. The horses' power surged through the leather in my hands. And I loved the feeling.

Mother had not been as pleased with her lessons and happily turned all future driving over to me.

"It's just as well, Mother," I said. "You know sitting in the sun only aggravates your health."

Her brows furrowed in annoyance, but she ignored my comment. She refused to discuss her headaches with me, even though they had increased since we set out this spring. Even back home, she was never without a bonnet to protect her eyes. Papa used to tease, saying she was like a mole, sensitive to light, but I thought he suspected her headaches were her own particular reaction to being displeased. Secretly, I agreed.

While Danny took my place next to Mr. Wilkins and the little ones napped, Mother and I plodded alongside the wagon, keeping within its shade. Hating to waste our moment of privacy, I ventured a new topic.

"I heard what the men talked to you about, Mother. You don't really mean to turn back, do you?"

We walked a ways before she replied. "There's nothing else we can do."

"But Papa wanted us to go on. We can't let him down."

"Marjory, please, he isn't here to help us. What do you think two women and three small children can do alone?"

Mother's comment distracted me. *Two women*. Did she finally value my companionship as Papa always had? "I'm not quite sure," I said, cautiously. "If we stop at Fort Bridger, will soldiers escort us all the way back to Fort Laramie?"

"There aren't any soldiers, Marjory. Fort Bridger is not a military post. It was built by a trapper to trade with Indians."

"Well, how . . . ?"

"It's a trading station." Her voice rose in irritation. "The Captain says it's a busy stopover for missionaries, trappers and others traveling between the Oregon and the States."

I searched my mind for reasonable arguments. "Wouldn't staying there have its own set of difficulties? How long would we have to wait for a party going East?" Before she could answer, an even worse thought occurred to me. "How would we even know if they were capable of guiding us? It could be dangerous. Besides, you know Papa didn't leave home without good reason." I paused and drew a quick breath, sensing her resistance. "He hated the thought of his sons getting trapped working for Grandfather's firm. I know if we try, we can come up with a sensible plan to go on."

Mother's tired sigh wasn't lost on me, and I rushed on, knowing I had to come up with reasonable options. "I can learn to drive the team. Even Mr. Wilkins said I show a firm hand. And we still have as much money as Papa thought we'd need, don't we?"

Mother pressed her hand against her forehead. "Oh, Marjory." Her voice carried a mixture of exhaustion and exasperation.

"For heaven's sake! It's high time you separated intentions from achievements. Papa's latest dream was to farm — but think about it. Think for yourself, for a change."

I was stung by her words. "I am. I . . ."

"Then face facts. Look around. We're not concerned with beginnings anymore. We're now trying simply to survive."

I stopped dead, staring at her, hardly hearing her words. The bitterness of her tone alone frightened me. I had never heard her sound so intense before. It even sounded as if she were angry — angry with Papa. But why? Surely, she didn't blame Papa for *dying?* When she turned back to me, I saw frustration, and yes, even desperation in her eyes. And I saw something more — something that frightened me.

Before I could say a word, she whirled around to catch up to the wagon.

"I have to lie down. Watch the children and tell Danny we need more chips for tonight's fire." She hurled her words at me across her shoulder without looking back.

Completely shaken, I remained rooted to the spot. The look on her face . . .

She — she hated me.

Three

July 29, 1847 — evening
Dear Friend,
The stars look bright and cold to-night, but they are not reflected in the Sweetwater River. It's a very dark night, which seems to suit my mood.

Mother's headache continues and she has retired, but I prefer sitting awhile to draw comfort from the fire. It has been a dreadfully long day. Though I know I should get along with Mother, now more than ever, I'm finding it more difficult than I thought possible to do so. If only she'd treat me as an equal — as Papa used to do. However, after today, I wonder if she ever will. Our argument ended so badly that it actually scared me. Perhaps she was just overly tired. I can do nothing but hope that was it. As for turning back, well, there is time for discussing that before we reach Fort Bridger.

I will admit, however, that she is right about one of her worries. We are two women, alone, responsible for three children, and I begin to realize the complications involved.

The second morning after Papa's passing, Mr. Wilkins helped me harness the team. I never dreamed I could do such a thing, for in the city, I had always been properly handed into a buggy without giving a thought to how it was to be pulled. But here I was, walking about the backsides of horses and shoving bits into their mouths.

It was a little frightening, especially when Ginger, the spookiest of the team, took offense at my nervousness. However, I would have turned back home before letting Mr. Wilkins see any weakness on my part. He said I must use a firm hand and show them who was in control. And that I would do. I'd do anything to get us through to the Oregon.

We left the riverbank behind about eight in the morning, and began crossing over a horrible, arid plain. Sage and greasewood struggled for life among the paltry blades of dried grass. Mother no longer seemed angry, and I was happy to put yesterday's argument behind us. Maybe it had only been a case of nerves.

As we walked alongside the wagon, flinty gravel and sand made the miserable trail trying even for the poor animals. Finally Mother took Sarie from me and hailed the wagon. She wouldn't admit she wasn't sure-footed enough to keep up the pace, but at least she did climb aboard to rest with the children in back.

On noticing the range of mountains in the distance, I quickened my pace to speak to Mr. Wilkins.

"Are those the Rocky Mountains?" I asked.

He looked ahead, then smiled down at me. "No. We got a ways to go yet, Miss."

I planned to continue walking, but to my surprise, he leaned down, reaching his hand to me. No doubt he thought I'd intended to take a turn at driving. It would have been awkward to refuse his gesture, so I accepted his assistance. I took his hand while trying to keep my skirt respectable, and readied myself to grab a foothold as he hauled me up, into the box. His rough hand felt warm and firm.

"See that gap? There, between those two dome-shaped rocks."

I searched for the gap that he pointed to, as the team continued their pace.

"Oh. Yes, I see it."

"Well, that's where we'll likely stop mid-day."

He turned the reins over to me and I drove on for several hours. I don't know why I was uncomfortable there sitting beside him, but for some reason I felt awkward. Probably because I had been taken by surprise.

We didn't talk after he showed me our goal. Without effort, he wrapped his arm around the front hoop and leaned against the sideboard to doze in perfect contentment. I found that sitting next to a stranger reposed in sleep, so vulnerable to public inspection, made me nervous.

And, I admit, just a little curious.

I couldn't help noticing a small white scar along his cheekbone and the dark curls crowding his ear. My boldness embarrassed me, and I looked away.

Mother had lowered the canvas sides of the wagon for protection from the dust, but not long after I began driving, she called out to me. She and the children wanted to walk again. I couldn't blame her. We'd hung a tin of cream — a precious donation from Mrs. Meyers's cow — on a hoop under the canvas. The jarring caused by the rocky terrain had by now churned the cream into solid butter. And as the sun grew higher, it became hot enough inside to bake biscuits to go along with the butter. Glancing back at the other wagons, I gave Mother a nod indicating that it was clear to swing down.

When I turned to check on the children's exit, my leg — up to my knee — collided against Mr. Wilkins's leg. I felt the firmness of his limb through my skirt and petticoats, and my cheeks burned with embarrassment. He didn't move or seem awake to notice, but I thought a grin flickered at the corner of his mouth.

The possibility that he was more awake than he looked left me panicky. I pretended to be unaware of our contact, but moved away from him the moment Danny made it down from the wagon safely. I was determined not to show a lack of sophistication by allowing unintentional improprieties to fluster me. Even more to the point, I refused to be a source of our driver's amusement.

Several moments later, our wheel bounced over a rock and he roused himself. Awake or asleep, I vowed that he would not see me discomfited, so I cast about for some casual conversation while glancing over the terrain.

"What a pity. There seems only to be sage and greasewood for as far as I can see. Do you think we'll soon come to better grasses for the animals?" I asked.

"Uhm. At the Sweetwater."

I felt him watching me from beneath the brim of his hat, and I held my head up, looking straight ahead. He offered no further comment. The team seemed to slacken their pace about then, as if they, too, no longer took me seriously. I stiffened my back and gripped the reins, giving the team a firm slap across their flanks, while the mulish beasts continued plodding along at their own leisure.

My mind searched for something to say that would show my indifference toward both man and beast.

"The animals look fatigued, poor things," I said in a dispassionate tone. "What a valiant effort they make on our behalf."

"That they do."

Surely, there was amusement behind his words. My cheeks burned, but I eyed him squarely, giving him my best well-mannered smile, and handed him the reins. "Indeed," I said, as casually as I could. "Yet, the horse is forced to haul its burden with very little food and, unlike man, has *no choice at all* in its traveling companions. That must be quite tedious for them." The words burst out of my mouth without forethought, leaving me sounding completely addle-brained. I had made no sense and, unable to justify my pique or even to understand it, I gave Mr. Wilkins a haughty *so there* nod, gathered my skirts and jumped down to join Mother.

I fell into step beside her as she trudged alongside, carrying Sarie on her hip and warning Jamie away from the wheels. As we walked along, I fumed at what a cake I'd made of myself. Either Mr. Wilkins had passed up a great opportunity to laugh at my expense, or he was left to puzzle over my odd concern for a horse's inability to choose its own companions.

What a to-do over nothing. And why? The answer was obvious. *Simple pride.* I was a complete novice around men outside the family, and I hated to have made my naïveté so obvious to Mr. Wilkins. Why I should care left me puzzled as well as humiliated. I would do better, I told myself, to put my mind to matters of greater concern — such as my dispute with Mother. That was a matter of importance.

It was also less painful to think about at the moment. Besides, I didn't want another argument with Mother, since I needed her to consider my opinions about our family's future.

In my heart, I knew her attitude wasn't entirely wrong. I was well aware that we faced the West alone, and of course, I knew we could not go to a strange land without being sure of our ability to survive. Therefore, I could only be patient and do my best to come up with a sensible option.

Just before coming to the narrow gap where the Sweetwater River pushed through the rocks, I took Sarie so that Mother could step behind some brush for privacy before joining us in camp.

As Mr. Wilkins pulled the brake, bringing our team to our nooning stopover, I noticed the sandy-haired younger Wilkins brother walking back toward us. His smile was broad and his eyes were brown.

"Walter, how's it going?"

Mr. Wilkins looked over his shoulder while climbing down. "Tad. What're you doing here? Why aren't you helping Pa?"

"No need to bellow like a bull with a bee up its nose. I thought it was about time I met the Turners, seeing as how I might be needed sometime, should you stumble into a gopher hole or something."

"Not likely," Mr. Wilkins answered, while chewing on the ever-present piece of grass. He knew I'd spent my free time with Papa and hadn't formally met many young people on our train, so he nodded to me.

"Miss Turner, this eager lad is my younger brother, Tad."

"How do you do?" I asked. The younger man responded with an easy laugh.

"Just fine. But don't swallow all that *younger* brother stuff. While ol' Walt acts like my father and looks like my grandfather, he's really only nine and a half years my senior. Apparently, at twenty-seven going on seventy-two, he has even failed to notice what a fetchin' female he's working for." He flashed me a quick wink.

The impropriety of his banter startled me. After all, we'd only just met. But his eyes were full of mischief and I knew his comment was meant in innocence.

While I fussed with Sarie's bonnet, I could not help comparing the two brothers. The younger one was a little shorter than Mr. Wilkins. They resembled each other in some ways, but our driver had thicker, almost black hair with dark brows that often looked intimidating. His brother's stature was, perhaps, a little less mature but certainly as becoming. His manner, of course, was much easier and his smile seemed a permanent part of his character.

Wanting to change the subject, I looked up. "We've been very grateful for the loan of your brother," I said.

"Really? Why, we'd gladly give him to you outright," he said, punctuating his delight with a brazen grin, "if it didn't smack of playing you a dirty trick. As it is," he continued with an exaggerated sigh, "we promise to take him off your hands soon as you've reached the Oregon."

"They aren't going that far," Mr. Wilkins said, wrapping our reins over the brake handle. "Now stop jawing and explain why you're pestering me instead of helping Pa? No, on second thought, don't. I'd starve while you spun out another of your explanations. We best be getting to eat before it's time to pull out again."

Our driver shrugged as though his brother was both a lost cause and an irresistible nuisance. As they turned to leave, Mr. Wilkins nodded to me.

"Tell your ma I'll be around before it's time to head out."

"Glad to have met you, Miss Turner," Tad called back.

As Sarie wiggled to get down, I could not reply. Mr. Wilkins's comment on our destination had just hit me. The whole camp must assume we are leaving the train. And still I had not the least idea about how to change Mother's mind.

By the next afternoon, it was a relief just to see the little group of willows ahead, with their promise that we'd soon meet the Sweetwater again. Mr. Wilkins left me to drive. The wagon rattled across the pebble-encrusted earth, slamming us against unforgiving wood with bone-jarring regularity, much like a stick being drawn across miles of picket fencing. But after walking for hours over marble-like obstacles, even the beating endured while riding in the wagon no doubt seemed preferable to Mother.

When she joined me on the box, the children played in back. We forced conversation, even over the noise of the road, rather than face the solitude of travel without distraction. I grabbed at the opportunity to forge common ground between us.

"I was thinking about Papa last night," I said, at last. "What made him decide to take up the law?"

Mother looked back at the children, checking on them.

"What brings that up?" she asked.

"I don't know. I've just been thinking."

"Well, as happens in many families, your grandfather chose the law for all of his sons, expecting them to join his firm."

"But Papa hated practicing law."

"Not always. In the beginning he was eager enough."

Mother's hands gripped the seat as if to ease the washboard effect of the road.

"But in the end," she continued, "disappointments, routine and dreams took over."

"Why didn't he just leave years ago?"

"I don't know. Your grandfather is very strong-willed, of course. And then, when your father did take a stand, your grandfather couldn't reconcile his notion of success with that of a farmer's life."

"Do you think Grandfather will expect Danny and Jamie to follow the law, too?"

Mother hesitated. Hoping to get an answer from the heart instead of her usual avoidance of important issues, I stared at the backs of the horses, down past the wagon tongue where the team's hooves sent bits of rock and crusts of sand flying.

"Maybe they will want to," she answered after a while.

"What if they don't, though?"

Again silence, but after a moment, Mother's tension eased and she became thoughtful.

"I suppose that's really the question, isn't it?"

I did not understand her meaning, but for the first time she'd dropped her pretense that Grandfather always knew best. Before I could speak, however, her mood changed again. "After all," she quipped, "what's so wrong with becoming successful and secure in a family firm?"

With a heavy heart, I gave up the fight — for now. Understanding Mother's reluctance to support my father's wishes would take time. Perhaps it didn't even matter. What Mother and Papa had or hadn't agreed on, had little bearing on what we needed to do now.

It was late evening before we camped and settled in for the night. I was tired, and yet my thoughts gave me no peace. I hadn't found a suitable opportunity to talk to Mother again. Worse, I hadn't come up with any logical ideas to persuade her not to turn back. Before I went to bed, I took up a blanket and stood at the river's edge once more. I thought of the home we'd left behind and of our front porch near Mother's bubbling fountain in the garden. Late evening talks that Papa and I had shared came to mind, as I leaned against the cool bark of a willow and listened to low gurgles from the river drifting lazily under the cover of night.

I yearned to go on, to go westward. I

found myself clinging to the idea of a new land for reasons that went beyond Papa. Yet I didn't quite know what they were or what drove me forward. All I knew was that no matter what dangers lay ahead, I wanted to go to the Oregon. I wanted to go for myself.

But how could I explain that to Mother? And if I could, would she even care? I wasn't at all sure that she would. In fact, I feared she would not. At least not the way Papa had cared. An emptiness sent shivers of loneliness through me. The night had turned darker and colder. I wrapped the blanket tightly around me, shut my eyes to the night's chill and slid down to sit at the foot of the tree before opening my journal to a blank page.

I missed Papa so much.

Four days later, after Walter hitched the team, I drove on my own most of the day. I gained confidence, even a sense of power, from directing the tons of horse flesh that pulled our wagon. While enjoying my success with the reins in the late afternoon, I heard Tad Wilkins holler to me from behind.

"Hey there, Miss Turner!"

I looked back to see him running to catch up. Before I realized his intention, he grabbed the box lip and heaved himself aboard. I yelped, clutching the leather in my hands, picturing the horses bolting out of control, but they didn't even flinch.

"Sorry. Didn't mean to startle you." He trapped a silly grin behind a near-perfect mask of decorum. "But I'm on a mission of the greatest urgency," he said.

I couldn't help but laugh. How could Mother expect me to maintain strict proprieties with such a tease, especially while on the trail? I gave way to his game.

"You're quite forgiven, Mr. Wilkins."

"*Mister!* Please. Leave the mister for my stodgy brother, Walter."

Unfortunately, I was aware that neither society nor Mother would tolerate such a lapse. He chuckled at my hesitation. He could afford to, I thought.

"You can't refuse," he said, grinning. "Just think of the tragedy if you hollered a warning to me — say, if a snake was about to strike — and I should pay you no mind, thinking you were warning my brother."

He bowed his head, mourning such a misfortune, forcing a smile from me. "I will be happy to avoid such devastating confusion. Hmmm, let me think," I said, tapping my chin. "How about Mr. *Thaddeus?*"

He threw back his head, his contorted

face the picture of agony.

"Oh, *groan!* How did you guess my name? Who betrayed me?" he demanded while clutching his chest melodramatically.

This enthusiastic performance almost lost him his seat, and an awkward recovery brought a sheepish grin to his face. I barely managed to maintain my own dignity and come up with a calm reply.

"No one betrayed you. I merely didn't think you looked like a Talmidge."

"Ugh. Thank heaven. That's even worse. How about Tad? Or even Mr. Tad."

"That sounds ridiculous. I'm sorry, but to avoid Mother's indignation, it must be Mr. Thaddeus. However," I added magnanimously, "I shall avoid bandying your name about unnecessarily."

"Such generosity. It's pure enough to be bottled and sold. Well, never mind. Now, are you ready for my big surprise?"

"By all means. What is it?"

"If I tell all, it won't be a surprise, goose. Just be ready to leave the minute we stop for nooning tomorrow."

"Leave? Leave for where? My mother . . ."

"Tut, tut. I have her permission already. And my mother's invited yours to sup with them, while we're gone. Also, Pa has given permission for you to use Ma's sidesaddle. So, be ready."

Then, as quickly as he'd come, he jumped down, adding, "Don't forget, be ready. We just have the nooning hour."

He ran back to his wagon, leaving me wondering what he had in mind. Where could we possibly go in this wilderness? I began to tingle at the prospect of a surprise. And, after all this time, I found myself delighted to have a friend on the train. I still missed Papa and our evening talks. We never tired of sharing the day's progress or future plans. But it had been a long time since I'd had someone my own age to have fun with.

Mother didn't have a mind for conversations anymore; Walter seemed too reserved to chat, but Thaddeus restored my spirits. He made me laugh and had a way of enjoying everyday life, like Papa had. Perhaps I might even find Thaddeus a trustworthy confidant. At least I could enjoy his company without worrying about what kind of impression I made.

As if by hurrying our progress I could hurry the day, I urged the team on. Yet, I knew that to be impossible. If only the many promising cool ponds that appeared scattered alongside the trail ahead would entice the animals to pick up their pace. But inevitably, as we approached, the bedeviling ponds dissolved into thin air, no longer fooling either man or beast. I would just have to wait for our nooning stop. I looked across the miles of desolation. What could possibly be out there for Thaddeus to show me?

Four

August 5, 1847 — noon
Dear Friend,
*   At last, we have come to our stop*
and are free — free — free from
chores. I am off as soon as he comes.

Thaddeus and I left camp behind. We abandoned the routine of over ten weeks on the trail and, throwing caution aside, galloped off in spite of the heat. "When are you going to tell me where we're going?" I shouted as we slowed to a trot.

"Soon. Are you getting thirsty?"

"Oh, yes. I didn't take time for a drink, and it's getting hotter all the time."

"In that case, how would you enjoy a nice cold drink of ice water?"

I shot him a well-deserved glare for being so provoking. "Well, *Mister* Thaddeus, I believe I would. Do you happen to have one in your pocket, *Mister* Thaddeus?"

"You mock me," he said. "And right when I'm about to share my secret surprise."

"Perhaps I'd be kinder if you got on with your sharing and did less of your talking."

"Fair enough. Truth is, I'm about to get you a supply of ice. How does that sound?"

"It sounds splendid. Did your father run on ahead and set up his mercantile already?"

"Hardly. And you'll be sorry for your sassiness," he retorted. "But, being of a generous nature, I ain't charging it against you."

He rode on with a disgusting smirk on his face, and I refused to yield again to curiosity. It was enough to be riding out on the rolling plains, away from the laborious shuffling of slow beasts, the drone of voices always at hand. Best of all, I'd been excused for a whole hour from the ever-present need to do chores. I was free. The dust lay low, the air smelled sweet and fresh. I felt alive.

"So, how do you like driving your own wagon?" Thaddeus asked as he waited for me to catch up.

"I love it."

"Ha! I did, too — at first," Tad added, with a strong measure of feeling. "You'll soon get sick of it, though. I wish I'd never let my brother teach me. Now I'm stuck. He, on the other hand, could drive all day. It must be the farmer in him."

"I thought your family was in the mercantile business."

"My dad is. Me, too, I guess. Although for now, I prefer the adventure of this trip to working in a store."

"What about your brother? Isn't he in the business, too?" I asked.

"Only till Pa gets set up. Walt's all fired to settle a farm. Always has been, since he was a kid, helping our granddad."

"And after your father's established, what then?"

"I guess Walter takes to the land, and I put on an apron. Ugh!" Tad made a face. "Work!"

"Don't you like the mercantile business?"

"Sure. I gotta do something, and the store's better than most jobs. But, like I tell Pa, it would help in the long run if I circulate around, once we get to the Oregon. You know, get the lay of the land, scout out fresh goods and drum up business. Pa understands, but Walt says that's a lot of bull . . . oops. Excuse me."

He flashed his grin. I suspected he knew that grin of his got him out of a lot of trouble.

"Walt's just in a hurry to get his own place," he continued, turning serious. "I say the land's been there all this time, and it ain't going anywhere this winter."

"Perhaps your father will decide that you

both can go out on your own," I said, thinking of my own father.

"Not likely. I'm afraid when Walt does pull free, I'm in for it. Of course, by then I'll be ready. I've got some good ideas about the store, which is more than Walt ever had. I'm just not in a hurry to start pitchin' wares yet."

Tad began scanning the rolling countryside surrounding us, and I was glad to let the subject drop. It made me uncomfortable to hear more than perhaps I should about his family. Besides, Walter's plight reminded me too much of Papa's. He, too, had hated working for his father. Papa's interests had been so varied, making new ventures quite appealing, while the law had become tedious for him.

I wondered about Walter. He seemed kind and considerate, like Papa. And he, too, wanted more than just to follow in his father's footsteps. But Papa had acted decisively. He'd decided to take up farming, and we packed up the next spring.

I couldn't help wondering if Walter lacked a little of Papa's determination. Although Tad could help his father get established, it sounded as if Walter had been influenced to delay his own plans by both Tad and their father. Thaddeus and I rode on in companionable silence, until I noticed that he had begun to crane his neck about, looking for something.

"Now the Captain said it should be . . ." Tad stared ahead. "Hey! That must be it. Wait here."

When he rode off a little way, his horse started to balk and shy away. Tad jumped down, letting his reins drop to the ground while he searched the area beneath him. For a second, I thought he'd gotten too much sun when he began stomping about in circles. Then, letting out a whoop of delight, he whirled around and came running back to help me dismount.

As he reached my side, we heard horses behind us. There were four riders coming fast. I tensed, but Tad waved his hat when they neared us. I recognized Walter first, then saw the scout and two other men from the train.

The three men held back, impatient to be on their way, while Walter rode up to his brother.

"Walter, what's going on? You horning in on my ice?"

"Don't worry, Tad. It's all yours. Our scout just came back with a report of buffalo. This might be our last chance, so we're riding out to see what's to be had."

"No fooling? Wait for me. I wouldn't miss this for the world."

Walter gasped and looked at me uneasily, as Tad started for his horse.

"Tad! You forget yourself."

Startled, Tad stopped dead, then turned to me.

"Oh please," I rushed to assure him, "I understand your excitement, Mr. Thaddeus. Really." Trying to look unconcerned, I patted my mount's neck.

He hesitated, looked back at the men waiting restlessly and flashed his charming grin. "You're swell. Really you are. Would it be all right if Walter took you back?" Without waiting for an answer, he turned to his brother. "You wouldn't mind missing the hunt, would you, Walter? After all, you got to go on the first one. This will be my only chance."

I held my smile in place while Walter looked as if he'd like to thrash his brother on the spot. Obviously, nothing short of an argument would stop him from joining the hunt. Walter turned to me with a show of sincerity. "I'd be most happy to take Miss Turner back to camp."

As Tad made an inelegant rush to escape, the older brother shouted out, "Watch yourself, boy. It's not a turkey shoot out there. They have horns."

Walter watched the men ride off, then dismounted.

"Well, I see you didn't get your ice yet."

"No, and I'm afraid I have no idea of how he intended to find any out here."

"Hmmm." He tied off his reins and walked around in a five-foot square, testing the ground. It shook like jelly. "Let's see if this works," he said, pulling a long knife from his saddlebag. Walter knelt down and worked for some time, cutting a large square of sloppy sod and digging it out in layers. I watched as he dug deeper and deeper, over a foot down. At last, he struck something solid. He pounded the knife down again and again, with solid blows, using a stone as a mallet. Rocking the knife's shaft back and forth, he pried a piece of ice loose.

"Ah ha. Here we go," he said, breathing hard. "See? The plain is so high here that the ice stays frozen beneath this thick turf. Would you mind getting two blankets and the saddlebags from my horse?"

He rolled out the blankets and put several blocks of clear ice on each one. He rolled them up in layers of the wool. "This will slow down the melting." Then he tied the bundles over his saddlebags.

After balancing them on his horse, he brought my mare around and cupped his hands to help me mount. This time, I was glad to accept his assistance.

Just as I steadied myself in the saddle, we heard the faint report of a gun. Walter mounted and stood in his stirrups to look about. More shots came from far off. We could easily have missed the sounds had we been riding.

Walter settled into the saddle, smiling. "Shall we head back?"

"What do you think those shots were?"

"Probably the hunt. I just didn't expect them to find game so soon."

We rode back, sharing pleasantries, and he didn't appear the least perturbed at missing the shoot. Perhaps I'd been unfair to suspect him of being amused at my expense a few days ago. He had been nothing but considerate to Mother, patient with Jamie and quite even-tempered with me.

I glanced over as we rode, noticing his straight back and his dark hair bobbing in and out of his collar. He had a very pleasant profile. At that moment, he turned in the saddle and looked skyward, obviously listening.

Then I, too, barely caught the sound of far-off thunder. But other than a little dust storm off the horizon, the sky remained clear. The last crest came as we neared the train, less than a mile off. Walter turned again, scanning the distance behind us. He frowned and suddenly dismounted. Dropping to his knee, he felt the ground, then put his ear down, listening. A slight echo of rolling thunder hung in the air, but mostly the sky was still clear and blue.

Just as suddenly as before, he jumped up and mounted. He turned to me with a grave expression. "Can you ride? I mean *really* ride?"

"Yes."

"Then do it. We have to get back to camp *now*."

I didn't know what he meant, but I didn't waste time asking. I spurred my horse to follow him and concentrated on riding as I had never done before. We saw some of the wagons already pulling into line on our side of a small stream that wound through the low ravines.

"We told them we'd catch up with them later," he shouted over to me. "Gotta get their attention." He took his gun out and shot into the air. "They won't make it, if they don't hurry."

I took his urgency on faith as fear gripped me.

"Wagons ho!" he shouted. "Get to the hills. *Stampede!*" As we neared the train, he waved and pointed. "Get up there. Stampede!"

I looked to our left. Across the little creek, bare rolling hills led toward the pass. The moving wagons lurched forward at top speed. They rumbled across the small stream and headed straight up the hillside. Others, still in line, broke rank and also wheeled toward the high ground, going five and six abreast. Only Mother's wagon and one other remained where they were. As we neared, a man jumped aboard the second wagon and whipped his team, chasing after the others. Mother flung Danny inside and moved to take the box. She had just got hold of the reins when Walter rode up. He motioned me to keep going and swung aboard our wagon, into the driver's seat. How he made it, I didn't know. I looked back to make sure they were moving out. He stood in the box cracking the reins over the horses. "Ha-yah," he shouted. "Yee-hah!"

I rode ahead. Crossing the creek at breakneck speed, I rode up the hill until stopped by the wagons stalled on the steep incline. Walter followed, pulling the team to a skidding, turf-shredding halt near me.

Breathless, we sat and watched. The

steady low rumble echoed in my head. My pulse raced as the building crescendo of thunder grew to a rolling roar, louder and louder. A great dust storm rose up from the land. We were safe, I told myself, yet the noise pushed me into near-mindless panic. A blanket of bobbing, brown heads appeared within the huge cloud that rolled up from beyond the ravines.

A crashing herd of wild beasts headed straight for us. I glanced at our wagon. A little creek would never stop those animals.

We held our teams back with tight reins. The slower stock had lingered behind, near the water, but now they scattered in frantic terror. Most crossed the creek toward us, but a lame ox and a frantic cow veered northward and ran along the far side of the stream. I looked to Walter. He glanced my way and gestured reassurance. But his confidence did not seem to reach his eyes.

I no longer had the choice of flight or courage. Fear seized me. The massive herd came on, their large horn-bearing heads dipping, weaving and slashing through the dust. Beyond escape, I stared ahead, waiting.

The dusty brown wall moved on like thick molasses, flowing down the gentle slope of the lowlands.

But the deafening brown tide didn't quite reach the creek; instead, they veered north, following the bank that formed a natural path of least resistance. I choked on the thick air. It seemed hours before the violent noise dulled as the last of the herd passed by. Finally they were gone, off to our left, dipping out of sight.

In the growing quiet, the dust began to settle.

A nervous laugh tested the silence. Then a few high-pitched, thin voices sprang up. Shaky testimonials swelled, sounding their relief. Just as quickly, they subsided.

Walter handed me down and assisted me into our wagon without speaking. I was thankful for his gentle silence. My insides were so shaky, I would have burst into tears at a word.

He tied my horse to our wagon, reclaimed his seat and quietly clucked to our horses, directing them to follow the creek until we came to an easier slope. Slowly, others followed. In solemn gratitude, we took our places in line, continuing our journey West — all but the foolish cow and sluggish ox. Their journey had ended.

For the rest of the day, the slow pace of climbing one gentle rise after another, leading ever onward toward the South Pass, worked its magic, restoring my confidence. I had never been so close to disaster, nor had I ever tasted such fear. Following Walter, even though unsure of the reason, had been frightening, but nothing touched the stupefying horror of such brute force advancing upon us. It took firm discipline to remind myself that we had been spared.

A rider stopped to tell Walter the rest of the hunting party was safe and would join us later. I saw the relief in his eyes and realized what he must have feared. He nodded his thanks to the messenger and we moved on. Walter's ease with the reins soothed the team and, sitting next to him I, too, bathed in his calming presence.

Behind me, Jamie and Sarie remained fretful from their fright. Poor babes, they must have thought the earth was opening up beneath them. I listened to Mother's effort to console them.

"It's all right; there's nothing to be afraid of now," she soothed.

Danny left her side and sat on the trunk, looking out the back. "I wasn't afraid none. I would'a just got Papa's gun and shot them all if they'd come any closer."

At that, Jamie buried his head deeper into the crook of Mother's arm. "I no like those cows. They make too much noise," he cried.

"The buffalo are gone now, sweetie, and we're safe. We'll reach the pass soon," Mother promised. "Then Fort Bridger."

The relief in her voice at the mention of the fort drove all other thoughts from my mind. I slumped back against the lazy pitch of the canvas frame and sank into concerns of my own.

She meant we would be turning back. Heading home. Was that where our future lay? I wondered. I thought of the dreams that Papa and I had talked of. There was so much to look forward to. And I thought of the past months of hardship, of laborious effort. Would it only end in our retracing our steps?

Maybe I was wrong to push our family to continue. Maybe everyone would be better off returning home. Yet I couldn't help thinking of Papa's reasons for leaving. He had wanted Danny and Jamie to have choices, choices that hadn't come easy for Papa.

Also, I wondered what Mother really wanted. She had never seemed to quite fit in with Papa's family. Yet Mother preferred comfort and familiarity to change. But had she always been this way? If only I understood her better. Was it really doubtful we could make it on our own in the new country, or was this an opportunity to become independent? Mother was qualified to teach. Perhaps instead of a farm, we could even buy a small business. There seemed to be so many possibilities.

When we finally camped for the night, Walter and I hobbled the horses beyond the circle of wagons. When he finished with Ginger, he stroked her mane thoughtfully.

"You were quite exceptional today," he said. "No questions, no arguments, just a lot of hard riding. You may very well have saved your family, as well as others."

His words caught me by surprise. Fumbling with my horses' tether, my heart raced with pleasure. Never had I been praised for common-sense behavior. Mother always found me wanting for practical judgment, and Papa disagreed only because we so often thought alike — always seeing the future as an adventure, so unlike Mother. "Thank you. But I did nothing more than do as you asked."

"You chose a fortunate time to become biddable." He ruffled Ginger's mane and gave her a last pat. "You also sit a horse nicely. Well," he said, barely concealing a yawn, "I believe they're set for the night. See you in the morning."

"Night, Mr. Wilkins." My stammer fell into the darkness, as his long strides took him toward his own camp. It was as well, since my emotions were such that I would not have made much sense.

Our campfire, though dying down, cast a shadowy yellow glow along our wagon's canvas. Against the flickering light, the black sky blotted out the landscape beyond.

"Marjory, is the team settled already?" Mother asked. "Here, come by the fire. Would you like this last biscuit before bed? I saved it, along with a spoon of butter."

"That would be nice." It truly seemed my cup runneth over this day. First, escaping the onslaught of rampaging wild animals, then praise from Walter, and now this.

Could I dare to hope for a new beginning between Mother and myself? Perhaps surviving a great danger unscathed would make us all the stronger. As I leaned back from the glowing embers, for the first time that night, I felt the fire's warmth.

We sat in silent companionship, watching the stars. The night air smelled sweet, and the creek sang musical lyrics in the gentle darkness.

"I put your shawl there next to you. It's getting a bit chilly."

"Thank you." Dutifully, I draped the

shawl over my shoulders.

"I see young Mr. Wilkins and the others made it to camp safely."

"Yes," I said. "His brother was worried, but Mr. Thaddeus got out of the way of the stampede in time."

"Mr. Wilkins had every reason to worry. It was a terrifying experience, and we were lucky for your warning. I feel faint thinking of how close those beasts were behind you."

"We sure did scramble, didn't we?" I tried to laugh the ugly memory away.

"Marjory."

Mother's eyes caught mine with an intensity that took me aback. "You must be careful," she said.

I saw her eyes glisten in the firelight. Tears? Surely, not now. "I will," I all but stammered, confused by her sudden agitation. She held my gaze a moment longer, then hugged her own shawl around her and returned to staring at the dying coals.

"I'm glad the children came through our wild ride across the creek without losing their appetites," I said, trying to ease the tension.

"But don't you see, Marjory?" she asked. "They were terrified. They shouldn't be here, out in this godforsaken wilderness with no one to protect them. None of us should be here."

Her eyes were wide with a fear that seemed odd now. The danger was over. There had been time to get out of the way, and we were safe. I did not know what to say to ease her fears.

"The children have us to protect them. And anyway, we are just days from the fort."

"Yes. That's true. And you must see that we have to turn back. We need the safety of family. Oh, Marjory. Please don't fight me on this."

Suddenly she jumped up and hurried to the river's edge. I suspected she wanted the flowing waters to cover the sound of tears. Instead, to my horror, she became sick. I rose to go to her aid, but she waved me back. I didn't understand. She had been so calm since the stampede. A moment later, she came back toward the wagon. I put my coffee down, ready to assist her.

"Just nerves. I'm all right, now."

"Is there anything I can do?" I asked.

"No. It's getting late. We've so much to do tomorrow." She looked back toward the gurgling waterway, watching its rippled reflection of pale silver with a sad expression. She seemed intent on the rapid flow of the water rushing past our clearing and then out of sight, into the night.

"Tomorrow . . . yes, there's always tomorrow." She sighed as she turned back for the wagon. "Don't be long, Marjory."

When she left, the burning chips crumbled into ash, almost burying the embers. My body sagged with sudden weariness. I leaned toward the fire trench, trying to soak up some warmth. I should have gone to bed, yet I knew sleep would be too hard to come by.

Five

August 5, 1847
Dear Friend,

Tonight, the doldrums have returned. One day my spirits rally, only to sink the next with the prospect of turning back. Yet how can I possibly try to change Mother's mind, when she seems so low-spirited herself? Sometimes I think she is troubled by more than Papa's passing. Of course, that could be just more of the same old thing, our inability to agree on anything.

At least we had a great time at our impromptu prairie picnic earlier. We made a rest stop near a small creek to quiet the livestock after the stampede. It was a great opportunity to celebrate our survival with a toast of "prairie lemonade" (as I call it). With the rare treat of ice, no one seemed to mind our substituting essence of lemon in our sugar and citric acid mixture. It was delicious!

Walter and I even received a toast from the Captain. But after praising us for our warning, he scowled at the

*hunters, blaming them for not consid-
ering the train's location before
shooting. Poor Thaddeus stepped forward, confessing that he was the one
who'd been too eager, which took
much courage.*

*Unfortunately, I need more than
courage, for I fear I shall never come to
terms with Mother. She remains so distant most of the time, and then often
breaks into hostile fits of irrational fear.
Somehow, we must work it out. I just
pray it does not have to mean giving up
and turning back.*

Writing did little to comfort me, and after
burying the coals and returning my journal
to its cache, I crawled into bed with a heavy
heart. I scooted under my blanket, desperately wanting to escape through sleep. Instead, I found Danny waiting for me.

"Marjory, I can't sleep."

"Well, try, Danny."

"I did, but I can't stop thinking."

"About what?" I asked, yawning. Then,
forcing myself, I rolled over to face him in
the dark. Danny had suffered a tragic loss
for a boy of eight, and still he'd been helpful
and undemanding. If he wanted to talk,
surely I could listen.

"Well, I was wondering," he said. "Why do people want to sign their names on Independence Rock?"

His solemn voice left me wondering what lay behind his question. "Well, they probably want others to know they have passed by."

"Is it like leaving your name on top of a mountain? To prove you were there?"

I nodded. "People want to be remembered. Especially in history."

He was very still for several moments. Then he lay back, and I heard a sigh.

"Papa is going to be remembered," he whispered.

"Of course he is, Danny."

"I mean even years and years from now, people will know that he passed this way. They'll know he was going to the new country."

I sat up to catch his words. "How's that?"

"You know, when I went with the Meyerses?" he asked.

"Yes."

"Well, I carved Papa's name on a huge rock, Marjory, just like others had done before us. It wasn't as big as Independence Rock, but it was really big, and right by the Devil's Gate. Mr. Meyers said it's a very important landmark, too. He lent me his knife. But I did it all by myself."

Danny lifted himself on his elbows. "Papa has a marker now, Marjory. People will know where he is. Even if it isn't exactly over his grave. It's pretty close."

A chill closed over my heart. "Danny, did you see the wagons . . . when we left?"

Through the dark, I barely saw his nod. *Dear Lord,* I thought. He'd watched the wagons roll across Papa's grave. I'd thought he'd been spared that. To leave Papa behind was bad enough. But to trample over his resting place and erase all sign of his existence was more than any child should have to witness. I wanted to cry. Both for him and for me. Swallowing hard to clear the ache in my throat, I sensed his eyes on me, waiting.

"It's all right now, though, isn't it, Marjory? God will know where he is."

"Oh, Danny." I scrambled over and scooped him into my arms, rocking him. "Danny, God knew all along. When Papa left us behind, he went with God." Then I remembered Danny's efforts at the rock and added, "But Papa will be happy that others will always know that he'd been on his way to the Oregon."

Danny hugged me back, then wriggled free and settled under his blanket. Satisfaction lightened his voice. "Yeah. Now they'll know," he said sleepily.

I slipped under my own blanket, drained yet somehow restored. *Strange,* I thought to myself as my body relaxed, *how Danny's gesture to Papa gave me peace, too. In a child's scrawl, his name was chiseled in granite.*

God knew where Papa was.

Yesterday, the Captain told us we'd lay over to roast and jerk all the meat we could from the buffalo downed by the hunting party before the stampede. The chance to restock our dwindling supplies came as a relief to everyone. Enjoying a change in routine, we began the day at a more leisurely pace. Just after breakfast, each wagon got their portion of meat.

All morning, the camp hummed with activity. The men mended wagons and equipment, the cattle rested, the children played and the women worked. I got the unenviable chore of doing laundry. Washing clothes is never fun, but in a creek . . . Ugh.

As I laid out my first load of scrubbed wash among nearby shrubs, I noticed Mother. Between trips to check the stew pot, she sorted through Papa's clothes, taking most of them over to Mr. Meyers's wagon. He and Papa were about the same size.

I was resentful at first, but I soon saw the sense in it. We could use the extra space and, I assured myself, Papa had always shared what he had with others.

Mrs. Meyers brought her share of buffalo over to our fire pit. She helped Mother add extra stakes over the trench, then they busied themselves slicing and hanging long strips of meat over the hot embers. Working together made the task more pleasant. Others around camp were doing the same.

While hanging Danny's pants over the wagon tongue, I heard Mama and Mrs. Meyers visiting. Apparently making an effort to keep Mother company, Mrs. Meyers talked about her family back home. She encouraged Mother to do the same. To my great surprise, Mother began to share her thoughts freely.

"My husband's family was the same," said Mother. "Horrified at our leaving for the Oregon. But last year that's all Jack talked about."

I heard a splat of raw meat as she threw another cut onto the board and began pounding it thin.

"Soon nothing would do but to build a new life with his own hands in a new place. I didn't mind him farming, but I worried at his beginning so far away."

"Beginning? Surely, you don't mean your husband had *never* farmed before, do you?" asked Mrs. Meyers.

"Indeed, I do! Jack had been trained for the law, but he grew tired of it. He spent all of last winter studying farming methods. Jack meant to learn everything he could. He was quite thorough. But still," Mother added with a sigh, "I hated to go so far from home."

At that moment, I glanced up. Mrs. Meyers stood gaping at Mother with a strip of meat dangling from her hand. "Well . . . my land. Imagine that. Learning to farm by the book." Hot coals brought her attention back to her meat. "Ah . . . what do you think you'll do now?" she asked, resuming her questions.

"Oh, we'll turn back at Fort Bridger."

I stopped pretending to work and listened in earnest.

"I'm afraid, however, that Marjory wants to go on," Mother continued.

As she spoke, she energetically whacked the flat of the knife's blade against a freshly sliced strip of meat. "I don't understand the girl at all. I guess she's too much like her father. They were extremely close."

Returning to my own work, I puzzled over Mother's tone. Had she been jealous of our closeness? Yet she sounded more troubled than angry. Why couldn't she be happy that I was like my father?

Finally, Mrs. Meyers took up the conversation again. "Marjory seems to be a fine girl. I'm afraid the good Lord never saw fit to bless me and the mister with children. You're mighty lucky to have those fine younguns."

"Yes," Mother answered slowly, "I have the *children*."

Again I looked up. Mother sat back on her heels at the pit's edge. She stared ahead as if she didn't see the fire, the meat or anything. She just stared into space with a distant look.

"Shall we hang the rest along the canvas to dry in the sun as we travel?" Mrs. Meyers asked.

Mother came to herself and nodded agreement. They divided the last slab of meat to cut into strips. I took a dipper full of water and rested against the wagon wheel, before spreading out the rest of my laundered petticoats. I was hot, and Mother's sudden confidences hung in the heavy air like a cloud of gnats. When I'd finished, I noticed they had taken up their conversation again. I wasn't sure I wanted to hear more, but by now it was hard to avoid.

"Jack wouldn't hear of anything else," Mother continued. "He bought the best horses money could buy."

"Well, now, my Charley did wonder," said Mrs. Meyers. "He was right surprised they was accepted on this train. Horses ain't too reliable on the long haul, I'm afraid."

Mother snorted. "On the long haul, I fear, the horses proved more reliable than our luck did."

There was an awkward silence. A slight breeze swept away some of Mrs. Meyers's reply.

"I'm sure 'twas hard . . . all that comfort left behind."

Mother murmured agreement. "However, comfortable living didn't make it easy for Jack to swallow his father's Sunday dinners."

At least, I thought, Mother recognized Papa's boredom with tiresome dinners that included extra helpings of business with every course. Mrs. Meyers's response drifted in and out of earshot as words were lifted away by the capricious breeze.

". . . God's will . . . acting with prudence, as the Good Book says."

"Prudence?" Mother cried out. "Was it prudent to die so far from home, leaving children at the mercy of this God-forsaken wilderness?"

Her sudden distress alarmed me. Her voice grew shrill. She worked herself into anger as easily as she built on her fears. Then Mother glanced about, as if suddenly aware of her lapse. She laid her knife aside and sat back on her heels. Softly, her next comment drifted my way.

"There are times I'm really not sure what to do."

Mrs. Meyers tried to console Mother with a dose of prayerful encouragement.

Mother sighed. "Sometimes, Mrs. Meyers, I wish there was a way we could go on. But there isn't. And it's vital that we return. I must get the children back home soon."

Mrs. Meyers looked at Mother questioningly, then patted her arm. "I'm afraid it is for the best. I didn't want to alarm you, but my mister has expressed his concern. And he ain't the only one to worry about you. Others do, too. I'm afraid them horses of yours . . . well, they just ain't the kind to tolerate such a trip. It's best that you turn back before the mountains."

I didn't want to hear any more. I grabbed

my basket and rushed back to the stream to finish my last load of laundry. There had been more than frustration and disappointment in Mother's voice. I'd heard anger, restrained only by a sadness that I didn't want to think about. The whole conversation disturbed me. And Mrs. Meyers's comments only added to my distress.

Danny joined me moments later, offering to help, and I no longer had time to reflect. His assistance included reporting his morning's activities. I could hardly complain, however, since it was the first sign that his natural exuberance was returning. He chattered about trading marbles and how he had scouted the camp with several other boys. Morning adventures tumbled off his tongue like swift currents scrambling over the rocky riverbed before us. His high spirits had a cleansing effect on me. How could anyone, I wondered, hold on to hurtful frustration or anger against the onslaught of a child's enthusiasm? We'd burned what little wood Mr. Meyers had been able to find, plus the buffalo chips Danny had gathered yesterday. After lunch, Mother sent me to look for more chips. When I headed away from the wagon, Tad joined me.

"Let me help," he said, pointing to my basket. "Otherwise I'll be too available for the chores that good ol' Walt is sure to think up."

"You really are a rogue," I said, with a reluctant grin. I handed him my basket.

"True, but I think you, more than most, appreciate my quest for adventure. My guess is we have much in common."

"Oh, really, Mr. Thaddeus? How so?"

"Well, for one thing, you seem bent on going to the Oregon. How many other young women would be so enthusiastic? Not many. Certainly not the fairy princess Walt was engaged to. She wouldn't even consider leaving *all decent* society behind, as she put it. But you, you're adventurous — like me."

News of Walter's broken engagement seemed too private a subject for his brother to share. Fortunately, I had no need to think of a response, as Tad quickly moved to interests of his own. "Don't you sometimes wish you could just ride ahead, and leave the wagons to their own slow pace?" he asked. "At this rate, there are times I fear that I'll be too old to make it over the mountains."

"If that happens, I'll share my cane so we can hobble forward together in mutual support."

His teasing chuckle left me self-conscious,

and I wished I hadn't spoken so intimately.

"Hmmm," he drawled, giving me a sweeping glance. "No, you're too pretty ever to get old. Yep, too pretty and too downright adventurous."

My cheeks burned and I averted my head. Tad laughed, but he didn't understand. How could he? I wasn't used to the idle flattery bantered about between friends. I hadn't been with many people my age since Grandfather insisted, several years ago, that I share a tutor with my younger cousins. Also, during the last year, Mother became less inclined to compliment anyone, and, while Papa admired my amiability rather than my appearance, my cousins delighted in calling me carrot-top. Though I was more blonde than redheaded, their taunts left pride little chance of ever becoming my downfall. So, although Tad's words left me a bit unsettled, I had to admit, I was not altogether displeased.

When Tad and I finished gathering what chips we could find, we stopped to rest. The afternoon sun beat against us unmercifully. I sat on the ground, tucking my skirts under my legs, with the sun at my back. He sat alongside, facing me, tipping his hat to shade his eyes. He leaned back on his arms, with his legs sprawled out before him.

"Did you leave a beau back home?"

"No, of course not. Besides, that isn't a question you should ask."

He laughed. "I'll bet you've never been kissed either. All right. All right," he said, putting up his hand in a gesture of surrender as my indignation rose. "You're perfectly right. Walter's always telling me I will get myself tongue-lashed someday."

When his familiarities once again breached acceptable limits, I found even his grin to be annoying. I was never sure if he laughed because he'd overstepped himself, or because I lacked sophistication. Had he not been so contrite all the way back to the wagons, I would have banned him from my company for the rest of our trip.

While we didn't travel that day, we were still busy with chores, and the rest of the afternoon passed as a blur. The exhausting day ended at last, with the children bedded down a little early. As I started to join Mother for a cup of coffee by the fire, I heard Mrs. Meyers approach. I didn't feel up to company so, wrapping myself warmly, I climbed up to sit in the box.

I heard Mother rummage about for a cup in which to offer Mrs. Meyers some coffee, but their sporadic conversation drifted away from my perch. I had heard more than I had wanted to hear earlier, and was glad to be hearing only the night sounds. I had been surprised at my mother's frankness with Mrs. Meyers at the fire-pit. Considering the topic, I didn't much appreciate it. Even with family, Mother had generally kept her own counsel.

My mother's distress worried me, but Mrs. Meyers's words of criticism about my father angered me. Who was she to judge the prudence of a man like Papa? But, of course, as Papa would have said, "Poor Mrs. Meyers was rooted in ordinary soil." *Visions* came from very different stuff.

With a heavy heart, I realized that all efforts to convince Mother that it would be best to continue with the train would now be twice as hard.

Soon I heard Mother saying goodnight to our visitor. This was followed by sounds of her scooping dirt over the coals before her weary tread drew near. The gritty scrape of her skirts brushing across uneven mounds of crusty sand foretold her approach. I drew back, into the shadows. Softly she stole into bed without noticing that I was still up.

When the wagon's gentle sway stilled after she'd prepared for bed and settled in, I allowed myself to examine my various concerns.

Mother's determination to return home came from some sense of urgency that was beyond my understanding, so I concentrated on some of the feelings she'd shared about Papa. Although she had never encouraged him to go West, she'd never hinted it was because she doubted him. Had she lost faith in Papa? If so, why?

He'd scarcely been unprepared for our trip, as Mrs. Meyers had implied. I knew this well enough, because Papa had put me in charge of organizing his notes on advice and research. He'd planned everything in detail.

As for Mother, I had to remember her situation. With Papa gone, she only had me to depend on. Of course she would be frightened. I just needed to give her a little more time, I thought. It'd be close to ten more days before we got to Fort Bridger.

Too tired for my journal, I slipped through the canvas flap and into bed.

Six

August 6, 1847
Dear Friend,
   Another day gone and I still struggle
for valid reasons for going on that
would help Mother change her mind. If
we can't farm on our own, perhaps we
can claim land when the Homestead
Act passes. Papa felt certain Congress
would soon adopt such a plan. Danny
will be of an age to help before too
long; and I could perhaps tutor chil-
dren, or do sums in a store, or hire out
as a mother's helper.
   So far, these are my best efforts, but
I know I will find better ideas soon.
However, tonight my immediate
thought is for sleep.

The evening of the eighth we camped on a
hillside above the Little Sandy River. Two
days before, we had crossed the gentle
slopes of South Pass — the halfway point.
It had been a cheering event until we
thought of having that much farther to go.

We found good grass for the stock along
the hill, though the hordes of mosquitoes

peppering the soggy shoreline were horrible. After watering the horses and setting them out, I stopped by the wagon to check on Sarie as she played with a large wooden spoon and a string of buttons. From behind the wagon, I overheard Mother greet Walter and invite him to take supper with us. I held my breath as I waited for his answer. When he politely refused, I stepped back, feeling somewhat disappointed. Not, of course, that I cared. Mother had begun to rely on Walter without question. And I had to be glad for that, because I knew we needed him and felt we could trust him. I just didn't want him to think I put her up to the invitation, simply because he had paid me one casual little compliment. Surely, I assured myself, he wouldn't be so vain. Thankfully, as we readied to go the next morning, it became clear he hadn't given Mother's invitation a second thought. Once again, I had fussed over nothing — unraveling a whole sweater just to pull a thread, as Grandmother used to say. I resolved not to be so sensitive again.

Walter and I started harnessing the team when we got word of a delay. A lady up the line had taken sick. Mother and Mrs. Meyers went forward to see if they could help. When they came back, their expressions were somber, even though they said we would be able to leave within the hour.

We decided to continue, and while picking up the trace and pulling it through Ginger's collar, Walter began talking about the day's destination.

"If we can hit the Big Sandy in a couple of days, we ought to make up some time."

"Make up time? Are we behind schedule?" I asked.

"Not really, I suppose. But before we left Missouri, I heard it was best to reach Independence Rock by the Fourth of July. Gives us a better chance of missing snow in the mountains."

"That means we're three weeks behind."

"Yeah, but like the Captain says, it's just a general goal. We'll be fine."

I wasn't too happy with this vague reassurance. Mrs. Meyers's ready pessimism was enough for Mother to worry over.

"At least there's good grass at the Big Sandy," he continued. "It'll give your horses a much-needed lift." He gave Ginger's rump a firm pat as he moved on to the next animal.

"*Our* horses. Why just *our* horses, Mr. Wilkins?"

"Because they're having a hard time of it now. And it will only get worse."

Mrs. Meyers's earlier criticisms came back to taunt me. "Oh, more so than for those wretchedly slow teams of oxen? Not likely." I bent to my task with fervor. "Just what do you think is so wrong with our horses, anyway?"

He looked a little surprised, but I didn't care. I heard enough innuendoes about Papa's choice of teams. From Mrs. Meyers, her husband and now from Mr. Charming, himself.

"Nothing's wrong," he answered. "At least nothing that an early retirement to pasture wouldn't cure. Just look around. How many other teams of horses do you see? Especially fancy stock like yours."

I snapped the trace into place on the whippletree and tromped back for the next line. "My father spent a great deal of money on picking out the best thoroughbreds available," I spat out angrily. "He had no patience for being stuck with clumsy oxen at the end of the trail."

From the sound that came back to me, I guessed that Mr. Wilkins had bit back his response. And it was a good thing too, because I had enough steam built up to pull our wagon to the Oregon all by myself.

As I stalked off, I was angry and yearned for solitude. A place where I could scream my head off. Somewhere private. Instead, a babbling circle of unending routine surrounded me: oxen being secured to their yokes, children scrambling back to their wagons, women putting out their fires. The pot of simmering activity closed in on me, suffocating me.

Because of the gradually increasing descent, Walter insisted on driving when we finally started out. I sat beside him, entombed in silence. When I at last noticed that my silence held no special message for him, I pondered my wounded spirits instead.

Weariness and sadness were becoming a part of my life. The loss of Papa, the criticism of him, Mother's doubts and fears, the tedious trial of walking or driving on and on, began to weigh on me.

I questioned my determination to go West. Mother didn't want to go, the Captain wanted us to turn back, even Walter assumed we'd leave the train at Fort Bridger. Why did I persevere? Was it willfulness, vanity or selfishness? It became easy to doubt myself.

I sat beside Walter, swaying with the beat of wheels grinding their way over the rocky trail, feeling alone and in strong need of prayerful guidance. I decided if a change of heart was needed, it would have to come from Him.

By the time the sun rose high, Mother and I had eaten, leaving time for the children to play. Mother had been having an unsettled stomach lately, but today she kept her meals down without a sign of her headache. Her color looked better, too.

Danny returned from a walk, eating a handful of berries.

"Where did you get those?" I asked.

"Out yonder." He pointed back beyond the river's edge.

"Go get a pail, and tell Mother we're going out berryin'."

I knew we had at least an hour before we broke camp. Danny came back, pail in hand. His eyes were bright with enthusiasm.

We started off just beyond the spindly willows along the river, and followed the shoreline upstream. We found a few bushes nearby, but saw more up ahead. The berries were a little firm but sweet. It was easy to forget the time, as we stuffed ourselves and tried to fill our pail. Finally, I looked around me with a start.

"Danny, we've been gone long enough. We best get back now."

"Okay. Just let me finish this bush."

I went over to help. He looked up as he picked.

"Gosh, Marjory, which way did we come from?"

"Which way do you think?" I asked.

He studied his surroundings, then pointed. "I can hear the stream over there. And we came upstream. So . . . that way," he pointed.

I laughed. "Right. You'll make another Davy Crockett yet. But we must hurry. Mother will be angry if we aren't ready to go when the others are."

We passed a familiar bend in the river where the water churned past the narrowing, and I caught glimpses of white canvas through a clump of trees. While Danny enthusiastically explored ways Mother could best use the berries, I thought I heard something behind us. When I turned, I froze in place. My breath caught in my throat. My mouth went dry.

Danny, as if sensing my fear, turned to look. I felt his shock from almost a foot away. His breath came out in a long, quiet hiss of disbelief.

Behind us, about three rods upstream, was a large party of Indians, coming up slowly. When we turned, they hesitated, their horses prancing nervously, before they continued to advance.

My mind raced, and I tried not to panic. I kept myself from looking back toward camp. Could we make it before being overtaken? No, never. What if I screamed? Would anyone in camp hear me?

Danny edged near me. "Shall we run?" he whispered. His voice sounded hoarse.

Mine was all but gone.

The Indians advanced, still slow and uneasy, watching for signs of our people.

"No," I whispered back. I relied on sheer instinct. "Act as if we have nothing to fear."

Danny took in my words, swallowed hard, then set the pail down deliberately and stood up straight, facing their approach. I tried to stand as firm.

The party stopped about one rod away. The last few horses carried large bundles draped across their backs. Three Indians in the lead came forward, wearing unpleasant smiles. I watched them as they neared us.

The one in front eyed me steadily, but the others scanned our position — behind us, to one side, then the other. Furtive, nasty glances. A quick surveillance of our strengths. Our weaknesses. All the while, the first man held my eyes without blinking.

My throat was too dry to speak. I raised my hand in greeting, wondering if that really meant peace. The rider in front hesitated, glancing around.

A friendlier look slowly replaced his earlier challenge.

He spoke, but I didn't understand a word. I racked my brain, frantic to respond. From instinct, I pointed to Danny and then to myself. With a picking motion, I pointed down to the pail and turned toward our encampment.

I'd been right. He had noticed the wagons off in the distance. He nodded. Not being sure of what to do next, I smiled, picked up the pail, took Danny's hand and walked away at a steady pace. It worked. The three waited and then began to follow. Not aggressively, but at a comfortable distance.

As we came into camp, the Captain saw us only seconds before noticing our entourage. His weathered face became a mask. I didn't know if he expected trouble from them, or simple trading negotiations. My first impression was that, after spotting our well-protected train, the Indians decided to be friendly. The Captain had spoken of generous tribes — and of dangerous ones. It appeared this group posed no threat, at least under the circumstances. The Indians stopped, waiting for the Captain to come forward and greet them.

The relief I felt in reaching safety made my knees weak. Danny wanted to watch as the Indians addressed the Captain, but I knew Mother would be frantic. Quickly I took Danny back to our wagon. I still felt shaky inside, but I couldn't let Mother see my fear. Danny broke loose of my grip and ran to her.

"Did you see them? Did you see them, Mama? We met them upstream. Wow! It was something!"

She'd been watching our visitors steadily, but looked down at Danny as he demanded her attention.

"We thought they were going to scalp us right there and then. They were fierce-looking, Mama. But we weren't scared." Danny hesitated. "Well, leastways, not too scared. We didn't run," he finished defiantly.

Mother turned her attention back to me. I guess the look on my face must have stamped truth to Danny's claim. She looked as pale as I felt.

"Marjory, what happened?"

Her hand slipped upward to her throat, nervously fingering her collar. I saw her hand tremble, and I wanted to go to her, but something stopped me. Maybe it was her outward calm.

"We've seen Indians before, Mother. The Captain has talked with bands lots of times."

"You met them while you were off alone?"

Her voice low, almost a whisper, alarmed me more than if she'd been angry.

"Yes, but they didn't bother us. They just seemed curious about where we came from." Mother looked pale. I wondered if she'd been sick to her stomach or if her headache had returned.

"Marjory." Her voice remained low but held a hard edge. "You will not put yourself or one of the children in such a dangerous position again. Not ever." She picked Sarie up, then turned back, catching my attention and holding it. "You can't run off doing as you please, as you used to do with your father. You have responsibilities now."

Her eyes glittered, but I couldn't tell if from anger or from unshed tears. She massaged her forehead in an all too familiar gesture, her hand shielding her eyes.

"These children need you. I need you."

I barely caught her last words before she took Sarie into the wagon.

The Captain spent some time with the Indians, and it was another half-hour before we left the camp. I began to unwind from the fright I'd had, only then realizing how terrified I'd been. The Indians we'd met around Fort Laramie had been curious, sometimes pesty, but most often quite helpful. Many stories described acts of generosity on their part. But these Indians had been different. Perhaps it only felt that way because we were alone out here on the prairie.

However, Mother had seemed more than surprised or even frightened by our encounter. There'd been a sense of desperation about her that I didn't understand. Her moods seemed to change from one moment to the next.

If only she'd seen how brave Danny had been. Eight years old, and he'd held his ground like a trooper. Then, sudden realization slammed into my consciousness, turning my knees to mush.

That sweet little eight-year-old boy could have been killed . . . and it would have been my fault.

By the time we started on the trail again, I realized I'd not only been foolish to lose sight of the wagon train as I'd done, but I'd also made it even harder to ease Mother's worries. I would have to think ahead more often, foreseeing consequences. Feeling better about my resolution was a short-lived phenomenon. It began to rain. I sat up in the box hunkered down, tightly wrapped in a wool cloak, trying to see through the downpour as I drove. Strands of hair hung down plastered alongside my face. Dampness crawled up the hems of my petticoats and I pulled the cloak tighter against my legs. Walter came by and asked if I needed help, but the mud was not deep enough to cause serious sliding yet, so I said no.

Soon after that, the Captain rode up and swung from his horse onto our wagon, his coat showering me in the process. He'd come to see how we were doing and to assure Mother and me that there had been no real danger once the Indians had seen our wagons. They were just bringing meat back from a buffalo hunt, he explained, and were too weighted down to cause trouble. Besides, they were Shoshone, who were most often friendly. Once they'd been assured we hadn't seen a Sioux party, they seemed relieved and in a hurry to be on their way, he told us. Then he left as quickly as he'd come. I could only hope his reassurance helped ease Mother's worries.

The rain poured down, pelting the canvas, the horses and me. I began to feel both the wagon and the horses slip on occasion. But we plodded through the mud into the rain-shrouded afternoon. By supper-time, the skies had lightened and the rain dribbled to an end. Walter rode over to say we'd be stopping ahead.

He still didn't trust me to circle for the night's camp and always took over the reins to close in behind the front wagon. It was a challenge to keep tightly behind the wagon ahead. When the circle was complete, the wagons were chained one to the other, leaving no gap. Today's adventure gave everyone a new sense of reassurance about this custom.

Walter helped me take the horses down to the river before hobbling them for the night.

"Your mother looked upset by your little escapade with the Indians."

"It wasn't an escapade," I retorted.

"I'm glad you realize that. It could have turned out very differently, you know. If they'd been Sioux, your being close to the train wouldn't have mattered much."

"Are they so much worse?" I asked.

"The Snakes and Shoshone call them the cut-throats."

I couldn't restrain a shiver.

"I don't mean to scare you, but I was upset to hear about your close call."

I looked up, startled.

"It was upsetting to all of us," he clarified quickly. "You and your brother could have been hurt, and an incident with Indians would be bad for all of us." His smile reminded me of his brother's teasing grin. "But these happened to be pretty amiable fellows, all things considered."

"Amiable? They didn't look amiable," I countered.

"I don't suppose any of us would either, under the same circumstances," he continued, his smile fading. "Finding your territory overrun by armies of white folk traveling through it and shooting up your buffalo could be a mite irritating. Reverse the situation and we might be a little testy, too."

I really wasn't thinking of anyone else's situation at the moment. Instead, my thoughts returned to something else he'd said. *He'd been upset.* The knowledge left me with a strange, tumbly mixture of feelings in the pit of my stomach. However, I made sure not to show how I felt, donning the best of my haughty expressions.

"Well," I said, "I'm glad my brother and I didn't cause any fuss by getting ourselves scalped or something. It being in the middle of a dinner break and all."

He looked at me and grinned. "I am, too.

I was having myself a good nap." Then, laughing outright, he added, "I'll give you one thing. You may have some impractical notions in your head and get yourself caught in the thick of things sometimes, but you're pretty game when it comes down to it. Most females would have taken off screaming, instead of calmly leading a band of Shoshone back to camp."

He tied off the last horse, winked and added, "Mighty generous of you, too, I'd say." He shot me a salute and walked away with a cheery, "See you tomorrow."

I never knew with that man when I'd been complimented, insulted or plain laughed at. I felt like an angry mule with a sore tooth being fed sugar, not knowing whether to nibble it up or to plant a well-aimed kick to Walter's backside.

As I headed for our wagon, I hoped Mother had put the children down. I was tired, but still I wished Mother and I could talk to each other. I wondered if anyone had ever made *her* feel mixed up and uncomfortable and what she had done about it. I heard soft voices as I stepped over the wagon's tongue. Mrs. Meyers stood talking to Mother, who shook her head sadly.

Mrs. Meyers soon left, and Mother came to sit by me. She poured herself a cup of coffee from the pot resting on a hot rock near the dying fire and sipped a few swallows before speaking.

"If you'd like to wait up, I'm going over to Mrs. Trent's wagon in about an hour. It would be an act of kindness if you came, too."

"Is she the lady that took sick day before yesterday?"

"Yes. I'm afraid she got worse. She's passed on."

I sat in the flickering light. There had been a quiet sharing between Mrs. Meyers and my mother. A woman's sharing that made me feel young and inexperienced. I caught Mother looking at me. Tears deepened the pain in her eyes, but they didn't dampen her cheeks. Mother held them back as she looked at me, and I sensed that she wanted to talk to me about Mrs. Trent's passing, but then she turned away.

I wanted to cry out, *Mother, not this time. Please don't pull away! Tell me the things I need to know. Talk to me. I'm grown and of an age to marry. Tell me the secrets that sadden you. The secrets I, too, will have to share.* We sat in silence until it was time to go.

Seven

August 11, 1847
Dear Friend,

Tonight we put Mrs. Trent to rest, and her newborn with her. That tiny form under the shawl was a mournful sight resting in his mother's arms, so dreadfully still. He'd lived just two hours longer than his mother. Poor little soul. Sometimes I feel we have traveled so far from home that we've left God behind.

Mother does not feel well again; even the smell of food bothers her, and her nervous headaches shadow her most days. But she seems more dispirited than ill, which is easy enough to understand, especially after this evening's funeral. So soon after Papa's. And now, to mark its end to this long, dreary day, thunder promises another soaking.

Tomorrow, we follow the Big Sandy and should meet with the Green River by early forenoon. It is the last major river before the fort. I don't know what will happen then.

Early the next morning, I pulled our team into line, and once again we were on our way. Mother still had the headache, and yet she walked in the mud with the children for several hours to give them relief from the constant jarring they endured while riding inside the wagon.

The rain finally slowed to a drizzle. Beads of water turned to shifting rivulets as they snaked down the horses' backs. By mid-morning Mother flagged me to halt the team so that she could climb in back, and I noticed how pale she looked. Yet minutes later, I heard her shoving boxes around above the steady rhythm of horse and wagon. Her energies sounded relentless. I worried she might overtire herself and wondered if I should say something, but before I could decide whether or not to speak, her voice cut through the monotonous din of the wagon.

"Marjory! Did you leave your sister's sweater behind when you washed it the other day? It's missing."

"No. I've seen it since then." I turned to tell her I would find it later, when I spotted the bright pink sweater. "There it is. In front of you."

She had sorted the laundry from the trunk into individual stacks.

"Where?" she asked.

"Right there. In your hands." It lay on top, the only spot of color in the pile. She looked down, first surprised, then irritated, as she stuffed it back into the trunk.

"Well, I asked because it is not the only thing that I haven't been able to find since then," she snapped.

I turned back, angry and frustrated as I struggled for patience. Perhaps as we neared Fort Bridger, the idea of turning back made her anxious. Having to depend on passing trappers or missionaries to return us to the States would worry anyone. Merely the complications of waiting for a return escort would be enough to affect her nerves. Also, the fort was beyond the halfway mark by more than three hundred miles.

Three hundred miles closer to the Oregon. To Papa's dream. Lord help me, but it just didn't make sense to go back after making it so far.

We traveled on for awhile before I noticed the quiet behind me and glanced over my shoulder. Mother had piled all of the bedding beneath her and slept soundly while the children, jostled unmercifully about in their cramped quarters, played next to her. I hoped the nap would restore her spirits — for both our sakes.

An hour passed beyond the time we usually stopped to noon. Ahead, I saw a large river cut across the browned landscape surrounding us. Clumps of cottonwoods and willows grew along the water's edge. When the first wagons neared the bank, they spread out, and the rest of us stopped behind them. Mother poked her head out as I waited for instructions.

"Good heavens! I thought this was to be a shallow crossing. Look at that water," she said.

I *was* looking. While the Green was known to be wide, it was also considered a shallow river, but the current looked swift and frightening. "Perhaps it's the rain," I said.

"Hello!" Walter hollered, as he approached our wagon. "You can make camp over there." He pointed to our left. "Captain says to sup, while he decides what to do about that." He nodded toward the river.

"We aren't going to cross *here*, are we?" I asked.

"I don't know what the Captain plans. It's nothing to worry about, though. I'll let you know soon as I hear anything."

Mother frowned at the river, then turned

to collect a few remaining dried carrots and rutabagas to add to our buffalo stew. She cleared a pit near a small cottonwood that grew back from the river, and fixed dinner in subdued spirits. Danny tied a rope around the tree and then around Sarie's waist, before taking Jamie with him to gather twigs to add to the fire. Word came that we wouldn't be moving for several hours, so I helped Mother by making quick bread and frying it in buffalo fat.

We were ready to eat when Walter returned from the group of men gathered around the Captain.

"Mr. Wilkins. Please, come supper with us. Let me give you a plate while you tell us what's going to happen," said Mother.

He nudged a rock into place and sat by the fire trench.

"Thank you, Ma'am."

"Marjory, serve some of your bread. It goes so well with the stew, Mr. Wilkins." She smiled sweetly as she dished it up. "You couldn't do better than Marjory's cooking. She has the gift."

I stared at Mother, unable to speak. If she believed that, she had certainly kept the fact a secret from me until this minute.

"Hope you enjoy this," she hurried on, handing him a full plate. "I don't know what

110

we'd have done without you."

What on earth has gotten into her? I wondered. Worse, what ever would Walter think?

"Marjory, pour some coffee for Mr. Wilkins." She sat facing him, attentive, as though expecting him to produce a magical riverboat to take us home. "Now then, what has been decided about the river?"

He took his coffee and wedged the tin cup into the dirt beside his boot. "We're going to chain the wagons into a line and begin crossing soon," he answered, between gulps of stew.

"Oh dear." Mother's face fell and she fussed with the fire, poking at the coals. "I don't like this. Some of the other rivers were much deeper, some even swifter, but this one looks so angry. I just don't like it."

"Mother, it's all right. Mr. Wilkins will see we cross safely."

Her smile was strained. "Yes, I'm sure he will." She looked up, set the poker stick aside and fixed her attention on him. "I must admit, Mr. Wilkins, I'm very glad you've agreed to help us. Marjory has all manner of faith in you. It's a comfort to me to know you'll be there for her and the children should anything happen. It's heartening to know you two get on so well together."

I almost choked on the bread I'd just swallowed. "Mother. Nothing is going to happen. Mr. Wilkins agreed to help us as far as the fort, and I'm sure he'll do all that's necessary until then."

"Of course, Mrs. Turner," Walter said. "This river's no worse than the others. It's only three to four feet deep. Stacked right, your goods won't even get wet. It just sounds fierce because of the extra water from a few days' rain."

I kept my eyes lowered as I ate, hoping Mother wouldn't say anything else.

Walter ran the last of his bread along the edge of his plate, before popping it in his mouth. After a few more sips of hot coffee, he stood, offered me his tin and turned to Mother. "Thanks for supper, Ma'am. I'll be back in plenty of time to chain up."

Mother's behavior with Walter embarrassed and angered me beyond anything she'd done before. Between her flamboyant praises and efforts to stuff him with my marvelous bread, I could have crossed the river without any help just to get away from them all. Maybe it was worry that made her act so out of character, but I didn't care. I'd had enough.

I slammed my plate down beside the other dishes and took my coffee to the front of the wagon. There I watched our team nibble on their first green grass since the Black Fork with great gusto. They, at least, looked contented, and although my coffee was hot, I swallowed a large gulp to hold back my tears of frustration.

How I missed Papa.

Just as I finished the last of my coffee, Tad walked toward me, carrying a coiled line draped over his shoulder.

"Hi. Wanna go down to the river and see what's up?"

Forgetting my earlier pique with him, I didn't hesitate. "Sure." Without a word, I left Mother with the children and the dishes.

Tad and I went down to the water's edge together. We walked along the bank and speculated about where they'd put the rope across. Danny followed us.

"Look!" Tad suddenly ran upriver and shouted back at us, pointing. "That willow over there. It looks strong enough. I'll bet I could cross with this line and then pull the heavier rope over and attach it to that tree."

"You wouldn't catch me trying to wade across," I said, made nervous by his bravado. "Listen to that current."

I saw Danny edge toward the water. "Stay back, don't get so close!" I yelled above the frenzied waters.

"Hey, Danny," Tad called out. "Tell Walt I've found the perfect place to tie off a line. Have him bring the rope they're going to use to guide the wagons."

Danny took off at a run. I turned to see Tad removing his boots. "What are you doing?" I asked. A coil of fear wound its way up from my stomach into my chest. "You'd better wait for the others. Maybe the Captain won't want a rope there."

"Sure he will. It's perfect. He said that as soon as they got the teams lined up, we'd get a rope across as a guide to keep the animals from panicking."

Already Tad had tied the line to his waist. He secured the other end around a small tree on our side, leaving the rest lying on the ground, then walked to the river's edge, dragging the rope behind him.

"Now hang on to this about here," he instructed me. "Play it out as I need it. If I fall and drift too far downstream, haul in some slack until I get my balance again. But don't let the end of the line come loose from this tree, or I'll have gone across for nothing."

"*Please* don't do this," I pleaded, staring at the treacherous water. My panic grew. "Wait for your brother."

"He'll be here by the time I get this tied to

the other side. Don't worry. I can probably walk most of the way."

He waded into the water while I watched in disbelief. What could I do all by myself? I gripped the line tight, praying for Walter to come.

To my surprise, Tad managed to stay on his feet for quite a ways. He made it a quarter of the way across before the water covered his knees. I could see the current affect his balance. Then I saw him wobble. I screamed, but he stayed upright after all.

He picked his way forward, carefully selecting footholds. His movements were deliberate, until his next step took him in past his thighs. Before I could open my mouth, he slipped and went under.

For several seconds he completely disappeared. My heart stopped. I looked around, but no one was coming. I hollered as loud as I could while trying to tighten his line.

Maybe no one could hear me. I screamed again and again. Panic almost caused me to drop the rope and run to the water's edge. But I forced myself to hold tight and prayed fervently. With all my might, I gripped the line and pulled at the slack. Desperately I hauled the rope in, my arms straining under the tension.

Tad bobbed to the surface. With only a

second or two for a gulp of air, he began swimming. He didn't appear to be struggling, and his stroke was strong. I prayed harder. I tried to draw the line taut until I felt it pull against his weight, but I wasn't making any headway. Tad had long since been swept past the tree he'd aimed for.

Often the swift current washed over him. He was losing ground in his effort to get to the other shore. I was terrified. What would happen if he ran out of rope? I visualized him pitching downriver until he came to the end of the line, where it would anchor him mid-stream, leaving him helpless, to drown. I hollered again. *Where was Walter?* I had to think. I had to do something. Should I let the rope loose?

My eyes were glued on Tad. Then, a sharp shove broke my grip. Walter had come. He yanked the rope from my hands.

"What the devil do you think you're doing?" he shouted.

Several other men ran up and joined him. They hauled the rope hand over hand.

"He's up!" said one of the men. "Looks like he ain't played out yet."

"Keep some slack. Maybe he'll make way if we steady him," said the other.

"That's mountain water," Walter shouted. "He'll tire soon. Keep it tight. If he

don't make it now, I'm going in after him."
As he kicked off his shoes, Walter's eyes
never left his brother's struggling form.

"Ah! There. Hold on, Walter. He's
making it," said the man nearest me.

Tad's arms broke through the thrashing
water as he made for the other side, but his
movements appeared heavy and awkward.
The fast current alternated between washing
over him and dragging him down, pounding
him against the rocky bed. Still, his flopping,
desperate strokes pulled him, inch by inch,
closer to shore. The men kept the line firm,
while carefully letting out just enough for
him to make it across. I glanced at Walter.
His gaze was fastened on Tad's every move. I
knew the moment Tad had made it. Walter's
face broke into a pained expression of relief.

"He did it!" the two men shouted in
unison.

"Even though he dang-nigh got hisself
killed in the bargain," the man closest to me
said, laughing.

The other man threw a friendly punch at
the first and they sauntered off toward the
wagons, laughing off their tensions. Neither
one looked my way or even seemed to notice
me. I stood there, shaking. Yet I knew how
scared Walter must have been. It was easy
to see there was a close relationship between

the brothers, in spite of their feigned indifference to each other.

A strange desire to hug Walter came over me. Instead, I walked to the rope lying in a heap near the tree and nervously rewound the wet line. Walter had stooped to retrieve his shoes.

"Leave it alone," he snapped, looking over at me.

"I . . ."

"What . . . what *were* you two thinking of?" His voice cracked. "That was a fool stunt to pull. He could have been killed."

I heard his fury, then. The unsteadiness of his voice was far worse than any shout. "I know . . . I didn't . . ." My stammer faded under his penetrating scowl.

"You should have stopped him. What was Tad doing, trying to show off for you? It almost cost him his life."

He dropped to the ground and pulled his boots on. I stood there gaping.

He had no right to blame me. I had watched Tad's struggle in horror, alone, not knowing what to do. And I hadn't encouraged him. But, Walter hadn't asked; he had assumed.

"You . . . you judgmental, stuffy . . . hypocrite," I shouted at his bent head. "How dare you?"

Walter's head snapped up, meeting my glare, as he held his boot midair. "My brother could have been killed," he hollered back.

"And that's *my* fault?"

"*You* were the crowd he was playing to."

For a full two seconds, I stood there, speechless. Then I whirled around and stalked off, seething with indignation.

Still, though I hated to admit it, sadness ate at the edges of my anger. I had counted on Walter, trusted him, and I thought he had trusted me. But without waiting for a word of explanation, he had accused me of egging his brother on to a rash act, and the trust was gone.

As I neared our campsite, I looked back across the turbulent waters. Beyond the ribbon of green that banked the river, life struggled dearly. In that solitary moment, a sad reality settled into place. Before me, the land appeared barren and forlorn, the future uninviting and the past unacceptable.

I returned to camp alone.

Eight

August 12, 1847 — noon
Dear Friend,

Friend. Yes, I surely have need of one today. Papa was right to give me this journal. It is friend enough and blessedly unable to turn false. Still, all the while I helped Mother to prepare for crossing the Green, I felt loneliness wash over me like the current that had swallowed Tad. As we wait now for the men to chain the other wagons, I could return to the States without protest.

Of course, I won't. I would not let Papa down and will still encourage Mother to go on. My reasons for continuing have not changed. I could never let Papa's dream die so easily. And I know that I, too, will enjoy the same freedom from others' expectations that Papa had wanted for himself and my brothers. I see Walter coming this way. It must be time to cross. God willing, I will write from Fort Bridger in a few days' time.

I replaced my journal and climbed in back

with the children. Mother wanted Jamie and Sarie to ride between us, so I had an excuse to avoid Walter. Once settled for the crossing, Mother began rubbing her forehead, and I knew she had worried herself into another headache. There was a delay ahead, which kept us pinned inside the wagon. It didn't help our dispositions.

"What's wrong?" Mother asked Walter.

He ignored her cross tone. "One of the forward wagons cracked a wheel. They're hooking a second team of oxen up to help pull his load."

"Has he another wheel?"

"Yes. He'll be all right. They'll change wheels on the other side of the river and fix the broken one at the Fort. By the time we get there, the blacksmith's shop will be a welcome sight."

Mother closed her eyes, tightened her grip on Sarie and leaned back to wait. The chain lashing the wagons together rattled against the running gear as we started up. When we made our way into the water, we found ourselves tossed about unmercifully. The current slammed the wagon bed against the chain, jarring us at every start and stop. The wheels rode the rocks beneath us like wash on a scrub board.

I glanced up at Jamie's giggle. He enjoyed

the tossing about as a welcome diversion, but Danny looked wide-eyed at the sight of the churning water visible from both ends of the wagon.

Sarie cried in frustration at her confinement within Mother's rigid grip. Both of us kept watch over the rolls of clothing that we had wedged along the sides of our wagon to keep the water out. Some rolls darkened from seepage, but our floors and goods remained dry. Mother caught Danny glancing between the water stains and the bank up ahead.

"Not much farther," she said, forcing a confident smile. "See, here we go." Not until we heard the sound of wheels against dry rock did Mother's worried eyes match the lightheartedness of her voice, yet she had kept the children calm throughout the rough crossing.

Sarie crawled off Mother's lap, happy to be set free. Immediately, Mother bustled about, wringing out wet garments and restoring order.

"Boys, get your shoes," she ordered. I was surprised by her tone. Instead of sounding relieved, her voice had again taken on a sharp edge. "We can walk once they've changed that wheel. Marjory, if you're going to take over driving, watch Sarie. I'd rather not have to carry her for awhile." She looked around, tied the back canvas flaps together and checked for dangerous objects that would tempt a baby.

While waiting for the boys, she poked about in Sarie's toy sack. "Oh Lord! Marjory, did you leave Sarie's new doll at Grandfather's?"

At first, I doubted that I'd heard her right. Sarie had never taken to the new doll. It was too fancy and we had deliberately left it behind. "I'm sure we did. Remember, she didn't care much for it."

Mother frowned, pressing fingers across her brow as if I'd tired her out with excuses. "Of course I know she didn't like it. But I asked you to pack the toys, and I'd hoped you would consider how impossible it would be to buy a new doll when her favorite one wore out."

It was all I could do to hold my tongue. Should I be expected to drag along a doll that Sarie wouldn't play with anyway? It made no sense. Long before we left home, I had heard nothing but "pack only the things you cannot do without." Mother hadn't fussed about leaving her furniture, fancy clothes, or even her fine china. What was behind this sudden concern for Sarie's doll? The crossing must have alarmed her more than I had thought. I could not help wondering why.

For three long days we mounted bluffs, crossed streams and passed a multitude of tall, oddly shaped columns resembling grotesque figures carved in stone. On the fourth day, through rotation, we became lead wagon again. We crossed a barren plain and came into a ravine, bordered on both sides by timber. Word spread quickly that Fort Bridger was not far ahead.

Walter hauled his horse in beside our wagon and asked if he could join me on the box. We had not spoken, unless it was absolutely necessary, since the incident at Green River, and now I gave him a wary glance before I moved to allow him room to join me.

He swung off his saddle and onto the wagon.

"Fort Bridger is up ahead."

"Yes, I heard," I said, stiffly.

"Oh." He paused, as if thinking of what to say. "There's a few wagons that are going to roll in on their last wheel."

When I didn't respond, he plodded on.

"I guess your mother will be relieved to get there." He paused again. "You do still plan to return, don't you?"

I choked back anger with an abrupt laugh.

"How eager you sound to have us off your hands."

"I'm sorry. I didn't mean it that way. The fact is, I'm sorry about the other day at the river. I shouldn't have taken my anger out on you."

"I would have to agree."

He twisted a piece of grass and stuck it in the corner of his mouth. After a prolonged study of the horizon, he tried again.

"Tad scared me the other day. He's pulled a lot of stupid stunts, but that one could have been fatal."

"And you blamed *me* for *Tad's* folly?"

"Yeah. Guess I did. In fact, I've come to realize I often blame others, rather than Tad, for his foolishness."

He stared ahead, and one hand unconsciously worked the knuckles of the other until he finally looked at me.

"I really am sorry."

I concentrated on the trail ahead. Hostility died away. Still, I felt hurt. With Tad, I'd only been embarrassed; I hadn't felt this sense of betrayal. Walter had turned on me without hesitation. Yet his sincerity stirred relief, hurt, gladness and caution all together, leaving me uncertain as to how to respond without risking even more disappointment.

As my silence drew on, Walter said, "Truth is, I've felt downright ashamed of my outburst. I've really enjoyed your company, and I don't want you to think badly of me. I've been wondering just how best to make my apology to you. With my *hat* in hand — or my *head*?"

The blade of grass that he chewed stilled, and he glanced at me. I couldn't help but smile. And then, I found it impossible to look away. His eyes were dark brown, highlighted with a flourish of gold flecks, making them penetrating, and yet warm. As if he had searched deep into my soul, and approved of what he saw. Approved, without so much as a smile to let me know. Our gazes locked in that mental embrace, and I believed he did care. And suddenly I was glad.

I wasn't sure how to act or what to say then. Even if I had known, I couldn't have uttered a word.

Walter was the first to collect his thoughts, and he arched his brows. "Forgiven?" he asked.

Trying to sound unaffected, even indifferent, I stammered. "F-Forgiven. And of course, I don't think badly of you. I'm . . . we're very grateful to you."

He looked at me again, brown eyes

touching my soul, making me shiver inside.

"Thanks." His voice was soft, deep. He shifted his legs and stared at the horizon, but didn't make a move to get down. Taking off his hat, he wiped at the brim and settled it back on his head.

I found his uncertainty pleasantly satisfying. With a rush of heat flushing my face, I riveted my attention back to the team.

He tugged his watch out, checked it, then squinted into the distance.

I anxiously waited for him to break the silence.

Finally he cleared his throat and seemed about to speak, but again stalled. The moment came and went. Again, I waited, wondering what was in his heart.

At last he found his voice. "I promised Danny," he said, "that I'd let him try driving before you left the train."

I had so expected something else that it took a few moments to make sense of this declaration. So that was why he had hung about, stalling. Making good on a promise. I lifted my head under a crown of pride. "Oh?" I said, unconcernedly.

"Yeah." He turned away, spitting out the mangled blade of grass. "This will probably be my only chance," he continued. "Would you mind?"

"Of course not." I gave him the reins. "He's walking behind. I'll get down and tell him."

In my haste for a dignified escape, I stood, gathering my skirts, preparing to jump to the ground as I'd done many times before.

I don't know exactly what happened. Most likely, as I attempted to clear the wheel, my hem caught on the axle-handle.

From somewhere, I heard a loud yell. Then, I felt a sharp pain and found myself on the ground, not knowing how I'd got there. I had a sense of Walter hauling the team in, but I wasn't quite sure if I'd landed in the way or not. Horses, wagons and harness ground to a stop, seemingly over my head. Voices came from all directions. Then Walter bent over me.

I looked up. His eyes were shadowed with concern.

"Are you all right?"

"I . . . I don't know."

His hands, searching for injuries, skated lightly over my limbs, warm and gentle. He touched my forehead, smoothing back my hair. His eyes canvassed my body, returning to search my face.

"Where do you hurt?"

"I . . . I'm not sure that I do." I tried to move, but his arms restrained me.

"Easy. Move your feet first. Good. Now move your arms."

"Ow!"

"What's wrong? What hurts?"

From a distance, I heard Mother reassuring Danny. "It's all right, she'll be fine." Then she called to Walter. "Mr. Wilkins, what's happened? Is she hurt?"

"I'm trying to find that out. Marjory," his gaze touched me again, "where do you hurt?"

"My elbow. My elbow hurts."

"That's all?" His face lightened. There was almost a smile.

"That's all." I tried to struggle to a sitting position.

"Easy does it," he cautioned. "Don't try to get up; just move your arm carefully."

"It's just my arm that hurts." The other wagons had stopped, but then continued on around us. Mother urged the children back inside ours.

"Please," I said. "Let me get up. I feel foolish lying out here."

"Better to feel foolish than sorry. You still look shaky. Put your good arm around my neck."

I stiffened.

"Don't argue. I'll get you back inside."

I did feel shaky. I gave in and did as he

told me. At first, when he scooped me up, I tried to avoid the intimacy of being held against his chest. It was not only impossible, but as he lifted me a whirling sensation hit my stomach and my head felt like a top, prompting me to sink into the comfort of his arms. Papa had once said, "Caution can sometimes be too costly." This seemed a good time not to risk making such an expensive mistake.

Through my dress, I felt the powerful glide of shifting muscle against me. My head settled against Walter's shoulder. The woodsy scent of smoke mixed nicely with the faint evidence of a man who has labored hard. It was an intriguing scent.

When he stood and gained his balance, the beat of his heart was strong and steady. I felt protected, a bit lightheaded and there were a whole lot of mysterious flutterings going on inside me. And I enjoyed every shameful moment of it.

Walter lifted me over the backboard and placed me onto the bedding that Mother had laid out. She took over then, and as Walter went back to the reins, Mother wiped my face with a dry cloth and wrapped my elbow tightly. Pain shattered my short-lived reverie, then settled into a dull ache. My elbow had already turned vibrant with color.

For the next hour, I was coddled and not allowed to get up. I enjoyed Mother's attention and yet, in spite of myself, I couldn't stop thinking about Walter. I was as knowledgeable as any girl my age about what the future held for women. I had read about courting, but it had been mere words. Words and giggles between school friends.

I didn't feel like giggling now. I felt fearful, uncertain and wonderful, all at the same time. I wished that I could talk to Mother. Had she ever felt this way? Were my feelings proper? Then I wondered what Walter would think if he'd known my thoughts.

Walter. I couldn't bear for him to become uncomfortable around me. I enjoyed being with him. The same way that Papa had said he had enjoyed Mother's company when they were young. He'd said they were the best of friends from the moment they'd met.

Then it hit me. Not a new realization, but a realization with new impact. If we left the train at Fort Bridger, I would never see Walter again.

My arm hurt even more. Firmly, I closed the fort from my mind.

Soon after my fall, Walter had regained our position as lead wagon. I should have expected it. He wasn't a man to lose out on our turn at being lead.

For that one sweet-breathing day, the dust was behind us instead of ahead, and I wanted to sit up front and enjoy it — with Walter. However, Mother insisted I rest till we stop. The miles rolled by, until at last Walter yelled back that we were nearing a clump of cottonwoods. I heard the Captain calling for us to hold up.

When the strain of brakes and harnesses slowed the forward motion of wagons, I worked my way to the box, dodging Mother's spinning wheel, climbing past trunks, sacks and bedding to look out as we stopped.

A keen disappointment shot through me. Fort Bridger consisted of a rickety-looking bunch of picket stakes, held up by spit and mud, enclosing all but the chimneys of two or three crowded buildings. Nothing could have looked less like a fort.

Glints of sun revealed a stream just beyond the scraggly fence. No one was about, but we waited, as if for some kind of formal invitation. This couldn't be a fort, I thought. But the Captain had motioned for the wagons to stop while he rode ahead. A crudely carved sign over the gate read "Fort Bridger." He went to the entrance and hesitated before riding inside, where he disappeared from sight. I watched anxiously for his return.

No greeting or raised voice carried over the eerie stillness. Tall trees stood guard, to the side and behind the fort, as though protecting secrets. Distant birds twittered nervously. Even the stream seemed to slip along its silt bed in silence.

The Captain, at long last, rode out the gate of the mud-daubed fencing and cantered back toward the wagons. He stopped about midway down the line, at a distance where he could be heard by all, and nudged his horse to face us. Glancing around, he took off his hat, wiped the inner rim with his kerchief and then leaned forward, almost standing in his stirrups. We waited, wondering if the fort had refused us hospitality, or if it might even be in quarantine.

"Folks," the Captain shouted up and down the line. "I'm mighty sorry to have to tell you — the blacksmith shop has been burned to the ground. The fort is deserted."

Nine

August 16, 1847
Dear Friend,
We are staying the night at Fort Bridger, but I do not like it here. This silence is unnerving. Even while the Captain tells us we are quite safe, he herds us inside the fort, leaving the wagons near the gate. And we are allowed no campfires.

The men water the horses and we prepare for tomorrow's pre-dawn exodus, moving like silent ghosts under cover of darkness. I have to ask, if all is so safe, why have even the animals been brought in to share our cramped quarters? It can only be from fear of attack, as if this wobbly fence of daub and sticks could stave off anything fiercer than a hungry pup.

They say that the burned smithy shop does not necessarily mean an Indian raid, but I tell you, dear friend, I am torn between relief at not having to turn back and fear of what danger may lurk nearby.

And through all of this, there is poor

Mother. The look on her face when we learned we couldn't turn back — I've never seen her appear so defeated. Maybe it would have been better if we had been able to return home. I just don't know. But I do know I will be grateful to see the dawn and be on our way.

The main building housed half of the people in our train. We bedded down in an atmosphere of cautious shuffling and shushing that emphasized our sense of danger. When the first guard left us to stand watch, the lovely thunk of a solid door closing out the wilderness comforted me before I drifted off to sleep. I had forgotten the security offered by a wooden door.

Hours later I woke to a pitch-black room, surrounded by a noisy orchestration of exhausted sleepers. But it had been hushed movements that had disturbed my sleep. Fully awake, I heard strained whispers as the Captain shook several of the men sleeping near the door. He cautioned them against making undue noise as he told them of an Indian encampment spotted just downstream. I sat up, trying to decide if I should wait for instructions or try to find Walter.

Moments later, word passed quietly for each family to gather their belongings and make their way back to the wagons. Walter had collected the animals and, as silently as possible, readied our team while Mother and I guided the children to the wagon and their own beds.

Under a cloak of darkness, we flinched at every sound that broke the stillness of pre-dawn. Traces jangled in spite of all our efforts, and animals shuffled about, snorting nervously, as we hastily prepared to leave. Not a soul gave a thought to departing without benefit of breakfast.

Walter drove when we at last pulled out. As we cleared the fort, I braced for the sound of attacking Indians. But only the noise of our ponderous progress rent the air.

The children went back to sleep the moment we had put them down. It would be hours before we'd stop to eat. When dawn filtered through the canvas, I could just make out my mother's outline. She sat on her covers, hunched beside the trunk. Her head was bent, not in rest, but in despair. I knew she'd not meant for me to hear the sound of her muffled sobs above the noise of creaking wood, grinding wheels and rattling harness.

"Mother." I picked my way to her side.

"Please don't feel so bad about our having to go on."

She hid her face behind her hands, shutting me out. "Go to bed, Marjory. I'm fine."

"Please. We're a long way from home. We *need* each other. You said so yourself." I waited, hoping, praying. "Mother, please talk to me."

She lifted her head and straightened. Her attention focused on me for a moment, then fell away. Her shoulders sagged, and she asked in a dull voice, "What do you want to talk about?"

"What do I . . ." I stopped, wanting to consider my words carefully, wanting to ease her worries. Instead, I blurted out my own fears. "Please, Mother, please don't hate Papa for dying and leaving us here alone."

Stunned by my outburst, I waited for her indignation, her wrath. She sat stone still at my outburst. Then, in the graying dawn, I sensed an unbending, a softening, almost as if the memory of my mother as she used to be emerged before me.

"Why do you think that I could ever hate your father?" she asked, her voice barely audible.

I avoided facing her, afraid to break the fragile thread between us. "I don't know.

It's just that you got so quiet." I twisted the frayed edging of my dressing gown. "I know you never wanted to come West. And you always seemed to discourage Papa's ideas . . ." My words trailed off in confusion.

"Discouraged? What did I criticize or disapprove of?" she asked, sounding genuinely surprised.

My throat tightened and I pushed away painful stirrings. "Well, there was the time Papa wanted to invest in Mr. Findley's new corn fertilizer." Only I had noticed the sad decline of his tenacious enthusiasm. "And remember, two years ago, how much Papa wanted to join Mr. Whitney's promotions for extending the rail system westward?" I brushed at my tears under cover of darkness and struggled to keep my voice steady. "It was Papa's big chance for an exciting new venture. But even I knew you didn't want him to do it."

"Oh, Marjory." She pulled her knees closer to her chest. "Do you think the rails were never laid because your father didn't leave Grandfather's firm and invest in them?"

I looked up, straining to see her. She sounded weary. "No," I answered, considering her question. "I guess not, but every time Papa wanted to discuss new opportunities, you weren't very . . . encouraging."

"Perhaps," she replied, "but I always accepted the decisions he settled on." After a long pause, she sighed. "I guess I found it best just to wait it out. His interest didn't tend to stay fixed for long."

She sank back against the trunk. Exhaustion seemed to claim her, like a fog bank absorbing light and shadow.

"It'll soon be safe to stop for breakfast. We must rest now." Her voice, feathery light, carried only an imitation of its usual authority.

I leaned forward. "Are you all right, Mother?"

"Yes, dear. I'm fine. Even my head is better." She set about straightening her bedding, so I got up from where I'd rested on my knees.

"Marjory?"

"Yes."

"I could never hate your father. I loved him. And I understood his ways."

I crawled back to my own blankets, needing to sort out my reactions. Yet I dared one more question. "Mother, if you weren't crying because of Papa, why were you feeling so bad?"

A long silence hung between us. I thought perhaps I'd gone too far, but she at last answered.

"I'm afraid, Marjory, terribly afraid. And I don't know why."

Her words were barely audible. I struggled to formulate a response, something with which to comfort her, but I could think of nothing. She mumbled a good night and settled into an exhausted sleep within minutes.

Long hours of driving the next day gave me time to think. Perhaps Mother had been right to wait out Papa's plans. As I looked back, I realized there had been quite a number of them.

"Life's an adventure," Papa used to say. "It isn't the success or failure as much as the trying." I couldn't help but remember that Mr. Findley's venture into a revolutionary corn fertilizer had taken place right in the middle of the terrible depression that led to so many farm bankruptcies.

And in truth, if Mr. Whitney's rail plan had succeeded, we'd be traveling West by train rather than by these miserable wagons.

Perhaps Mother had understood Papa better than I'd realized. And perhaps I'd understood him far less well than I'd thought.

I had never questioned Papa's enthusiasms before. The realization troubled me. I hated doubting Papa. Yet, if I hadn't seen

Papa clearly, had I done any better by Mother? Then I remembered Mother's comment. She had loved him, understood and accepted him.

I mopped my brow with my sleeve, released a breath I hadn't been aware of holding and set aside all choosing and judging. Acceptance. It was a good word. For surely, no father had been as much fun as Papa. But, as I contemplated Mother's circumstances, I realized I would much prefer sharing life with a man of a little less imagination. Papa's fascination with new beginnings must have finally lost its appeal for Mother. I realized now how tedious fresh starts could become after awhile.

The sun blazed down, growing hotter as we traveled on. I lifted my chin to catch whatever breeze might cool my neck. As I drew my thoughts back to the road and team, I became suspicious about the lack of activity behind me. Glancing back, my smile faded. Once again Mother napped soundly while the children played about her. She never used to do that. I wished I knew what was wrong.

I slapped the reins against our team's dust-coated backs as if it would clear my worries away. The horses neither noticed nor cared. They plodded on with little thought for anything, save their next meal.

After two weeks of tiresome progress toward the next fort, we circled up beside the adobe walls of Fort Hall. Upon our arrival, a fast-talking little man greeted our train, offering plenty of potatoes, coffee and dried beef to any wagon that would turn toward California. He swore that a Captain Sutter offered six sections of land to every family that settled near his fort. I was glad for his peskiness, because he greatly irritated Mother. His relentless recruiting brought some color to her cheeks and seemed to energize her.

The fear of our train breaking up raised images of disaster in her mind. Walter painstakingly assured her that only small parties of Mormons were headed for New Hope in California, and they had planned to do so from the beginning.

Even the man running the Hudson's Bay Post added his assurance. "Ye got a good train, Ma'am. There's not many that arrives with the same wagon master as what they'd beginned with."

By now, I also needed encouragement, for doubt had begun to cloud my own enthusiasm. Overhearing some traders speak of a new route to the States brought home to me for the first time that somewhere near Fort Boise we had left our own country and were now traveling in land claimed by Mexico. We weren't just following Father's dream; we were alone, heading for a new frontier among strangers.

I also grew more worried about Mother. Even shopping within the tall, strong adobe walls of Fort Hall had failed to raise her spirits as I'd hoped. I thought surely the chance to purchase fresh supplies would help, and it did, but only a little.

Our stay at Fort Hall lasted one night. We left the last week in August. The Captain said we couldn't afford any more time because of the threat of snow in the mountains. There was quite a scramble to get the blacksmith to take care of our repairs by then. Some of the men simply rented his equipment and made their own repairs.

The possibility of Mother's being seriously ill had become, by then, more obvious. Realizing that sheer arrogance had prompted my dismissal of Mother's concerns about venturing West shamed me. Even though part of me still rejoiced at going on, I saw the true folly of my naïveté. I'd asked her to take such a risk with little thought beyond my own wants. Not that it mattered now; after twelve hundred miles, the choice was no longer ours to make.

Mother was not feeling well again, and I was glad for the late start the next morning. I suspected that her nausea had returned, but she said it was just the headache.

I had assumed she suffered the same stomach ailment that plagued many travelers. But when I realized she had been sick, one way or another, most days since we crossed the pass, I wondered. Any mention of my concern, however, made Mother more irritable. I finally decided to speak to Mrs. Meyers at my next opportunity.

My chance came when Mother asked me to take Sarie over to the Meyerses and have her ride with them for the morning. Mrs. Meyers agreed to take the baby with unrestrained enthusiasm, and she showed concern at my mention of Mother's illness.

"She does seem a mite peaked to me, too. Is she sleeping all right?" asked Mrs. Meyers.

"Not too well," I answered. "She doesn't like me to fuss, but I am worried. She seems edgy. And now she's upset to the stomach. In fact, she gets sick more days than not."

"Really!" Mrs. Meyers's brows arched, then furrowed in deep thought. A sadness came into her eyes. "Perhaps I should stop by to see your ma later today. I'll bring the baby back when she's ready to nap."

"Mrs. Meyers, do you think it's serious?" I asked. She hesitated. My stomach tightened.

"No. I doubt it's serious. I should say it's just . . . troublin'. Very likely it's nothing to worry 'bout. But I should be 'specially helpful to your ma, if I were you. She should rest as much as possible. Now, now," she said, noticing my frown. " 'Tis most likely nothing uncommon, and you mustn't worry."

She gave me a smile and took Sarie up in her wagon. As I returned to ours, I wondered at the sad look of recognition that had come to Mrs. Meyers's face before worry had replaced it. It was a look exchanged by women when they shared private concerns among themselves. Like the night Mrs. Trent died.

I remained uneasy, until I decided these thoughts would do little to cheer either Mother or the children.

The next night, I sat by the fire after long hours of driving over a rocky terrain that was especially hard on the animals. Tad stopped by. He stood beside me, then dropped down on his heels and poked at the waning fire with a stick. I was tired, yet glad for the company. Mother had gone to bed early with the children. Tad sat for awhile before heaving a long sigh.

"Sure hasn't been much to see since the waterfall, a ways back," he said. "Ain't much grass for the animals, and too often we can't even get down to the water. I hope the rest of the trip isn't going to be this bad. It all gets to be a bit boring." He jabbed at the coals, sending a spark flying skyward.

"I think following the Snake River is beautiful and exciting, at least when we're close enough to look over the canyon's edge."

"Yeah, but the Snake's brought up a bunch of palaver from Walt. He's not going to let me live down my swim in the Green for some time to come." Tad tossed the stick into the brush. "How's it been going for you? I'm surprised to see Walt's been driving a lot. Thought you were set on taking the reins yourself."

"I am, usually. It's just that my mother hasn't been too well lately. So I spend more time watching the children. Your brother has been kind enough to drive whenever I'm busy." I sat near the heat, twisting a strand of hair that had gone astray.

"Oh, I don't imagine he's being all *that* kind."

"Why . . . what do you mean? Has he said anything? Do you think he minds?" I asked.

"Naw. He ain't said nothing. And he doesn't mind, far as I can tell. Fact is I suspect he likes driving for you more and more. Seems in a big enough hurry to get here."

Tired as I was, Tad's sour look piqued my curiosity. "What makes you say that?" I asked, taking renewed interest in our conversation. "I'd suppose there are a lot more interesting things that he'd rather be doing."

"Well . . . would've been once. Don't seem to be none anymore."

"Why not?"

"Ha! Guess I ain't the one to ask. 'Sides, none of my business." He picked up a pebble and flung it into the night. "I just wished it wasn't so blamed dull around here. Guess I'm about ready to *get* where we're going. Day after day, all you see is the rumps of oxen, and all you get is dust in your face. I hear tell we got some mountains coming up. A bunch of them."

"I'm ready to get where we're going, too, but I'm not anxious for any mountains. Or excitement."

"Well, sure. But then, you're a girl. To be expected."

He stood up, pulling out a small box. "I brought over some checkers. Are you interested in a game? Can't count on Walter anymore. Appears he's too tuckered from playing Sir Lancelot."

I colored at his comment and, even though minutes before I'd been dead tired, I felt cheered, even exhilarated. Tad's hints about Walter's feelings made me wonder if his assumptions were accurate. What had Walter said concerning me? I couldn't help myself. My pulse pumped a little faster and I grinned foolishly. "Sure, Tad. Only one game, though. There's little enough time for sleep as it is." His face brightened with the prospect of competition, as he placed the board between us.

The next morning Mother woke looking better than she had for a while. She had breakfast with us and when we started out, she wanted to walk with the boys. It was an encouraging sign.

Walter insisted on driving, even though I could have done it. I played with Sarie near the driver's box, relishing the opportunity to visit with him. I saw no harm in taking pleasure in his company. Walter was a real help to our family.

Sarie was in a decidedly playful mood. As we jolted over a gopher hole, she squealed with delight when I toppled over on my side in an exaggerated roll.

At the sound of her laugh, Walter turned back toward us. "She sure is a happy young one."

"She has a full tummy," I answered over the rumble of our progress. "Bounce her around when she's empty or tired, and you'll hear a different song."

"I'll bet." He moved over to one side of the seat and turned so he could better talk while handling the team. "Glad to see your mother feeling better," he said, settling against the first hoop.

"So am I."

"Now that you're going on, do you know where you'll settle and what you'll do? That is, if you don't mind my asking."

"Of course, I don't mind. Mother hasn't said much yet. I understand there are several settlements near the Columbia River. Know anything about them?" I couldn't help wondering if he really cared about our plans.

"Not much." He glanced ahead, checking the team as he continued. "Other than missions, I heard of some settlements called Vancouver, Portland and Oregon City."

"Papa talked of the Willamette Valley. He mentioned heading for Oregon City first. A town would offer us more opportunity in the long run."

"I agree. You know, Marjory, I've come to know you and your family and if I could . . ."

A loud holler interrupted Walter. Danny ran alongside, waving and asking to ride on the box. As much as I cared about my little brother, for a few intense seconds, I toyed with the notion of locking him in a trunk for the rest of the trip.

Ten

September 3, 1847
Dear Friend,
    I am sorry I did not have a chance to talk to Walter again today. How wonderfully at ease I find myself with him. Not that it makes any real difference, however, for I am well aware that I have all I can do just to help Mother. Besides, Walter is already committed to helping his father. Still, his friendship is a source of strength.

We left the riverbank to follow a straight western course. The dreary days went by, one after another. I sometimes thought my whole life would be spent walking. Walking . . . in the dust if I was lucky, in the mud if I was not. And when I did ride, it was usually to drive.

The sun shone without a break during the week after we left Fort Hall. Again we followed along the south ridge, where the canyon's bed cradled the Snake River far below us, well beyond our reach.

During a particularly hot afternoon, Walter took the reins while Mother and I walked alongside. I had Sarie tied to my back with a large shawl. Danny insisted on walking ahead, but Jamie plodded along clutching Mother's skirt while dragging a stick. I tried ignoring a trickle of sweat that ran down the back of my neck and began a conversation as a distraction.

"You'll have to write to Aunt Marian," I said, trying for a comfortable topic. "We can assure her that she hasn't had real flat bread until she's baked it over a hot rock. She'll think we've indeed gone savage."

"I suppose so," Mother replied. "Likely, cooking our own meals will be enough to brand us so in her eyes."

Her voice sounded flat. She sighed, rubbing her forehead as we followed the canyon's edge. Far below, the river snaked its way alongside, taunting us with its bright sparkles whenever the sun danced on the water. From up the line I heard Danny shouting at us as he ran back, pointing toward the canyon. At the same time, Walter shouted down from the box.

"Look at that!"

"Wow!" Danny cried, reaching us. "Did ya ever see anythin' like it?"

I looked over at the canyon and caught my breath. A myriad of waterfalls cascaded down the other side of the rocky gorge into the Snake. From top to bottom, big and small streams spewed forth, seeming to bleed from a multitude of wounds cut deep into the steep embankment beyond, while straight across from us, water spilled over the edge from the top of the shrub-encrusted plateau. Covering the entire face of the north embankment, springs burst forth, as if forced through a sieve.

All of the wagons slowed to a stop. The whisper of cascading water had been muted by the noise of our creaking wheels and shuffling hooves. This awesome display should rouse Mother's spirits, even on her worst day.

I glanced at Mother. The sun was down to our left, just a few hours before setting. She stood with her hands shielding her eyes, leaning forward, squinting as if trying to make out the features of a small object some distance away. A chill ran through me. The panoramic sight filled the entire landscape, and still she squinted and strained forward.

"Mama, can't you see the falls clearly? They're huge."

"Of course I see the falls. I'm not blind," she grumbled. "But what's one more water-fall? A lot of good it does us anyway, being so far beyond our reach." She motioned to my brother, as he stood riveted by the sight.

"Don't get so close, Danny. Stand back with us."

Danny retreated, even though he'd been a good two rods away from the edge. We both wondered at her caution. Could eye trouble cause a case of nerves? I wondered.

I resolved to speak to Mrs. Meyers again the next day. She'd told me that Mother would speak up when she wanted me to know anything. But if Mother was having trouble with her vision, I should know.

Then, a few hours after being unimpressed by the waterfalls, I found Mother in a good mood, sorting buttons and easily stringing them on waxed yarn to make a toy for Sarie. Her sight seemed improved, but her actions confused me.

I tried to remember how life had been back home. For some time, headaches, feeling poorly, and retiring early seemed one way Mother handled unpleasantness with Papa. She avoided conversations about the Oregon by pleading fatigue. Perhaps these days Mother simply felt overwhelmed by Papa's death. Illness and headaches could be temporary reactions to the disaster that helped her cope. If so, I wished she would find a better way. For all our sakes. Later in the day, I drove while Walter took over his father's second wagon. I had the feeling Tad had somehow talked Walter into taking his place. Sure enough, less than an hour after Walter left, Tad showed up.

He rode into camp at breakneck speed, slowed his mount as he approached the train, and headed for our wagon.

"Mind if I come aboard?" he asked, pulling up alongside.

"Of course not. Where have you been off to?"

"Giving old Blazen a chance to stretch his legs."

"Fifteen miles a day isn't enough?" I asked, pitying the poor horse at the mercy of a restless boy bored by the pace of oxen. I moved over as Tad swung onto the box with me.

"You sound like Walt. Traveling at a snail's pace is killing Blazen. He's used to real runs. 'Course, Walt just thinks I'm trying to get out of driving for awhile."

I looked over at him. "Aren't you?"

He grinned. "Yes, but I think it's kinder to let him think I'm on a mission of mercy."

"Poor Walter," I said. "I wonder how he gets his fun."

"He doesn't need fun anymore. He's nearing thirty. Anyway, he's too busy planning for a place of his own. Then he can collect himself a female and kids."

"Is that what your brother wants?"

"Blamed if I know. He's sure bent on his own place. And he's gettin' downright crotchety about it," Tad complained. "He finally agreed to sell Grandpa's farm so's me and Pa could use our share to set up out West, but now Walt's even setting limits on how much time we'll be needing him to help out."

I always felt uncomfortable when Tad discussed private matters so carelessly, especially concerning Walter. I searched for a new subject, while Tad struggled to get a pebble out of his boot.

"I sure hope Sarie is behaving for Mrs. Meyers," I said. "She offered to take her for awhile, so Mother could get a nap."

"You mean that old lady I've seen with your ma? She sure seems to buzz around the little ones, doesn't she? Ain't she got any of her own to fret over?"

"No. She told Mother she'd never had children. Seems kind of sad to me."

"Don't know why it should. But she certainly does fancy your brother and sister. The other day," he said, shaking out his boot, "I saw her showing your little sister off to some lady up ahead. 'I could just keep this little angel forever,' she said. And all the while she's talking, the other one's got two younguns hanging on her and is hollering at a third. You should have seen it. The mother looked sorely tempted to hand over a couple of her own kids to the ol' lady's care, since kids seemed all it took to make her so all-fired happy."

Tad chuckled, but I was tired, and his sense of humor was beginning to wear on me. I wiped sweat and grit from my callused hands onto my skirt. From the corner of my eye, I spotted Tad eyeing a loose piece of yarn in his sock.

"Don't pull it!" I said, but it was too late. He'd yanked a broken strand of yarn at the ball of his foot, unwinding about a quarter inch of sock. The toe of his stocking came free, dropping at my feet like a wool cap for a small pup.

"Now, you've done it," I said, looking up at him. He sat there with a surprised look, wiggling his exposed toes as if to validate their escape.

"Well, I'll be. How did that happen?" he asked, seemingly fascinated by his own toes.

Watching those grubby, thin toes with knobby joints wiggling in the sunlight suddenly threw me into a fit of giggles, in spite of my sore hands. Never would I have been so indiscreet back home. But then I would never have watched a man take off his boot, nor would I have wiped sweat from my own hand. I wouldn't have acknowledged sweat in the first place. However, at that moment, in the middle of nowhere, it all seemed funny.

"And just what's so hilarious?" Tad cast me a suspicious look.

"Nothing. But your toes sure could use another dunking in the nearest river." He studied his toes and I began to laugh at his surveillance. He looked up, then laughed with me. Unfortunately, we forgot Mother had been sleeping.

"Marjory! What on earth?"

Tad jumped up, leaped from the wagon and made a hasty retreat, boot in hand.

Mother struggled forward, snatched the reins from my chapped hands and told me to collect Sarie from the Meyerses, "quickly, before they tire of tending her." My brief release faded.

The next two days dragged by. The misery of the wastelands threatened to creep into our very souls. The dust, so fine that it billowed up overhead, stung our eyes and clogged our noses, while encrusting our hair and clothes. It was even more tortuous for the poor animals.

I grew weary of our travels, and if I hadn't

had Tad to laugh with and Walter to talk to, I do believe I'd have gone quite mad. Late one afternoon, Mother and the children were napping while I walked doggedly beside the wagon.

"Why don't you come up and ride awhile?" Walter asked. "The horses haven't much of a pull here."

"It doesn't look much freer from dust up there, but maybe I will anyway." I grabbed the hand he offered and braced my other against the side of the box.

"One, two, *three!*" He hoisted me to the seat. "That does it. You're getting pretty good at this. I don't even need to slow down anymore."

"Yes, but by the time we get to the Oregon, one arm will be twice as long as the other."

"Now that should get you special notice right off." He chuckled. "You might get work washing second-story windows."

"Very funny," I replied, taking my bonnet off to brush sweaty curls from my face. "I'll be sure to tell Mother that I have a real future."

Smiling, he watched me retie my ribbons. Then he turned serious.

"Speaking of your ma, how's she been feeling? I heard her playing with the children when I came back from dinner."

"Sometimes she's better, but it doesn't seem to last. Yet, every time I wonder if it could be the stomach ailment, she improves again."

Walter glanced at me.

"She's been having an upset stomach?"

"Yes."

"Oh." He hesitated. "How long has that been going on?"

"Since before South Pass. But she's better now."

For some time, he made no other comment. I wondered if I'd been indelicate to mention Mother's illness.

"Do you have any close family back home?" Walter asked after awhile.

"Papa's family. But I'd say they weren't close, since they had a lot to do with Papa coming West. As for my mother's parents, they've passed on."

He frowned. His elbows had been resting on his knees, but he sat up, shifting his weight back against the seat.

"You really didn't want to turn back?" he asked. "Farming's a rough existence. It must have been a shock when your father decided to homestead, especially since you've been raised to city living."

"Not really. I knew Papa was weary of

being an attorney with Grandfather's firm. He wanted to try working with his hands."

I leaned back, pondering Papa's decision. "But I wonder, in the long run, if the solitude would have appealed to him. For me, it was the best part."

"Oh? I'm surprised. I enjoy the quiet, but it's not often that a woman feels the same, especially a young, attractive one. Sure you won't miss society and your friends?"

I laughed. "Do I miss pretending to have an interest in things that bore me and faking ignorance of things that don't? Hardly. I'm afraid I'm a terrible misfit — somewhere between being bookish and unsuitably drawn to rooting around gardens in a less-than-dignified manner. Poor Mother. She has been at a loss in preparing me for society," I said, trying to swallow a small lump that settled in my throat. "I think that I have been a great disappointment to her." I caught back a nervous laugh and was grateful that he refrained from pursuing the matter. Yet I found my mind racing on, one thought chasing another. Without a doubt, Papa and I had been kindred spirits in many ways: he, hating the boredom of working for Grandfather, and I, chafing against my fate, resisting a colorless future of simpering modesty.

I was reminded of my friend Lisa during last year's social, when Papa and others had discussed the newly published guide, *Route Across the Rocky Mountains.*

"We might be making just such a trip, next spring," I boasted to a group of friends.

"Marjory," exclaimed Lisa. "How awful for you. They say you travel months through dust and dirt, without so much as a bar of soap or a pail of water."

"But think of the countryside that I'll see," I countered.

"The sun will simply ruin your lovely skin," said another friend, Charlotte.

"I shall have my bonnet. And just think, I will stand atop real mountains, see new lands and meet people of all kinds."

"Yes, and some of those people may throw you in a pot and cook you."

"Oh, Charlotte," I cried, growing impatient. "We are not going to the Amazon, but to the other side of this continent. Wouldn't you like to see what such a vast land is really like?" But my challenge had been met with morbid groans.

"You will be lost among savages, Marjory. You'll never again shop, your clothes will become dowdy and you'll soon have to go native." The words were said with a distinct shudder. I had looked at my peers, feeling utterly alone. The last straw had been Mr. Perry's valiant attempt to rescue my spirits.

"Ah, Miss Lisa," he said. "But our Marjory would be the prettiest little savage on the whole frontier."

That was the night I gave up trying to conform to society's edicts and turned away from all pretense with my charmingly contented friends. That was Grandfather's life and perhaps Mother's, too. I had sided with Papa. Papa's decision had offered me freedom.

As I grasped the sense of peace that thought gave me, I barely caught the last of Walter's question.

". . . don't you think?"

"Pardon?" I sat up, again embarrassed. "I'm sorry. What did you say?"

"I said rebellion is a poor motivation for a hard life of farming, don't you think?"

I stiffened. "Yes, if that was my motive. But it's not." I turned my head to face him. "I'm not running away from anything. I'm running to . . . to a life that offers satisfaction . . . the satisfaction of sweating over a task that is . . . necessary. I do not shy away from hard work, Mr. Wilkins, and I think I would have done quite well on a farm."

My indignation quickly died. Why should I expect others to understand what my own mother did not? Only Papa had accepted me for who I was. Only Papa had accepted the duckling, instead of trying to turn her into a swan.

Walter bit off the mangled end of the grass he had been chewing and stuck it back in his mouth. "Maybe you could have made it. I agree with your sentiments, anyway. Not many folks appreciate the challenge. Still, the city appeals to most girls."

"It has nothing to offer me. I wanted our family to make this trip."

"You've got spunk; I'll give you that," he said. He turned to me with a grin, but his smile soon faded. As he studied me, his eyes softened.

A tingle began to creep up my spine, a warm sensation of acceptance and approval embraced me, and I met his look full on. His soft gaze seemed to darken, to deepen. The smiling warmth of his eyes turned to a strange, somber shade of brown that seemed to draw me into his soul. I found it hard to breathe.

Quite without warning, our universe seemed changed. Wagon, horses and others did not exist. There was just him and me.

A little frightened, I thought to turn aside, knowing I should. But I couldn't. I didn't want to. Before I could so much as draw a breath, however, a shutter lowered over his eyes, and his gaze fell away.

Even though neither of us had made a move, I felt the pain of his withdrawal. We'd shared more than an intimate moment; we'd experienced something new, something that couldn't be taken back or ignored.

For a moment, he was silent. His profile took on a sharp edge.

I looked at my hands resting in my lap, hoping to cover a growing uncertainty. Had I only imagined that intense moment? Or had he experienced it too?

"You might have spunk," he said, his voice hard and flat. "But, it takes more than that to survive in a new land."

His attention turned back to the horses. A frown creased his brow, and his voice sounded harsh.

"I had to say goodbye to a particular friend who quickly found reality had a sobering effect on a dream," he said. "Most women, when it comes down to it, find they have a real need for basic comforts." He glanced at me with a twisted smile. "It's only natural. If they don't have to move away, why should they?"

Chilling anger stiffened my spine. "I couldn't possibly speak for *most* women," I said.

Clearly surprised, he glanced at me again, before looking away. The stem of grass that he chewed moved vigorously, and he worked his jaw without saying a word.

As I calmed, I realized our spirits had touched and retreated, without a word, but it had been too much, too fast. The silence between us became thick.

"I think I hear Sarie," I said. "She mustn't wake Mother."

Eleven

August 13, 1847
Dear Friend,

Finally, with everyone in bed, I have time to think. It has been a confusing day. I fear I am becoming fonder of Walter than is wise, and even dare to wonder if he feels the same. Worse, I may be making something of nothing. And it's all based on a wordless exchange, a mere look, but nothing more. Yet I cannot seem to stop thinking about it, even though we each have our own responsibilities.

Am I courting folly? I wish I could talk to Papa.

I can barely see the ramblings that I am recording by firelight, but the soft whisper of lead gliding over my secrets lends a substance to my worries and cautions me, for I could well have misjudged our encounter.

Anyway, tomorrow we leave the Snake again and veer north. I think Mother feels better, but cannot be sure. In fact, there is little I am sure of these days.

Before breaking camp the next morning, Mother suddenly excused herself during breakfast, and rushed for the river. I hurried after her. Even before reaching the bank, I heard her retching, and the savagery of her spasms made my own stomach lurch in sympathy. When I neared her, she waved me back, leaving no doubt that she wanted privacy, so I reluctantly turned away.

A fear began to take hold of me as I packed our utensils. I knew Mother would not discuss this latest attack, so I determined to tackle Mrs. Meyers to find out what she had learned. If Mother was ill, she would need me.

After our train plowed through a long morning of miserable dust, I went to see Mrs. Meyers during our noon stop.

"Mother still can't eat properly, Mrs. Meyers. Tiredness, the headache and increasingly an upset stomach plague her. I need to know what she's told you."

Tucking a graying strand of hair under her cotton bonnet, Mrs. Meyers sighed. "I know, dear. I'm surprised your ma doesn't see that herself. Truth is, she's too proud to say."

"She told you nothing when you asked?"

"That's just it, I'm afraid. She avoided any reference to her health. As I say, your ma is a private person. Wouldn't admit a word about feeling poorly. It's as though ignoring the situation will make it disappear." She gave a sad little smile. "But I'm afraid, Marjory, *that* ain't gonna be possible forever."

"Mrs. Meyers, do you know what ails Mother?"

She hesitated, then shook her head. "I can only guess, mind you. But it don't hardly seem in much doubt."

I clenched my fists, as if bracing myself. First Papa, now . . . I couldn't bear to think of Mother being ill, too. Quite suddenly, I didn't want to know. But it was too late. Mrs. Meyers had decided that I should.

"I don't know how much your mama talked to you about such things, but you must remember *something* about before little Sarie was borned."

"Sarie?" I blinked back my surprise. "What about Sarie?"

"Nothing, dear. Except think back to how your ma was, seven, eight months before Sarie. Did she have trouble eating? Or did she have nervous headaches?"

I muddled through memories that seemed entirely irrelevant. One by one, I dredged up seemingly unimportant incidents from a lifetime ago. "Yes, she was sick. A lot. As for her headaches, I don't remember when they started. More recently, I think. About the time we were making plans to come West."

Her questions made no sense until a thought crystallized in my mind, turning me ice cold. "Do you mean . . . but . . ."

"Your pa ain't been gone all that long, dear. I think she'd been in the family way for a month or so before his passing."

"But, Papa isn't here to take care of her," I said, nearing tears.

She smiled. "That's true. That will be up to you now, child. I don't figure she'll be needing anything special till after you get to the Oregon, thank the good Lord. That will make things easier and give you time to prepare."

I left Mrs. Meyers's wagon numbed, wanting to walk awhile before returning to our camp. I needed to think — to think what this meant to us. If what Mrs. Meyers said was true.

A baby! Slowly, a sweet pain filled me. A new little life. It would have been such an exciting prospect if we were a complete family, if Papa were still here.

Two years ago, I'd been too young to take a hand in such things. But now, near sixteen, Mother could have confided her condition to me, and we could have had such fun planning . . . if only Papa had lived. But, he hadn't. And now I wondered what we would do. Without Papa, Mother had no one — except me.

I thought of my brothers and sister: Danny, so serious and stoic, yet vulnerable; Jamie, cheerfully, stubbornly exploring the delicate balance between Mother's comfort and his own new independence; and Sarie. Chubby, delightful little Sarie. I loved them so much. And I'd love the new little one, too. They needed us. Mother and I were all they had. The thought settled on me heavily.

Dear God! Please, please, let my mother be all right.

Walking back to our wagon, I spotted Sarie. She had crawled to the edge of her blanket. I watched her put her hand on the prickly grass, littered with sharp, gravel-like pebbles, before quickly drawing back. Again and again she tested the unfriendly terrain, drawing back, rocking on her hands and knees, measuring the distance to cover before reaching her beloved ball that had rolled beyond her quilt. She sat back, whimpered, looked around for Mother then back at her ball. In a moment of decision, she lunged forward on her hands and knees, striking out across gravel, weeds and dirt. She fretted at the discomfort, but never once took her eyes from her goal. When she reached the ball, she grabbed it, plopped down on her bottom and sat with her prize tightly secured between pudgy little hands.

Her eyes lit up when she spotted me, knowing I would come to her rescue. How could I do less? I scooped her up, feeling a rush of love. It swept me up in its power, like a leaf caught up in a rushing brook. We weren't alone in our time of need, any more than Sarie had been. And, after all, child-bearing wasn't new to Mother. She had been safely delivered of five children. I could work. Surely, between her experience, my energy and God, we'd make do.

I heard Mother inside the wagon and, wanting a few more moments to myself, I kissed Sarie and sat her in the middle of the blanket before wandering between the wagons ahead. It was time to confront Mother, but I wasn't ready yet.

To avoid a family taking their noon meal, I ducked behind their wagon, and walked between two larger ones. Through the turmoil of my thoughts, I found myself on one side of a prairie schooner with two men standing on the other side, their voices raised in anger.

"You know full well that Pa will find one reason after another for me to stay on," the first man shouted.

The other voice answered, more defensive than angry, "He's only asked for help to get started. What's the big problem?"

I stopped short, suddenly recognizing the voices. I hadn't yet been seen and, from the sound of things, Walter and Tad were no more in the mood for company than was I. If I walked on, they'd surely see me. As I looked for an escape route, they continued.

"The big problem *is*," Walter countered, "you're the one who should be helping him. You'll be his partner."

"So?"

"So, the store will be yours, and it's high time you earned your partnership," Walter said in a low, angry tone.

The growing hostility in his voice shocked me.

"I'll be earning my way soon enough," Tad shot back. "Dad understands. Besides, one or two months and the store's set up. So, if Dad don't mind my plans, what's your complaint?" he demanded.

"My complaint," Walter answered in a voice tight with anger, "is that *I* mind, and Pa can't work the store alone. He *needs* your help."

"He did all right back home without it."

"Because he had me. And I'm serious about not waiting on your adventurin' before going after my own land. From now on, your interests, or anyone else's for that matter, stop coming before mine. I'm not waiting on you or anybody any more."

With the sound of pebbles grinding into dried grass, someone whirled around and stalked off.

"Whoooeee," whistled Tad under his breath. "Big brother sure has a temper, after all!"

I heard him chuckling as he walked after Walter. I knew Tad wasn't heavily endowed with sensitivity, but how could he make so light of Walter's concerns? His anger hung heavy in the air, and yet Tad seemed surprised, even amused. I felt sure he cared for his brother, but obviously, Tad hadn't heard the desperation in Walter's words.

I turned back the way I'd come, confused, and with a new sense of distress. As I stumbled toward our wagon, Walter's words followed me, gathering energy. They slammed again and again against my mind. *I'm not helping . . . Not your problems, not anyone else's. I'm not waiting any more.* The words hammered at my brain, angry, resentful words. Words from a man trapped by his own kindness.

As I reached our campsite, the train readied to leave. I arrived just as Mother put Sarie in the back of our wagon.

"We'll walk," she said. "At least for as long as Jamie holds out."

I climbed on the box and pulled our team into line, grateful the trail didn't demand Walter's assistance.

Before long, we found ourselves traveling over the powder-fine landscape. The ride was even worse than before. By sheer endurance, our dehydrated teams scraped past the prickly sagebrush. Iron-rimmed wheels pounded over lava rocks. Sun-dried wagons lurched wildly through the dry, brown fog of dust. The desiccated earth, ground to powder and pitched heavenward by man, beast and wagon, billowed around us, making it necessary to filter each breath through a scarf.

The foul air was thick enough to lose one's self in. This I found somewhat satisfying. It gave me the illusion of isolation in which to quiet the ache winding its tight band around my chest and to sift through my thoughts . . . time to plan.

I sorted through my priorities with determination. First I considered the best way to deal with Mother's condition, having accepted Mrs. Meyers's guess as fact. It explained so much. I ached with shame at having suspected Mother of using her headaches and upset stomachs as a way of rebelling against Papa's trip. Poor Mother. For now, the kindest thing would be to allow her the choice of how and when she would confide in me. Until then, I'd help by taking on as much of the work as possible. Walter would have to . . . Walter!

The weight of his frustration, his sense of entrapment . . . I hated contributing to it, but I didn't perceive another option. We needed him. I could only be grateful for what assistance he could give us. We would get to the Oregon and, if I was lucky, I could still count Walter as a friend. That would be all I could ask.

Later that afternoon, when Walter rode up, I told him I would drive for the rest of the day. He asked about Mother, and I said she seemed better. It was true. She had walked a good bit of the day with the boys. He tipped his hat and went back to his father's wagons. Whether he was relieved or not, I couldn't tell.

We had thought the Plains were as bad as it would get for eating dirt and for boredom. But again we were tested. The flat, dry terrain over which we now traveled forced us to protect our faces from the dust that rose to a hundred feet above our canvases. We spread our wagons out across the desolate land above the Snake, each driver hoping to avoid the other wagon's cloud of grit.

As the days passed, I found it easier to talk to Walter again. He must have sensed my withdrawal, because I noticed that he, too, seemed awkward after our last encounter. We soon regained a comfortable ease with one another, however. Later, when I saw Mother hadn't really improved as I'd hoped, I shared my concerns with him.

He never offered opinions, but he always listened and encouraged my flagging spirits.

"Fort Boise is ahead, Marjory. Perhaps you could talk your ma into seeing a doctor there."

"I don't know if she'll admit to needing one."

"She still won't talk about what ails her?" he asked.

"No, she doesn't even agree that she's anything but tired."

"Have you talked to Mrs. Meyers?"

"Yes. She thinks that Mother . . . ah . . . that Mother's confinement won't come before we get to the Oregon."

"Oh." He hesitated, appearing ill at ease. "How long does she guess it would be before your Mother might require some attention?"

His gaze remained fastened on the team. Mine remained glued to the horizon. "Maybe not until after the first of the year."

He remained quiet for some time. When I felt his eyes on me, I looked up to meet them. His compassion warmed and comforted me.

"You mentioned going to a settlement. Do you still hope to get to the Willamette Valley?"

"I don't know. Is that where Oregon City is?" I asked.

"I think so. I know it's south of Fort Vancouver."

"I guess that would be best then, unless we come to a hospitable settlement closer," I said.

"I suppose so." He switched a shaft of dried grass to the other side of his mouth, remaining thoughtful for some minutes. A worried frown creased his forehead. "Do you have any idea of how you will get through the winter?"

I remembered his frustrations, his battle to be free of other people's troubles. "Papa had money to get us started. We won't be buying farmland now, but we'll get through the winter and still have something left to take advantage of any opportunities that come our way. Maybe we could start a rooming house. Mother's an excellent cook and I could do the heavy work."

His brow smoothed. Approval lit his eyes. "You are quite something, Marjory Turner. It's nice to know some city-bred ladies can do more than just sit and look pretty."

A grin touched his lips as he looked at me. "Not that looking pretty doesn't have merits of its own. But having a little substance under that mass of strawberry curls can only enhance a pleasant appearance." His cheeks colored, and he lowered his voice, as if unable to contain one last afterthought. "A handsome combination, golden red curls and large brown eyes."

I struggled to keep a tight rein on the horses as well as my spirits.

"I'm amazed," I said, trying to cover my lack of sophistication. "Your ability to distinguish the color of my hair is remarkable, considering all the dust it hosts."

"True. I just happened to notice earlier."

For a moment, in the privacy of my own thoughts, I soaked up the flattery and held it close. But I sobered soon enough.

That evening we met the Snake River once more. Bone weary and covered in grit, I helped Mother prepare supper and put the children down. Mother looked exhausted and left me to bury the campfire. The men had already lowered pails to the river to replenish our water. As precious as our supply was, I vowed that before my journal would so much as see the tip of my pencil, I would first take a small pan of water to the back of our wagon.

In the shadows, I scrubbed off as much grime as was possible, all the while trying to ignore Walter's earlier compliments.

Twelve

September 9, 1847
Dear Friend,
Today we suffered a tragic drowning at Three Island Crossing. Over half of our group had crossed safely and made camp, waiting for the rest of the group to join us. While some remained on the far island rather than brook the deep, fierce current at such a late hour, those on the second island set out to ford the remaining section of river that separated us

It was during this effort that poor Mr. Baker slipped and hit his head. He was taken by the treacherous current. His terror-stricken wife watched helplessly as he was swept away, out of sight.

It was over before anyone could react.

One more shadow cast itself upon our dreams of the Oregon. Needless to say, we retire tonight somewhat sobered.

The next day, after regrouping on the north shore of the Snake River, we set out again. I worried that Mrs. Baker's tragedy would renew Mother's own grief. We had not really known the Bakers, but surely such a loss must be a painful reminder. All day I watched her, trying to sense any change in her behavior. She'd been subdued, but so had most of the train. Since Mother hadn't been sick for several days, my hope grew, yet I watched for any possible setback.

Earlier, during breakfast, she had teased Sarie into eating her dried biscuit with surprising patience. Mother also ate with no apparent sign of nausea or headache. Perhaps she had passed through the last stages of her indisposition.

Even while happy for Mother's improvement, I found another day of merciless heat very trying. The team already had worked up a sweat in the harsh sun. I eased my skirts above my ankles to encourage a tiny draft. Moments later, I ducked my head just in time to avoid a swarm of gnats. How I hated the bugs, the dust and the eternal dryness. Could it have only been a matter of weeks since I'd cursed the rain?

Mother walked up beside the box.

"How are Sarie and Jamie doing?" she called.

I looked back into the wagon. Sarie had finally gotten her shoe off and was taking great delight in banging it against Jamie's back as he bent over his latest project. Not even being clubbed with his sister's soft shoe broke his concentration on the tangled laces in Mother's corset. I had to grin at Mother's ingenuity. What better toy for an imaginative four-year-old? Jamie bent over his work, carefully threading the long lace through a lengthy row of holes, leaving an erratic yet apparently pleasing trail.

"They're fine, Mother. Jamie should be busy for quite some time."

"Good. He needed a challenge," she said. "And Sarie?"

Mother's alert interest pleased me. "Sarie's busy, too. How are you doing?"

"Fine," she answered. "I can relieve you, if you're tired of driving."

Her voice sounded untroubled, and she even seemed to stand straighter. I shook my head in answer, unsure about the change in her, wondering if I was only seeing what I wanted to see. She moved off to the side to escape our dust.

The monotonous trail consumed the next few hours, until Walter rode by.

"I just heard something interesting about our next camp," he yelled from his mount.

"Oh," I said. "What is that?"

"We'll stop at some hot springs." The

dried stem of grass in his mouth danced as he talked. "I hear it's a great place for washing and bathing, and some say the waters are healing."

"Will we be there before dark?"

"No, but the Captain says we'll stay over a day to rest the stock and catch up on chores. Considering the shape of some of our animals, he thinks it'll save time in the long run."

Walter had been right about the springs. They were a most welcome treat; even Mother was impressed. Early the next morning, we baked bread and washed clothes, scrubbing everything in sight. Later, after allowing the water to cool, we bathed the children. Imagine, having to cool water before using it. The luxury seemed to invigorate Mother. She didn't fade the whole day.

However, poor Mrs. Meyers had an entirely different reaction to the wonders we enjoyed. We saw little of her after we first camped. Even the next day, she had hurriedly cooked her meals, only to disappear again inside her wagon. It seemed odd that she wasn't making good use of this opportunity to houseclean but, as we were busy, we didn't make overly much of it.

After supper, she finally made her way to our wagon. She appeared quite nervous. Within minutes she poured out her grievances. "The Captain couldn't have known of the fearsome disturbances yonder when making camp last night," she said. "Those unholy mists churning above the boiling waters. Surely, he'd never meant us to camp near such a bad place as this. And yet we have spent the whole day here."

All the while, her hands worried each other, and she cast distrustful glances over her shoulder toward the bubbling springs.

"What do you mean, *bad place?*" Mother asked.

Mrs. Meyers looked shocked. "One has just to smell those vile vapors. Why, the foul odors alone betray their origin. It's a place of unnatural doings. Mark my words, we're in a bad place, for sure, and I ain't restin' easy until we're on our way."

My first temptation was to laugh at the woman's superstitions. She peered at the rising mist as if Lucifer himself would step through its curtain to join us. Then I saw how earnest she was, and my heart softened. "I have read of such places, Mrs. Meyers. It has to do with the earth's inner heat. Oftentimes, such hot waters are used for medicinal cures."

I could see the hesitancy in her face. Medicinal benefits were not easily given up. But those hard-earned Biblical lessons, warning of the devil's lair, proved more powerful than any promise of mortal comforts. She would not be tempted.

"You're such an innocent, child. I know it's easy to be misled through too much book-learning," she said with renewed vigor. "But true is true. This ain't a good place."

Mother offered Mrs. Meyers a cup of coffee, resting a hand on her arm to reassure her. "God will watch over us," Mother said. "Try to enjoy our reprieve from the dusty trail. You must admit that at least catching up on our wash has been a good thing."

Mrs. Meyers did not look as if she agreed one bit, but she refrained from further comment, sipped her coffee and changed the subject.

After she left, Mother and I rigged a blanket behind our wagon for the luxury of a sponge bath. Oh, the wonder of having an unlimited supply of boiling hot water. Mother even teased about our brazen indulgences so near Mrs. Meyers's watchful guard. I could hardly believe the trouble-free aura that had settled over this day, and I embraced the moment. Like a child sneaking candy before dinner, I furtively smuggled pails of hot water past the Meyerses' wagon to our makeshift stall. Carefully mixing it with cooled water, I waited for Mother to soap down, then poured it over her head. She shrieked when the water cascaded down her body, undergarments and all.

"Shhhh," I begged. "Mrs. Meyers will hear us and we'll get a stern lecture."

"Shush, indeed. See how quiet you are, when I pour scalding water over your head."

I glanced at her, and she was smiling. She twisted her hair free of excess water and stepped from the basin.

"Here, use this to soap up while I peel off these wet things and hang them to dry for morning," she said.

When I'd been thoroughly rinsed from the second pail, Mother found a linen for me to wrap myself in. Shedding the grime of the trail was a real blessing. It was truly a wonderful evening.

I rubbed my skin vigorously in the night air, but when I brought the towel up to cover my hair, I bumped our temporary partition. The nail holding the blanket to the tree popped out just as voices neared our wagon. Midair, Mother caught at the rope, holding the blanket up while the men passed by, mercifully oblivious of the near-disaster.

"Marjory! Be careful," she said, in a hushed voice. "You almost exposed our heathenish bathing in the devil's waters." I heard a hint of laughter while she struggled with the blanket.

"More than that was nearly exposed," I said.

She laughed, and her laughter brought back the loving times I'd all but forgotten. We secured the blankets again, and I began rubbing my hair dry.

"Mother, do you remember my thirteenth birthday?"

She thought for a moment, then her eyes lit with shared memories. Plunking herself down on an overturned bucket, she leaned on her elbows, hugging the bundle of clothes she'd gathered.

"You mean the one Grandmother Turner planned?"

I shuddered. "Yes, that one." The shiver wasn't entirely exaggerated. That year Grandmother had ordered a dress for my party; an infantile dress so dreadful that I would have been unable to face anyone my age ever again.

"I could hardly forget," Mother responded. "You came to the table like someone awaiting execution."

"I *was* — a social execution. Until you determined to rescue me, that is." We both laughed. But it hadn't been funny back then. After our family dinner, my friends were due to help me celebrate. It was then Mother had executed my escape, as only she could have.

"I remember, all right. You were so incensed," she said, smiling at the memory.

"No wonder," I replied indignantly. "I hadn't eaten a bite. I could do nothing but anticipate my ruin. And then, as I saw it, you pounded the last nail into my coffin."

We had almost finished our meal, when Mother left me speechless with her abrupt accusation.

"Marjory!" she had exclaimed. "You have spilled on your new dress. How shamefully careless of you."

It wasn't that I would not have been happy to ravage it entirely. However mere moments before facing sure humiliation before my peers, Mother had suddenly jumped up to accuse me of something I hadn't done. It was too much. And before I could even muster a defense, she pointed to an imaginary stain, seconds before a puddle of lukewarm tea settled in my lap.

"To be honest, I thought it was an act of pure genius," Mother said.

"Well, it certainly took care of that dress."

Mother's pleasure was almost, but not quite, hidden by the pale moonlight as it spilled over the top of our partition. We lingered over our own thoughts for some minutes, before I noticed that she had sobered. She began fingering the laundry in her lap.

"It's been awhile since we've shared some good times, hasn't it, Marjory?"

"Yes," I said. "I guess it has."

"I'm sorry for that." Her voice turned soft and quiet. "I seem to have lost my sense of humor."

With a troubled look that tore at my heart, she folded the garments and rested her arms on top of the pile. "I wish I knew why. Snapping at everyone because I feel poorly only makes it worse. I wish things were different."

I wanted to say something, anything, but I couldn't. I just sat there, immobile.

"I'll try to do better, Marjory." She sighed. "I'd like to live this whole last year over."

I was not sure if Mother's thoughts had turned to Papa or not. Certainly he never struggled with regrets. He brushed them aside and simply started over. The problem for Mother was that she didn't have that option out here — a fact that, for the first time, captured my attention. *She didn't have any options.*

The next morning Mother woke in as good a humor as she'd been in the night before. She said not one word about bad dreams or suffering from a restless sleep. Yet I had heard her tossing about during the night. Sometimes she woke me by crying out fitfully, but she never responded to my whispered concerns. I welcomed her casual cheerfulness, yet I felt uneasy. Even with yesterday's rest and her general improvement, I began to wonder about her complete turn-about in attitude. There was little reason this morning for such a carefree mood, since the day promised nothing more than continued miles of dry, hot dust. And our prospects were as uncertain as ever.

"Did you sleep well, Mother?" I asked, wanting to reassure myself.

"Yes, quite." She turned to catch my brother on his way to play. "Danny! Take those pails of water over to the horses before they get the sulks and we have to put you into harness. And stay nearby. We'll soon be ready to leave."

Hurriedly we stowed the last of our things away, and I reminded myself I had decided to give Mother time before confronting her.

We were the sixth wagon to pull onto the trail, with the morning already bright and warm. The landscape allowed our wagons to spread out three, even four, across.

Just before the sun came on hard overhead, Tad rode up and joined me on the box. I was glad for his company.

"How did you get away from driving your father's rig?" I asked. Thinking of Walter, I couldn't resist reminding Tad of his responsibilities, even though I was glad to see him.

"I told Walter that I'd join the hunting party to search for game."

"You don't plan on shooting off any bullets near our wagon?" I asked, feigning horror.

"Not so you'd notice. I'm just waiting around. They're not ready to head out, yet." He flashed me a big grin. "So, I came over to keep you from pining away from sheer boredom."

"I am indeed grateful."

"So you should be." He leaned back, heaving a great sigh. "At least, neither of us will be bored for long. The most challenging part of our trip is still to come."

"Oh?"

"Absolutely. There are still the Blue Mountains and the Columbia River. Both are said to be much more exciting than anything we've been through so far."

I couldn't hide my irritation. "Oh, Tad! This is hardly a game of adventure," I scolded. "Surely this trip has claimed enough losses already."

His expression sobered. "I'm sorry. Of course it has. Especially for you. I didn't mean to be such a dunce. And things will be better once we get to the Oregon. Why, I hear the land is so lush that there's hardly time to weed before you must harvest your crop."

"Now that does sound fortunate." I couldn't help but relent a little.

"Well, it should please Walter no end." He glanced my way, looking repentant. "I'm sorry. There I go. Complaining again. It's just that Walter has me on edge. All I'm asking for is a month or so before settling into the store. Is that such a big sacrifice?"

"I don't know," I answered, remembering their earlier quarrel. "Perhaps he's tired of postponements."

Tad shot me an angry look. "Oh? Has he said something to you?"

"Of course not."

"Well, it's a little hard to tell with him

lately. When we left the States, he was grouchy as a bear with a burr under his tail. I thought sure he was soured on all women for good. Not that he'd ever admit it, but he was pretty disappointed back home. But lately . . . Well, since meeting you, who knows? One minute he seems to admire your persistence, the next he thinks you're crazy . . ."

His face turned bright red, as his hasty words caught up with him. "I . . . ah, I mean . . ."

His words drained what hope I harbored, and I felt foolish for presuming Walter's compliments meant as much to him as they had to me. Pride came to my rescue as I struggled to sound casual. "It sounds as if he's had a rough time." Although my self-esteem had suffered a blow, I couldn't resist knowing more. "I can't fault him for being impatient to get on with his life. It must have been someone very special to disappoint a man like Walter."

"Oh, she was that, all right. She had a fragile look to her, yet tall and graceful, like a thoroughbred, with long, silky, almost black hair."

Tad's relief at the shift in conversation fueled his enthusiasm. Walter's beloved had been blessed with warm brown eyes that could melt stone, if Tad was to be believed. Apparently she was a paragon of beauty. The more he talked, the lower my spirits slipped. Obviously, I was not of a cut to interest Walter, even if such a match had been likely.

Tad's preoccupation with Walter's ex-fiancée was innocent enough. He was simply bored — as well as dead to all sensibilities. "Tad, what is the game that you hope to bag?" I asked, in desperation to change the subject.

Without hesitation, he reversed topics and fondly patted his rifle. "My first hope would be a grizzly." His face was quite serious. "Trouble is, they keep hiding behind the jackrabbits."

I focused on a picture of Tad stalking a cagey rabbit. "Surely they can still be a challenge."

"True. And I have a great plan. I intend to recite one of Walter's lectures on responsibility. Likely before I can finish, rabbits from miles around will rush me, snatch my gun away, and bash it over their own heads."

"Tad. You are impossible! It's a wonder your brother hasn't boxed your ears years ago. No doubt, though, you have managed to tease him out of it."

"He does say I can talk a cornered wolf into fetching my gun for me. However, no matter how hard I try, I can't drag a smile from Walter, much less ask for the slightest favor, *unlike some nameless person* I happen to be seated next to."

"Me? Aside from his assistance on the trail, a request made by the Captain, may I remind you, I have not asked for the smallest favor. Nor would I dream of doing such a thing."

"I didn't say you did. I merely have observed that you seem to have some influence over him, because, in spite of his grouchiness, he looks exactly like the mutt hound that just fetched two ducks from one shot every time he heads over here. And I must say that's a most sorrowful sight to see in a grown man."

I burst out laughing in an explosion of conflicting emotions. Tad kept shifting the ground on which I built my reality. But, if it were true . . . *No! No more wishful thinking!*

Would I never, ever learn?

Thirteen

September 12, 1847
Dear Friend,

Only half a day from the springs, and again we must stop for repairs. More than ever I feel inclined to hurry on our way, yet delay seems to pile upon delay. To make matters worse, a cool head could have avoided our latest trouble.

We were headed down a butte when the last wagon came to disaster as one of the oxen slid on the loose shale slope and went down on its knees. The heavy wagon could not be stopped by its teammate and the great burden behind them caused the fallen ox to be dragged forward by its yoke over layers of sharp rocks. The wagon's owner, greatly overset by the accident, ran to the poor suffering beast and shot it.

That was not the thing to do, however. The other teams, exhausted, thirsty, some with bloodied feet, panicked and stampeded. You would never think such pitiful teams could go so fast. Because of the lay of the land, we were spread out some, and most children were safely in the wagons. By God's own mercy no one was killed, save the ox. There were casualties, however. Two broken wheels, one axle and three lame animals.

Since then, I see worried faces all around me, casting their eyes to the west. In spite of this miserable heat, we all are aware that snow lurks ahead for those who fall too far behind.

Thank God, Walter had been driving during the stampede. We were already halfway down the butte, but it still took a great effort not to allow the horses to spill us over. For a terrifying few moments, I thought Walter would never get them reined in, but slowly he brought them to a stop.

Repairs were well under way by supper. The men planned to work into the night. Danny watched Walter and the others, while I organized our remaining supplies to gain more space inside the wagon. Mother even had time to catch up on the mending.

After settling Jamie and Sarie down, I joined Mother. She bent over one of Danny's socks she was mending by the flickering firelight. I watched her needle glide smoothly in, out, up, over and felt its restful rhythm. Her silence added to a sense of contentment between us.

"You know," Mother said, finally pausing to watch the glowing coals, "your father and I met at an evening bonfire."

"Really?"

"Yes. Our pastor held a big potato roast on an All Hallow's Eve night," she explained. "He invited all of the young people in our community. We had a Bible study outside by the campfire, and then we talked and sang. We even told ghost stories . . . after Pastor left to join the adults for coffee."

"Hadn't you ever met Papa before that?"

"No. My parents had just moved from New England and I didn't know a soul. I sat on a stump near the fire, feeling like a toad on a log."

"Why? Didn't anyone talk to you?"

"The girls were too busy trying to outswoon each other, as the gentlemen's tall tales progressed from ghostly to ghastly."

"How awful for you."

"It was, a bit. But then your father introduced himself. I was shy with strangers, so he started telling me outlandish tales of supernatural doings, all the time sitting there,

199

both daring and encouraging a reaction from me." She smiled softly. "At last I gave him such a set-down, the others took up my cause and joined in the fun."

"Papa must have felt pretty sheepish."

"Not at all. He and I had a lovely evening."

By the waning glow of our campfire, I saw a softness come into her eyes that I had never before witnessed. She stared into the fire, apparently reliving that long-ago moment.

"Your father was my first true friend," she said. Her longing sigh drifted into the night.

We lapsed into a comfortable silence. It occurred to me that I had never thought of my parents as young people with concerns like my own. The notion gave me an odd feeling, odd but nice. Kind of warm. I didn't feel so lonely.

Mother sat absently winding her threads. When I looked over at her, she gathered the mending she'd finished, then stood and covered a yawn. "Perhaps you'd better check on Danny, Marjory. I'm done in for the night."

"All right. Have a good rest; we'll be quiet when we come in."

"Thanks, Marjory." She started for the wagon, but turned back. "Marjory?"

"Yes?"

"I just . . . I just wanted to thank you again for being so helpful." She fingered the wicker sewing basket in her hands. "You're a good daughter."

She looked up, eyes brimming with tears she wouldn't let fall. I thought of that moment I'd seen her with unshed tears in her eyes after Papa had died. I'd suspected her struggle had been for control of the situation. More likely, I realized now, it had been a quiet struggle just to hang on.

The play of light and darkness from our campfire danced about her face and her dress and reminded me of the bonfire she'd spoken of earlier. She stood, holding her basket close, still hanging on. She'd once had a tall, dark-haired youth with a teasing smile to relieve her loneliness. Now there was only me. My throat closed with the ache of wanting to help her. "Mother . . ."

Her hand lifted in a gesture meant to silence me. "Please, let me say it now. I haven't felt myself for quite sometime . . . until these past few days. At least, I almost feel like my old self. And I want to tell you how proud of you I am."

She set the basket aside, walked up to me and took my face between her hands. Her voice cracked as she continued. "I know your father would be proud, too. Very proud."

Oh, how I wanted to take the pain from her eyes as she looked at me. How could I tell her it was all right? That we would make our new life work? Together. I tried to speak. I tried, but couldn't.

She kissed my forehead. She knew. Somehow she knew we both wanted this chance for a new beginning.

"Good night," she said as she stood back.

Not until she smiled could I force the ragged sound of my voice past my throat. "Good night, Mother."

Once more Mother woke in fine humor. Her movements weren't as quick as they had been, but the whole train was getting worn down. By mid-morning, however, I noticed that she was massaging her forehead. She quietly curtailed her activities after we'd nooned. I watched her make a game of lying down with Sarie to get a nap. By dinner, Mother only pretended to eat. I hurried to help her clean away the dishes.

"You didn't seem too hungry," I said.

"Yes, I . . ." She stopped, frowned then turned to me with a sheepish smile. "I'm not really sparing you anything, am I? To be honest, my headache is back."

She stacked the last tin and turned to face me. Her eyes were tired, even pained, yet the warmth lingered, making my heart open to her.

"I've so enjoyed these past few days with you and the children. I hate even admitting that I feel poorly again. But I do see now that denying it isn't doing you a favor." She made a gesture to push back a strand of hair, as she caught a stray tear that had slid halfway down her cheek.

If only she could tell me about the baby, I thought.

"Be patient with me a little longer, Marjory."

This time I refused to remain tongue-tied. I took her hand up in mine, squeezing tight, searching her face. "Oh, Mother. I will do whatever you ask of me. Just trust me, please."

"I do. Really, I do. It's just that . . . that I'm not sure of myself right now. I'm used to keeping my own counsel, but things are so different now. And I am trying to do what's best."

Mother gave me a quick hug.

"Good night, dear."

She turned and climbed into the wagon. I wanted so badly to protect her, to make everything right for her. But the feeling grew that it wouldn't be as easy as I'd hoped, and I was suddenly terribly afraid.

When Mother said prayers with the children as she settled them in, I decided to ask Mrs. Meyers to take Sarie and Jamie tomorrow morning. Maybe if Mother got more rest, she'd feel better again. I could imagine how difficult it was for her now, being with child while on the trail. I didn't want her to expend any more energy than was necessary.

I stoked the fire and turned toward the Meyerses' wagon.

"Hello," I called.

"Why, Marjory." Mrs. Meyers responded with evident pleasure.

They both seemed cheerful and glad for company. Mr. Meyers smiled, nodded a greeting and excused himself. Mrs. Meyers patted a place next to her.

"Do come and sit. How's your ma?"

"Fine," I said as Mr. Meyers walked toward the back of the wagon. "At least she has been. That's what I came to see you about. I want Mother to rest a little more tomorrow. Could you watch the children?"

Mrs. Meyers's instant grin chased the wrinkles from her cheeks. "Of course I can. Be pleased as punch. Didn't I say anytime?" She shot a look of triumph toward Mr. Meyers, as if to say *see*, as he sat near the wheel, working on some leather straps.

"Did ya hear, Mr. Meyers? They would like us to watch the children tomorrow. I said we'd be more than happy to. Isn't that right?" she called to her husband.

He looked up from mending some leather straps and nodded. "I'd say that's true 'nuff."

I smiled over at him, eager to reassure him of our gratitude for all they had done.

Mrs. Meyers returned to our camp with me. Mother had bedded the children down by the time we joined her for coffee. She sat huddled over her coffee while Mrs. Meyers rambled on in high spirits.

"That young man you got driving for you sure can handle a team, can't he? Saw him during the stampede while we was a'flyin' downhill, right behind you." She shook her head in wonder, and took another sip of hot coffee. "I was plumb glad he could, too, as we was too close to avoid trouble. We're not likely to forget that thrill for a spell."

"I guess not," I said. To change the subject, I poked at the fire and said, "Mother? More coffee?" Harping on near-accidents would do little to help Mother.

"No," Mother replied. "Not for me." Her thoughts seemed to be elsewhere.

"I suspect you've noticed what a fine-looking man he is." Mrs. Meyers leaned forward for a coffee refill. "My mister and me couldn't help seeing how he looks at you, Marjory. Of course, I hear a girl has quite a choice out West. Not many single women, I'm told."

My cheeks burned as I returned the pot to the coals. Yet another subject to avoid, I thought, wishing I hadn't invited Mrs. Meyers to our camp.

"I was talking to his ma the other day," Mrs. Meyers continued. "They're going to open a mercantile. Imagine. They must be quite well off. But they're still just as regular as any I've met."

She turned to Mother. "Seems to be a fine family, don't ya think, Mrs. Turner?"

"What? Oh, yes, I'm sure."

"Yes, indeed. Now that Tad . . . well, he's a one, you know. Always out for fun. Nice boy, but not too dependable, I'd guess. Scared his brother half out of his wits when we crossed the Green, I heard. My mister says the older one almost had to go in after the boy."

"Tad made shore all by himself," I said, not knowing exactly why I felt called to defend him.

"True enough. But he is flighty. I guess I like the older one better because of him coverin' for Mr. Meyers. The night that my poor husband wasn't feeling too perky and overslept his watch. When he didn't relieve the older Wilkins boy, that young man took on my mister's watch without reporting him to the Captain. No one takes kindly to extra duty, or even worse, to finding the animals left unguarded. But Mr. Wilkins didn't say a word. Wouldn't accept nothin' for the extra duty, neither."

I felt pride in Walter's actions, but tried to hide it. "I suppose we all make an effort to help when we can."

Mrs. Meyers swallowed the last of her coffee and set the tin down. "Some do and some don't," she said. "Want to thank you for the coffee, but I'm tired and looks to me as if you're a bit worn too."

I followed her glance and saw the truth of her observation. Mother did look weary.

After Mrs. Meyers left, I told Mother I'd see to Danny while she finished her cup. I settled him down and started back to stow our things for the night when I saw Mother near the fire, folding a blanket. She'd given the quilt a firm shake, and I expected to see her flip it once more before folding it up. Instead, she stood frozen, staring dead ahead, with the top of the blanket gripped in her hands, the rest dangling in the dirt about her feet. Her eyes were fixed in the direction of the grazing cattle. At first I thought she saw something that worried her. Not a muscle moved. She just stared into the night.

I waited, too, half-afraid of what she might have seen. But after a full minute, I started to worry about her fascination with whatever held her attention. Anxious and even irritated, I wanted her to finish with the blanket. I stood there, holding my breath, determined to outwait her. At last, she gave her wrists another shake as if there'd been no interruption, and bent to fold the cover several times, finishing the task as she walked back to the wagon.

"What did you see?" I asked.

"See? What was I supposed to see?" Her voice sounded flat, uninterested.

"I just wondered what you were staring at out there?"

"I'm too tired to waste time staring," she said, sounding completely indifferent to my concerns. "Are you coming?" She climbed into the wagon without waiting for an answer.

Our exchange troubled me, but I was too tired to pursue it. I didn't lie awake long, but as I drifted off, I couldn't avoid a terrible uneasiness worming its way into my mind.

We had coffee, hard bread and fried mush with dried raisins for breakfast the next morning. Once more, Mother took sick just after the dishes were cleared away. Afterward, she didn't want to talk about anything, saying she'd do better to sleep while she could.

Danny wanted to walk with some boys up ahead. When Mrs. Meyers came for the children, there was nothing to do but mount the box and begin another day.

Still, Mother said nothing about the new baby.

Fourteen

September 17, 1847
Dear Friend,
Almost a week since my last entry, but I'm too tired and poor-spirited to manage much tonight. The endless days of driving through this hot, dusty country-side are tedious, but worry over Mother wears on me more. She tries hard to maintain an even temperament and good humor, but it is an obvious effort.

She now makes light of her illness to the children. "Mama's head is cranky," she tells them when she has to lie down. Or, after a hurried exit, she'll grin at Danny, saying, "My tummy is being cantankerous again." He may worry, but I see her tone reassures him some, so I, too, adopt a lighter attitude around the children.

However, this gives me an even greater desire to hurry on. We must get to the Oregon soon, so Mother can regain her strength in time for the baby's arrival, for I fear she will not fully recover until we are settled.

She still does not mention the baby.

Except for one evening of drenching rain, we have had no relief from the sun. It baked the dry land almost to the point of igniting the sagebrush. Yet the nights are cold, and we welcome evening campfires.

We pulled out earlier today, and Walter pointed out the Sawtooth Mountains in the distance. I was not convinced the change in scenery was worth the effort of climbing them, but for the moment I looked forward to a change, any change. Even more important, the mountains signaled a near end to our journey.

At day's end, Jamie and Sarie had fallen asleep, and Danny, Mother and I sat near our fire. Danny practiced shooting marbles while Mother and I finished our coffee. After draining her cup, she stored it away, and returned from the wagon with a hairbrush.

"Marjory, remove your ribbon and let me brush your hair," she said. "It'll relax us both."

Surprised, I slipped the ribbon off. Mother sat cross-legged behind me, lifting a handful of hair, and began working out the dust-caked snarls. Once the tangles were gone, my muscles began to relax with each long, hypnotic stroke of the brush. It was heaven, pure heaven.

After some minutes, she gathered my hair in her hands and fanned it out across my back. I opened my eyes and turned to see if she'd tired herself. "Ready to turn in?"

She smiled and nodded. "No. As a matter of fact, I've been waiting up for him."

I followed her direction and saw Walter walking toward us. For a moment I stared, wondering why she'd been expecting him. Then I remembered my hair, flying loose, without even a ribbon. Feeling as though caught in a state of undress, or worse, looking like an infant, I quickly lifted the thin shawl from my shoulders and draped it over my head.

"Sorry to be so late, Mrs. Turner."

"Please don't be. I appreciate your returning this evening. If you'll give me a moment, I'll be right back."

She rose and called to Danny. "It's time to turn in, Danny. Come with me."

Danny grumbled at having to go in just when Walter had come, but he followed Mother back to the wagon. Unexpectedly alone with Walter, I felt ill at ease with my hair in such a state, and tied my scarf securely.

"What did Mother want to see you about?" I asked.

"I'm afraid I'm in the dark, as to that. She

just asked me to come after the children's bedtime."

Before I could wonder at that remarkable invitation, I saw Mother return from the wagon, holding a small bundle.

Walter rose to his feet as she approached, but was waved back down.

"Ever since Mr. Turner passed on, I've been worried about this."

She unwrapped a holster and gun that I'd never seen before. "Where did that come from?" I asked.

"Your father thought it would be an absolute necessity once we were out on the frontier. Hating guns the way I do, I convinced him to pack it away until then. I understood the need for a rifle, but not the pistol." She turned to Walter. "I don't want the children to ever come by it accidentally. In appreciation for all you've done for us, I'd like you to take this."

Walter slid the pistol from its holster, holding the shiny steel up to the light of our fire. After a few minutes' examination, he returned it to the holster and offered it back to Mother. "This is a very fine weapon. You should keep it. I'm sure you could sell it, maybe at the next fort."

"Maybe. But I don't like guns, and I don't want them around my children." Mother's tone brooked no argument. "Besides, it gives me pleasure to repay even a little of your kindness."

She took a cup from her apron pocket, bent to pour coffee and offered it to Walter. I noticed she'd given him little opportunity to refuse.

"Marjory and I are very grateful to you for your help. And it's been good for her to have someone to talk to during the journey."

She turned, refilling my cup before I could speak. Then she set the pot down and stoked the fire with our last sticks.

"I hope you'll excuse me. I want to be sure Danny's down, and I'm tired myself. But do stay, Mr. Wilkins. Keep Marjory company while you finish your coffee." Turning to leave, she bade us goodnight over her shoulder.

If I'd been surprised earlier, I was downright baffled now. She had left Walter no choice but to visit with me. Yet she knew evening hours were a luxury not easily given over to idle socializing. There were always harnesses, wagons, even boots to mend and the animals to tend, leaving little time for relaxation. Walter held his cup, making no move to drink.

"That was very generous of your mother. To give me the gun, I mean," he added.

214

I didn't know how to respond, so I stared into the fire, hating the way Mother had trapped him.

He settled his legs more comfortably, turning toward me.

"I was talking to Danny today. He says your mother has been in pretty high spirits lately."

"Her spirits are better," I said. "She's making a real effort, and so am I. I'd developed some hard feelings earlier, but lately we've gotten to understand each other. It has been quite wonderful. I'd forgotten how much fun we could have together." As I stopped for breath, I felt my face heat. His manner was too inviting. My every thought seemed to pour out like heavy cream from an overturned pitcher. Walter smiled. The reflection of the fire caught his eyes.

"That's good," he said. "I'm really glad for you. If anyone deserves better times, it's you."

My cheeks burned hotter. I couldn't think of a thing to say.

"But is she feeling any better? I see Mrs. Meyers takes the children in her wagon quite often lately. If you prefer, I can drive whenever your mother needs your help."

"Thank you. But she rests better this way, and for now I think it's best." I looked in the direction of the mountains. "I fear you'll be taking over the driving soon enough."

"Those?" He followed my glance. "We don't have to worry about the Sawtooths. We'll pass well south of them. And it'll be a good week or more before we hit the Blue Mountains."

"Oh." I let the silence settle between us. The distant yelp of a coyote drifted across the whispering sage. Walter sipped his coffee and sighed thoughtfully.

"But the Blues will come soon enough. It's been a long haul. Any regrets yet?" He immediately raised a hand to stop my answer. "I know, you weren't much for society anyway. Wonder if you'll feel that way after the reality of frontier life settles in." He frowned, crumbling a little crust of dirt in his hands. He let it fall between knees that supported his elbows.

"I don't think I'm quite as fainthearted as you persist in thinking," I said crossly. "I told you, I'm not afraid of hard work."

"I'm not criticizing, believe me." With a restless energy, he shoved a half-burned stick into the middle of the fire. "It's no sin to dread losing your looks, to dread ending up old and tired before your time. It's not an easy life."

"Really."

"You can't just buy what you need. There's no sending someone to shop for winter preserves, or even soap, if you're sitting in the middle of a land grant."

"It's quite true that my father's family purchases their needs or relies on their day help for such things, but Mother was quick to insist we both learn the art of preserving and other homemaking necessities, once she realized Papa was determined to come West. Believe me, women are much more practical than men appreciate."

A smile softened the sting of his inquisition. "You just might be right about that. I humbly give way to your valid rebuke and salute your initiative. I do believe you are as prepared as any woman a man could hope to encounter."

I took pride in that admission, but once again I thought we were on subjects best left alone. What was the point?

Just then a large spark exploded. I jerked back. At the same instant Walter jumped up, snatched my shawl and flung it down. With his other hand, he grabbed a hunk of my hair.

"What —" I gasped. I tried to get to my feet, but he shoved me back, holding my hair and swatting at it with his free hand. The smell of burning wool hit me as I tried to push him away so I could stand.

"Hold still!" His voice was sharp, anxious. He kept slapping at my hair. "Your shawl. The spark . . . it's burnt your hair."

He brushed away the clinging cinders. The odor of singed hair filled my nose, and I instinctively reached up to feel for damage. My fingers covered his hand. At my touch, he stilled. He had bent down on one knee to check my hair, just as I looked up.

Our gazes met, and held. His lips were but a whisper away and yet I was unable to speak. Awareness danced amid the night's stirrings, inviting thoughts that the light of day would wear away. We were rescued from foolish dreams by the dying fire casting out a burning ember that flared, popped, then fizzled near our feet.

He stepped back.

"It's getting late, Marjory. Better go in to your mother."

I hesitated as he stood near the sputtering fire pit, then I turned and climbed into the wagon. As I sank onto my blanket, I heard the soft shower of dirt being poured over the coals. Silently, I undressed and bedded down. The cool night air chased the last remnants of the evening's campfire away.

I didn't have occasion to visit with Walter for several days, but when we forded the

Boise River, he drove again. He teased with Danny, as always, spoke reassurances to Mother and took the reins from me much the same as before.

His casual manner made it easier for me to maintain my composure. I had concerns enough to deal with, since the last few days reinforced my conviction that Mother was not improving as I'd hoped. Each day I noticed things about her that concerned me. I did not know what to do, so on the evening before we were to reach Fort Boise, I went to the Meyerses' wagon. As I neared the fire, Mrs. Meyers looked up from her mending. I approached hesitantly. "I'm worried about Mother, Mrs. Meyers."

She motioned for me to join her. "What's wrong, my dear?" she asked, while shaking a dried gourd into the toe of another sock. After securing the hole over her darning shell, she poked a needle behind the frayed yarn and made her repairs. I watched the gaping hole slowly surrender to a network of new yarn. I felt a little bit like that hole. One after another, worries wove around me until I felt that I, too, might disappear.

When I realized the needle had paused, I found Mrs. Meyers watching me, concern in her eyes.

"Speak up, child. You're worryin' me."

"Sorry. I'm not quite sure what to say. For a while, Mother really seemed so much better. We even had fun together. Then the headaches returned and now . . . well, it's just a lot of little things. Sometimes she seems so sad. She often stares off into space, but when I say something, she gets confused.

"Then, today during our noon stop, Danny came running to get me. He said Mother was acting odd and I should come. He was very upset. But when I got there, Mother had just put away the last of the tins. She was a little vague, but otherwise she seemed all right."

"What did Danny say had frightened him so?"

"I asked him later. He said that he'd come back to the wagon and found Mother muttering to herself while she kept wiping out the same tin with sand."

Mrs. Meyers smiled.

"Why, land sakes, child. I've let off a little steam myself, muttering away while I took out my frustration on a poor plate. Maybe he just ain't come across your ma's frustrations before."

I wanted to share her relief, but I couldn't. "But Danny said she kept rubbing the plate over and over, long after it was clean. And when he tried to talk to her, it was as if she couldn't hear him. As if she didn't even know he was there. She really scared him."

Mrs. Meyers's hands lay still in her lap as she spent some minutes thinking. "You know, Marjory, so much has happened to your ma. Being uprooted to come on this trip. Then your pa dying. Now the baby. There's a possibility she's a little melancholic."

Her suggestion came as a relief. Melancholy. Surely, that couldn't be too serious. "What should I do?" I asked.

"Your ma is a strong woman. Just give her things to look forward to. Reassure her. Tell her everything's working out for the best. Get her to rest often, and talk of happy times." Mrs. Meyers resumed her sewing. "I think it will pass. She just needs lots of rest, healthy encouragement and time. You'll see."

I felt some better and stood, saying I should get back to our wagon.

"Marjory, you might see if there is a medical man at Fort Boise," she added, looking up. "He might have something to lift your ma's spirits and give her energy."

"Thank you, I'll look into it."

"Good. If she balks, tell her I want to see

someone, too, and we can go together."

The next day, I talked to Mother. She had joined me on the box after we left our nooning spot. Her spirits seemed a little better again.

I approached her cautiously. "Mother, I don't mean to pry, but I am worried about you." She didn't say anything at once. I kept my eyes down, praying she wouldn't get upset, but I could see her hands twisting in her skirt.

"Sorry for worrying you," she said at last. Her hands clenched with determination.

"Mother, I didn't mean . . ."

"I know," she said, interrupting me. "I mentioned earlier that it's time for the truth between us. You see, sometimes I worry, too. Ever so often, I feel a bit odd. I don't know how to describe it. Even before leaving home, I felt a dread growing inside me. Not of the trip, so much, but of something . . . But I couldn't account for my feelings. And now, there are other things that worry me."

I looked over at her. "What things?"

"I can't explain them." She sighed. "Sometimes a queer feeling comes over me."

"Queer?"

"Yes. Sometimes objects can appear distant, and yet they still look too large. It's hard to explain. It's like a dream, and yet I know I'm awake and where I am. But I also have a sensation of everything being far, far off." She laughed nervously. "I guess that sounds crazy, doesn't it?"

"No. Of course not." I hoped my reassurance sounded more positive than it felt. Perhaps melancholy was taking too great a toll on her. I thought it could only help if she would share her feelings about the baby. "But it does sound as if you're under a strain," I continued. "That certainly is understandable, under the circumstances."

"Maybe." Mother stared at the horizon. "Have you heard what the next fort is like?" she asked. "Is it military?"

"It's another British outpost, the Hudson's Bay Company. But, I hear it's quite nice."

"I wonder if they have a medical man in their fort?"

"Very likely. Mrs. Meyers says she hopes to find one there," I snatched at the opening to encourage a visit.

"If I saw someone, it would be best for you to accompany me." She patted my hand, giving me a tired smile. "Remember? I'm turning a new page. We're in this together." With that, she climbed into the back, saying she'd grab a nap with the little ones.

Later that evening, we pushed forward — on into the growing dusk, knowing Fort Boise lay just ahead. As the sun hovered near the dry, barren horizon, I saw the outline of adobe walls, and the rise of a two- or three-story tower at one corner.

Tomorrow, I thought with great relief, I would find Mother a doctor, even if he came with feathers and a painted body, howling great chants and vigorously shaking rattling gourds about our heads.

Fifteen

September 18, 1847
Dear Friend,
It was late by the time we got the children bedded down after reaching the fort. Mother went to sleep soon after, exhausted. But I am wide awake tonight. We were told there is a doctor here, and Walter agreed to find him first thing tomorrow to ask if he'll see Mother. They say we are lucky to find him back at the fort this early in the year. Looking around, I can't imagine where else he would be.

He seems to have a good reputation, and that's all I care about. For the first time in weeks, I feel hopeful.

At last Walter returned and helped Mother from the wagon. "It's all set. The doctor's not military, but a civilian who has settled in this area for his health. Apparently he took to trapping in the nearby mountains because it kept him in the fresh air and provided enough money to live on out here," Walter said, as he escorted us to the doctor's temporary quarters.

"What's he like?" I asked.

"Seems a nice fellow. He's even been schooled somewhere back in England, where he came from. The fort commander puts a lot of store in him."

As we approached a small outbuilding, I saw Mother's hand clenching and unclenching within the folds of her skirt.

We entered the only door, finding several drab blankets screening off one end of the room. The room's stark mustiness confronted us. Stacks of boxes stood in one corner, while a rickety desk and three chairs lined the near wall. A cabinet with glass doors held dusty cartons of rifle cartridges, a tin marked "tobacco," an assortment of bottles and a large roll of cotton. The bottles and cotton were the only items not entombed by dust. A young, fair-haired man stepped from behind the curtain as Walter closed the door.

"Come in. Come in," he said cheerily. His manner was positive and reassuring. "You must be Mrs. Turner. I'm Dr. Dunn."

As he walked forward, he moved a stack of papers off a chair before extending his hand. "Sorry for the clutter. They let me use this storage room for seeing to patients when I come in to trade," he said, nodding toward the stacks of boxes. "Before fall sets in, I head for the fort and put out my shingle for the winter."

His lively blue eyes and warm smile encouraged confidence. The doctor gave Walter a friendly but dismissive nod.

"I have an errand to run for the Captain," Walter said, snatching at the chance to leave. "But I'll return in time to escort you back to the train."

"Please, ladies, do have a seat," said Dr. Dunn.

He pulled a chair for Mother alongside his desk and offered me another, before sitting down to face her.

"This must be difficult for you, Mrs. Turner. Please know that I am at your service. I understand this is your daughter." His warm smile swept over me, acknowledging my presence, before returning his full attention to Mother. "How many other children have you?"

"Three living. One died of measles ten years ago."

"And I understand you are a widow?"

Mother started. It must have been the first time that she'd been so addressed.

"Yes. My husband . . . met with an accident and was killed six weeks ago."

"I'm very sorry to hear that, Mrs. Turner." The doctor's voice managed to convey sympathy, but he quickly moved on. "I understand you haven't been well lately."

Mother nodded. "My most trying complaint is the bouts of nausea. Not keeping my meals down makes me weak and tired."

"And when did this begin?"

She paused again. "About a month ago. Maybe a little longer."

The doctor sat back, looking at Mother, a slight frown of concentration creasing his brow. "You do not feel this is a familiar pattern? Nothing akin to what you experienced before the birth of your other children?"

Mother's eyebrows shot up. "I'm quite sure *that* is not the problem, Doctor."

"There is no chance of it being the basis of your distress?"

Mother sat forward, her eyes steady. "I am very sure. Besides, the headaches started before we even left home."

A small knot tightened in my stomach. How could this be? If it wasn't a baby, why should Mother's illness last so long? Mrs. Meyers had been so positive.

"Headaches? Do they seem associated with your nausea?"

"Yes. They bother me more often now than they did before we left home. And they seem to be getting more severe."

The doctor picked up a pencil, leaned

back in his chair, and absentmindedly rolled it back and forth between his hands. "You say your headaches have increased. When did you first start having them?"

"As I said, they were an inconvenience even before we left home."

"How long before?"

"Oh, about six months or so."

"Did you see a doctor then?"

"Once. He gave me eyeglasses. They didn't seem to help much. For the most part, my sight has improved on its own."

But headaches had been her way of avoiding issues with Papa . . . hadn't they?

Dr. Dunn frowned in concentration. "Have you any other complaints? Anything at all?"

Mother looked at me, then at her hands. She kept them still in her lap. "It's hard to explain, but I have been feeling that something is wrong. Something I don't understand."

"For instance?"

He watched her closely, still rolling that pencil back and forth, while puzzling incidents flooded my mind. The morning we left Fort Bridger. Crying spells at night. Her reaction at the falls. And the blanket . . .

"Well . . . for one thing, I have been having other problems with my vision," she said, quietly. "There are still times when I can't see clearly, and occasionally I see one thing as if it were overlapping another."

The doctor made no comment, waiting for her to continue. Mother's thumb massaged her wedding ring, twisting it around and around, back and forth. Finally she spoke.

"I have had a few . . . misty experiences . . . where I felt strangely distant from the things around me."

"Do you speak to anyone during these occasions?"

"No. I don't seem to notice anyone else around."

"Does anyone speak to you during this time?"

"I don't think so."

I bit back a comment, but the doctor noticed and turned to me. "Have you been aware of any of this?"

My heart began to thump. This wasn't what I had expected. A baby was complication enough, but now, if not a baby, what? I didn't know what to think or what to say. I couldn't put my finger on what had been bothering me most. Perhaps I made too much of little things. I decided to withhold comment, even as I heard my fears put to words. "I'm not sure," I stammered. "I've noticed Mother staring off into space once or twice. Once she didn't answer Danny, as though she didn't know he was there. But she was fine moments later."

Mother leaned forward. "Why would I do that, Doctor?"

"Do you remember the experiences she's describing?"

"No. No, I don't."

"Is there anything else that concerns you?"

Mother frowned in thought. "No. I guess not. What do you think is wrong?"

For a long moment he just sat there, deep in thought, trying to sort it out, I supposed. Then he smiled, as if he'd come to a conclusion and had remembered Mother's question at the same time.

"Well, let's see. Headaches. You leave home on a trying journey, and your headaches increase. They cause nausea, which weakens you, and you experience visual incidents. Halfway to the wilderness, you lose your husband in a tragedy." He leaned forward and patted Mother's hand. "Offhand, Mrs. Turner, I'd say that was cause enough for anyone to develop the migraine."

Migraine! I suddenly felt like laughing with relief. People didn't die or lose their senses because of migraines. *We'll be all right,* I thought. For the first time in weeks, the terrible, silent fear drained away, like water on parched earth. *It will not be as it was with Papa.*

The doctor rose and went behind the curtain, returning with a much-worn black bag. "Mr. Wilkins tells me you are traveling unaccompanied by other family members. Since you have little choice but to continue on the train, I suggest you concentrate on resting all you can. Accept the headaches and the nausea as one more trial of the road, and above all, don't let them worry you." He rummaged through his bag. "Do you ever hear any noises in your ears, a ringing perhaps? Or any other sound, for that matter?"

"No. Not really. Except when it's very quiet, I fancy a little whooshing sound, like a pump that hasn't been primed properly, but I'm not even positive about that. It could just be my imagination."

The doctor smiled. "Well, a little imagination does no harm. As I say, all you can do for now is avoid chores and rest all you can."

He looked at me purposefully. "Will that be possible?"

"Yes, of course," I said.

"Good." His smile returned. "Now,

would you mind if I took this apparatus and listened to your heart?"

Mother looked at the fancy ivory funnel in his hand. The wide end narrowed, becoming long and slender, like a horn with a much smaller funnel at the other end. She loosened the blouse of her dress and fastened her attention on a point somewhere beyond the doctor's head as he leaned forward.

I frowned, wondering if she was getting the best diagnosis. He must have seen my nervousness and misunderstood.

"It's only a stethoscope. So I can check for healthy heart and lungs. It's completely harmless."

I nodded. He scooted closer to Mother's chair, placing the large end of the funnel to Mother's chest. He paused, then moved it again, listening each time. When he finished, he put his stethoscope away, giving Mother a chance to fasten her bodice. He looked tired, and his smile didn't return until he turned back to Mother. He guided her face to the light, holding each eyelid gently as he searched her eyes.

"I am glad to report that your heart and lungs sound very hardy," he said, sitting back down. "I can bleed you to give some relief from your headaches, and I have some powders you may take with you."

He had Mother sit on the edge of the table behind the curtain. I almost fainted as Mother suffered the experience of being bled. She never showed signs of distress, even when he opened the vein on the back of her foot. I thought he'd never stop the flow of blood. By the time he was satisfied, Mother had to lie down, too faint to sit up.

"It would be best if Mr. Wilkins carried her back to the train. I'll see if he is outside."

I put Mother's stocking on over the bandage.

"Migraine. It's only the migraine," she said. Her smile spread to the corners of her mouth and danced in her eyes. "It's hard to believe . . ."

"I know," I said, almost reeling from my own sense of relief. I had picked up her shoe before I realized she'd have to forgo it for the day, at least. She laughed and said that maybe Walter would give her a piggyback ride back to the wagon, but in moving her foot, she winced.

"Don't move, Mother. Walter should be right back." After some minutes, I went to the door, feeling greatly irritated to see both men standing outside in deep conversation, while Mother lay helpless. I called out to Walter, who added a few hasty words to the doctor before hurrying over. He seemed upset by my impatience, but I noted he was quite gentle with Mother.

The doctor walked out with us. "After a rest, she will feel some relief from her headaches. When you reach your destination, be sure to have a doctor check her again. Good luck to you both."

When we reached the wagon, Walter insisted on adding extra padding from his wagon for Mother to rest on. And, as we started out, he wanted me to remain with her, even though the children rode with the Meyerses and Mother slept for hours.

Mother didn't even awaken as we crossed the Snake River for the last time. It was just as well. That river had never pleased her much anyway.

We were on our way to the last real obstacle before finally reaching the long-awaited Oregon. Relieved, I thought ahead. Whatever could possibly be as bad as what we'd already survived?

Sixteen

September 20, 1847
Dear Friend,
Mother sleeps soundly as we travel on. She is pale, but appears to rest peacefully. Perhaps the worst is behind us. I pray it is so.

Nearing dusk the second day out of the fort, we finally reached the Malheur River. Mother again slept most of the day, but I woke her for an easy meal of coffee, common cheese and hard bread.

"I feel much better," she said, finishing the last piece of cheese.

She looked as if she had recovered from the bloodletting, and even went with me to the river that was warmed by hot underwater springs. It was too late to wash clothes, but some women refused to waste an opportunity to enjoy the bath-like waters. Shamelessly, we removed our shoes and joined those who waded into the shallow stream, getting our calicos wet.

"Marjory, if Grandfather saw us now," Mother said, shaking her head. "Most undignified."

She grinned while easing herself down onto a submerged rock. Swirls of warm water covered her knees as she hovered over the warmed waters that bubbled up around one of the spring sites. "Ummm. This feels wonderful. Get Mrs. Meyers to bring the children down, Marjory. They'll love it."

After asking another lady to keep an eye on Mother, I hurried toward the wagons.

"Warm water? It just ain't natural. Are you sure your ma wants the children there?" asked Mrs. Meyers. "It's almost sundown."

"I know. That's why we must hurry. Let them come in the clothes they're wearing. A little water will do both some good." She gathered towels for our use and even offered to help, but she left no doubt that any assistance from her would be administered from dry land.

The minute the boys spotted others splashing about in the waters, they ran to Mother. I carried Sarie in. Her eyes grew wide as I knelt beside Mother. The boys' wild thrashings didn't ease Sarie's apprehension.

"Boys, don't scare your sister," Mother admonished. It was too late to save herself from their exuberance. Water already dripped from her hair and soaked her sleeves. She reached for Sarie, who eagerly lunged forward into Mother's arms, almost pushing her over backward.

After making sure she could handle Sarie, I turned my attention to the boys. Accepting their challenge of a water battle, I lead them into cooler waters away from the others. I looked back to make sure we were unlikely to disturb those enjoying the springs, when I heard both boys shout my name. Alarmed, I turned just in time to catch a face full of water.

"Gotcha!" Jamie squealed. He bobbed up and down in the water so excitedly he almost lost his footing.

"Jamie did it," Danny said, laughing. And he sprinkled his brother's head in turn.

Jamie retaliated, but did more damage to himself than to Danny. He sputtered and redirected his attention toward me. "We get Marjory, Danny. Come on, Danny."

Laughing, I advanced, holding the heel of my hand just above the water, threateningly. "Okay boys. You really want trouble?"

"Yeah. Come and get us," Danny yelled, as he scooped Jamie up under the armpits and hollered. "Kick, Jamie. Kick."

Jamie churned the river, drenching me in a wall of water. I gasped and retreated to safety. Jamie laughed so hard, he swallowed water, and Danny had to stand him up and slap him on the back, only to find himself a victim when Jamie surprised him by putting his arms to work with as much success as his thrashing legs had achieved. I thought this a good time to intervene, and I shot a healthy jet of water toward them both. The exuberance of their retaliation left me drenched. I decided to take advantage of the fading sky, so I threw up my hands in surrender. "You win," I shouted. "It was a great battle and I surrender. Now it's time to head for shore, boys. Mrs. Meyers has some towels over by where Mother is."

Upstream, I saw that Mother had gained Sarie's confidence in the water. Danny left Jamie in his wake after one last shot at me. Wiping a sheet of water from my face, I looked up to find Walter standing on the bank, making an effort to restrain outright laughter at our antics.

While I struggled over the stream's rocky bed, Jamie slipped on the slimy pebbles at the shore's edge. Walter stepped in and scooped him up. Oblivious of the soggy little body he holstered on his hip, Walter stood back and waited for me. Heartlessly amused, he watched me wade through the water, hobbling over the rocks to the shallow bank. When I could finally stand upright to grasp his extended hand, I glanced up to find him staring at me in a disconcerting way. Then a sudden awareness washed over me. My water-soaked dress — I could feel it clinging to my body. I stood before him and the world as if I were a shameless hussy. I could hear Mrs. Meyers's words of pious horror, as if she stood beside me. I wished I could disappear. She would be right, of course. But to show embarrassment would only make matters worse. I had to brazen out my situation while I eased the layers of cotton away from my legs.

Walter avoided my eyes, mumbling something about my looking half-drowned while he pulled me up the slight embankment, and shifted his attention to Jamie. "That looked like a pretty good water fight. Who won?"

"Me and Danny. I kicked hard. I super strong. Marjory gived up."

"Whoa, there, young man. I gave up because it was getting dark," I said, laughing.

"No, you not. We won. We splashed good."

"You know," Walter said, looking at me, "I think this is the first time I've seen you really enjoy yourself. You look downright happy."

Taken aback, I mumbled, "Thank you. I . . . I guess I am."

"It's nice to see." He hesitated, added in a more serious tone, "It's so nice that I intend to do whatever is necessary to see that it continues."

I glanced up, surprised, wondering about his comment, yet not wanting to make overly much of it. "Would that include gaining us first-class passage on the nearest train west?" I asked, retreating to humor.

He grinned. "Well, *almost* whatever is necessary."

We saw Mrs. Meyers hurrying toward us with a large bathing towel.

Walter turned to me and spoke quietly. "By now you must know that I think a good deal of you."

This time his words caused my heart to race. Yet I dared not take him too seriously. Mrs. Meyers's untimely approach forced a hurried response. "I . . . I'd hoped you found me pleasant company." She was almost upon us.

"Well, I do, and you are. And much more," he added in a whisper.

I watched his face as Mrs. Meyers hailed us. I hadn't said at all what I'd meant. Or what I'd wanted to say. And I couldn't help but wonder what he had meant by *much more*.

There had still been time to explain, but he turned instead and awaited her approach.

She came directly to me, fussing about the chill and hastily wrapping the towel around me.

"Mr. Wilkins," she said, her tone sharp, almost biting, "the boy is half freezing, and Mrs. Turner will be waiting for him. If you'll be so kind as to get him to his mama now."

The only change in his amiable expression came from a hint of amusement. "Of course, Mrs. Meyers. Come on, lad, let's get you back to your mother."

Fascinated by the stubble he'd discovered on Walter's chin, Jamie was clearly free of any hint of shivers. In fact, the evening was unusually warm. But neither Walter nor I argued with Mrs. Meyers.

"My dear girl," she said, fussing over me when he left, trying to bury me in the towel. "This won't do. It ain't fittin'. Not a'tall. Standing there, soaking wet, in front of a man. I'd think such upbringing as yours would have you behavin' more sensible." As we returned to Mother, I tried hard to make sense of Mrs. Meyers's strict code of behavior.

The warm water appeared to have done Mother a great deal of good. Before bed, she managed to tuck the children in and even told them a story. When she finally said goodnight, she was tired, but her smile held a contentment that I hadn't seen for some time.

The sun continued to bake the land by day. And although the wagon lurched and pitched against the hard earth, Mother found it better to avoid the bright light by staying inside than to walk. When we stopped to noon and I brought her something to eat, I asked if she'd been able to nap any.

"Maybe a little," she said.

Before I could ask more, Mrs. Meyers stopped by and pulled a sack of flour up to sit near Mother's mattress. She seemed a little hesitant, but very much like a woman with a cause.

After a few pleasantries, she said, "I'm thinking, this rest is doing you some good, Mrs. Turner. You're looking a mite better. Marjory must be such a blessing." She looked at me for affirmation. I reached for Mother's plate, as she shifted the pillow against her back.

"Still, it's a pity to have to drag the two

younguns out so early every morning when we head out. They just never get back to sleep once we move on. Why not let them sleep in our wagon? It would make it a mite easier for everyone that way."

I glanced at Mother, to see her reaction to such a shocking suggestion. Taking the children during the day was a real help, but we weren't ready to give them away entirely.

Mother closed her eyes and didn't answer for several minutes. Of course, it was a scramble to dress the kids and get them over to the Meyerses' before leaving each morning, but for them to sleep somewhere else, to move some of their things to the Meyerses' wagon . . . well that was something else again.

She sighed and then smiled weakly. "I see what you mean, Mrs. Meyers. And I thank you kindly for such an offer, but I'm sure you can understand that I need time to think about it. And of course, I would want to see how Danny feels about it."

Before I could react, Mrs. Meyers jumped up. "Of course, my dear. I quite understand. This all must be so hard on you. And you've shown nothing but devotion to your family, and I do hope knowing it will only be till you're better will make it easier." She patted Mother's arm. "Now you just lie back and get some rest. I'm sure it won't be long before we're on our way again." She drew her sleeve across her forehead. "My, it does get warm under this canvas without a breeze."

Mother nodded. "Tying the sides up helps. You do get more dust when we're rolling, but a little breeze usually comes with it."

She closed her eyes again and I followed Mrs. Meyers down from the box. I busied myself with gathering up dishes, and soon Mrs. Meyers took the hint. I was not merely acting rude; my mind was blank. Cold and blank.

After a long dusty drive, we finally arrived at a bend in the Snake River, giving us one last view of its perverse waters. Hot and tired, I joined Walter as he circled the wagon and unhitched the horses. Only the memory of yesterday kept exhaustion from overtaking me. The warmth, the promise in his voice, the look in his eyes. And even during the long day, I felt his attentiveness. His weariness from the hard drive was obvious, but still he stayed to help me with the team.

"Good grazing here," he said. "And the animals sure need it. Tomorrow, I'll wrap some hides around their hooves." He let Ginger's foot drop from his grip after checking her bloodied shoe, then gave her rump a firm pat of reassurance. "How's your mother doing today?"

"She's better, but I'm still making her rest. What worries me is that she's *letting* me." My smile apparently didn't hide my concern.

"Don't let it bother you. That's what the doctor wanted her to do." Walter paused after he dropped the last of our traces. "I heard her groan as we hit some rough spots. Are her headaches worse?"

"She says they're better. The doctor's powders help." I believed every word of what I said, yet I still felt uneasy. Mother's appearance had changed to a pinched, gray pallor that marked her bouts with pain. Yet her spirits were up, her appetite almost normal, and the earlier strangeness in her behavior had abated.

Walter's voice broke into my thoughts.

"I understand Mrs. Meyers wants to have Sarie and the boys move their things into her wagon until your ma gets better." Seeing my frown, he hastily continued. "I know that sounds too permanent for both you and your ma's peace of mind, but they'd only be one wagon away. And it would be easier for Mrs. Meyers."

I had been at a loss to counter her arguments, but Mother had her own ways. I was sure she would not give over easily where her family was concerned.

My agitation must have been apparent as I recalled Mrs. Meyers's visit. I noticed Walter watching as I finished my task before we watered the horses. As I worked faster, I tried to calm myself. Try as I might, the idea of moving the children's things to the Meyerses' wagon grated on my nerves. Yet all the while, I knew we were lucky to have been given the offer.

I peered over the horse I was unharnessing. "I know she means well," I assured Walter. "We do appreciate her help." I snatched the bit from our lead horse's mouth, and he reared his head back in protest. "We just don't want the children upset." Walter gave me a concerned look, but was wise enough not to pursue the matter. This was something Mother and I would have to work out.

Dropping the gear in a heap, I grabbed several halter leads and, with Walter, headed for the river. I stood back to watch the horses drink their fill as they lined the bank. The soft sounds of their long draws of water soothed me. A fading glow blanketed the row of sun-warmed brown haunches, and the horse nearest me shifted his weight from one hind leg to the other without pausing to lift his head. The weary beasts lazily swished their tails at the occasional intrusion of a fly. A gentle breeze brushed my face and I breathed in the refreshing peace of day's end, allowing my mind to settle. I dropped the halter ropes and went to sit a little way off, under a spindly willow. Walter joined me.

After several moments of listening to the soft camp sounds drifting to us, he plucked a blade of grass and began to chew on the end of it. Sweeping it to one corner of his mouth, he looked out over the river.

"Take a good look. It's the last time we'll see her. The Snake, I mean. We swing northwest now to the Oregon — in dead earnest."

"Can't say as I'll miss this river," I replied as I stretched my feet out. "Seems as if half the time it's been below our reach, teasing our thirst, and the rest of the time it's been thundering out of control or half drowning us."

"That might not sound so bad in the dry days ahead. We've got twenty-two miles to make in one day, with only the water we can carry."

He saw my worried frown and smiled.

"It's inconvenient, but not deadly. We'll do all right. Sorry I mentioned it." He tossed off the piece of grass. "You looked peaceful for a change. Happy last night and peaceful today. It's a sight I like to see." Then he hesitated before going on. "I meant what I said last night. I hope to make things easier for you. And I hope you'll come to me for anything you need. Any time."

"That's very generous. I appreciate your concern."

He sat forward, wrapping his arms around his knees, looking over at me. "It's more than concern, Marjory."

I stared at him for a second, then looked down at my hands, not knowing how to reply.

"I guess I'm not being very clear about my meaning," he continued. "I feel I can be honest speaking with you. Say things outright, you know? Under the circumstances, it's a little difficult to do a proper courtin' and all. But you must know I have come to care a great deal for you."

"Care for me?" I gasped.

He looked surprised. "Of course I do. How could you think otherwise?"

I didn't think otherwise, but somehow the thought of the man I cared for above all others, hoped would care for me, the man whose arms felt so safe, so pleasurable, could actually be speaking such words to me so left me confused, even frightened. I hadn't wanted to risk hoping for too much. I looked at Walter, wanting to laugh, wanting to cry, wanting to hide. "I'm sorry. I just don't know what I should say."

He smiled and reached for my hand. "What do you want to say?"

Blinking back tears, I answered before caution stopped me. "That I, too, care. I'm glad you spend your time with me." I let my free hand sink into the cool grass beside me, and I glanced back at the Snake. I watched the soft, lazy surface swirls that spoke only to the wise of the river's deep waters and turbulent currents running below the visible calm. Was I being wise or foolish?

Letting out a long breath, I turned back to Walter. "I'm glad you've spoken up. But I'm afraid, too. I know you have your own dreams, and I have my responsibilities. They're responsibilities that mean as much to me as your dreams mean to you."

He gave my hand a squeeze. "Marjory."

His voice was almost a caress. Off in the distance, I heard voices and sounds of animals heading our way for water. But the only thing I wanted to acknowledge was the sureness of Walter's feelings.

"Marjory, I never expected to meet anyone as forthright as you. Perhaps it's your honesty that I love most," he said as he stood, then pulled me to my feet.

Love was the only word that registered with me. For only a moment, he held me close. I laid my head against his chest, and his voice rumbled beneath my ear as he held me tighter.

"As for your responsibilities, you won't be alone, Marjory. I promise. I'll always be there for you."

I barely listened to his words. His arms, his nearness, the beat of his heart all felt too good for me to think of anything other than this precious small moment of heaven.

Several boys led a team into view as they sought to water their animals. Others followed with their stock. We stepped apart, took our teams and walked them to grass near camp.

It had been a long, trying, yet exciting day. The concern for his good opinion, the thrill of his nearness, the fear of his attention coming from friendship rather than love, had finally been laid to rest. He cared. He would always be there for me. We would work it out, and I would never be alone. He did love me. When I finally drifted into sleep, my dreams were pleasant.

The next morning, we left the Snake behind, after three hundred miserable miles of its company. However, it seemed bent on sending us on our way with yet a new trial to endure. We turned from its banks and found ourselves traveling over miles of medium-sized stones. This was the worst test yet that we'd set before our exhausted animals.

Mother paled at the pummeling she received from the slamming of ironclad wheels against small, unforgiving boulders. And our poor, belabored beasts' split and battered hooves soon bloodied the rocks as they trudged on.

At one point an anxious driver's ox staggered, fell and lay in its yoke, taking all manner of punishment rather than to struggle back to its feet. With no grass to feed it, no water to tempt it, the distraught man unyoked the fallen creature, brought in another and drove his wagon around, leaving it behind to die.

Mother stared out the back as we passed it. I had to look away from the sorrow in her eyes as we left the faithful, yet mortally stricken, servant that had drawn its load so many miles, only to die alone on a scorching bed of rocks. Alone, with those ever-present scavengers waiting to devour it. Desperately, I wanted to distract her with small talk as she leaned back on pillows against the trunk. But her wet, tear-smudged cheeks left me silent, with haunted thoughts of my own.

Even though they traveled with the Meyerses, the children always nooned and supped with us. I encouraged Mother to sleep as long as possible in the morning. But she wanted to have the children visit her whenever we traveled over less violent parts of the trail. I insisted on only one at a time. Jamie stayed after our noon stop.

According to my little brother, Misser-My, as Jamie called Mr. Meyers, had lots of fun things. "I play rimbull," he chanted happily. Unable to make head or tails of this new toy, we were at least able to gather that he viewed his stay with the Meyerses as simply an extended playtime.

Mother gave him the rare treat of sorting through her "shineys" from her velvet jewelry box. For most of an hour he played, content within the crook of Mother's arm. Soothingly she stroked his hair. "Are you a good boy when you go to bed for Mrs. Meyers?" she asked anxiously.

"I not go to bed," he boasted, as he

threaded a strand of pearls through a ring. "I on'y put my nightshirt on. Then Missy-My tell me a long, long, long story. All night long," he added, delighted to share this new experience. Then, another shiney fully captured his attention.

Mother's relief held a sweet sadness, not unmatched by my own. The children were getting along quite well. And I knew Mother and I were thinking the same thing. We couldn't get to the Oregon fast enough.

Once there, Mother wouldn't be battered by our travels any longer, and would surely recover faster. In a place of our own, we could keep the children with us, yet Mother could rest, when need be, in her own bedroom.

Bedroom. What a sweet, but faint, memory.

Jamie picked and sorted through the jewelry, thoroughly enraptured. When I noticed Mother's energy wane, I took him back to the Meyerses' wagon.

"You know," Mrs. Meyers said as I walked alongside her and Danny, "I think these short visits with your ma make the children feel special. I mean, not having to always share your ma's attention." Bored, Jamie scooted after Danny, who walked on ahead of us.

"Yes, I'm sure that's true." I smiled and tried to feel grateful. What we'd do without her generosity, I didn't know. But I resented our need for so much of it. If only Papa . . . "You've been very kind to the children and to us," I said, my jaw set with determination.

"Bosh! I'm doin' what any Christian would, including yourselves. Besides," she continued gruffly, "you know what joys they are to have around. Now, how does your ma be?"

"Better. She still tires easily, but she's better."

"That's real good to hear. I'm sure she just needs rest, like the doctor says. She'll be right as rain, you'll see." She cast me a glance before continuing. "You know the children is quite content, as long as they know their ma is right behind us. They look at it as a camp-out. Just a short-lived treat, which it is, of course."

"Sarie, too?" I asked. "She's so little."

" 'Course it's different for her. If it weren't for that smart little Danny, we'd of had a time. But he is a marvel. Knows just how to amuse her and put her at ease, whenever her ma can't get over at bedtime. Your ma's done a fine job with those younguns."

I returned to our wagon, feeling kindly

toward Mrs. Meyers and wondering why I worried so much. It had not been so very long ago that I had accused *Mother* of always needing to be in control of everyone and everything. Now I seemed to be doing the same thing.

During the next week, the trail grew worse rather than better. Our trek through Burnt Canyon was a five-day ordeal. The walls towered over us on both sides, in some places leaving only a narrow creek bed to travel, which left us baking in a coffin-like passageway. Walter and I had no further opportunity to talk as we battled the terrain. At times, I feared we'd turn the wagon over on ourselves as we struggled around obstacles.

The animals were nearly spent. So were we. Man and beast alike had little left to give in the miserable heat. I feared this brutal pounding of wagon and passenger would all but split Mother's poor head open. Her pain returned with a vengeance. Often I'd see her grasping her head between her hands.

When she felt strong enough, she preferred trailing after the wagon to riding inside. But on our fifth day of struggling to make it out of the canyon, Mother said she had to lie down. Walter urged the team over the rocks that littered the ruts, walking alongside the team, slapping their haunches with the reins. There was no room to avoid obstacles or to ease the jolts as the day wore on. Later, with the sun still beating down on us, I heard a strange thrashing sound coming from in the wagon. I could detect it even above the clatter of animals and wheels.

"Mother?" I hollered. "Are you all right?" Hearing no response, I panicked. Stumbling over rocks, I caught up to the wagon and scrambled up to the box. I heaved myself over the bench and fell beside her. Mother lay on her back, all askew, like a rag doll flung to the ground by an angry child. She lay very still, half on and half off her bedding. A trickle of blood ran down her chin.

Seventeen

September 29, 1847
Dear Friend,
I can do nothing but watch over Mother as we struggle to reach our destination. I felt such terror, seeing Mother lying there, blood down her chin, unconscious. Thank God for Walter's presence of mind. He checked her pulse and her breathing, and then moved her back onto the mattress. Now I can only watch and wait. What has my determination to go on to the Oregon done? I fear my willfulness has cost too much, and I pray to God that Mother doesn't suffer for it.

I put aside my pencil with the prayer fixed in my heart. I heard water splashing against our wheels as they grated over the rocks. We lurched once more into the canyon's narrow creek bed that was the only trail left to the wagons. Mother rolled with the pitch, but didn't wake. She still looked pale.

The train stopped often to allow a short rest and extra water for the teams, but it was hot, with no room to camp and no feed for grazing, so we pushed forward as soon as possible. During hard pulls, Walter handled the team while he walked alongside. Where the trail leveled, I rode inside for as long as I could.

I frequently squeezed a wetted cloth against Mother's lips, then laid it across her forehead. The heat had gathered under our canvas, turning the wagon into an oven. Raising the canvas sides did nothing to help. I mopped my brow with my skirt and leaned back, hoping for a breeze. The next incline wasn't severe, and Walter returned to the box after awhile. Late that afternoon, he poked his head back.

"The end of the canyon's just up ahead. Finally!"

"Perhaps at last we will feel a stir of air," I said. "The weather's been so oppressive."

"True." Walter looked about the wagon. "Keep things secured. The hills up ahead are steep."

The front of his shirt was dark with patches of sweat and I was ashamed of my complaints. I, at least, had shade.

"Has she spoken to you?" he asked.

"No. Not yet. I just can't understand what happened. I heard such strange noises, as if she were thrashing about or struggling with something."

"Perhaps something began to fall and she tried to catch it. We were on pretty rough ground."

I didn't argue the point, for I was too weary to think. Yet, his explanation didn't reassure me.

"Word has passed down. We're keeping on till dark, trying to make up for the days we lost in the canyon," he added, when I didn't respond. He turned back to the team, his neck red from the heat even under the shade of his hat.

Later, as Mother slept on, I moved up front. Leaning against the side rail, I could talk to Walter and still keep an eye on her.

"Any change?" he asked

"No. Her breathing seems regular, but she shows no signs of coming around."

He looked back at me. "It'll be all right, Marjory."

"I know." I desperately wanted to believe his encouragement. Mother and I had finally become close. We were even beginning to understand each other, and there was so much we could share. We had already lost Papa. And with my sister and brothers so young, she had to recover soon. Surely God would see that.

"I had a long talk with Tad," Walter said. "My father, too, the night we stopped at the Malheur River."

"Oh?" I twisted the hot, thick hair that was held back with a ribbon, and pinned it up off my neck.

"Yes. I'm staking a claim this winter, and I've convinced Tad he should take over from me within two months of our settling in Oregon City."

Thoughts of Mother still lay heavy on my mind, and his words drifted away, until I remembered that I was not the only one with problems. I sat up straighter and said, "I don't suppose Tad was very happy about that."

Walter chuckled. "No. He wasn't real thrilled." Then his voice took on an edge. "But he sees my point of view now. I also settled things with Pa."

I wanted to react with enthusiasm. I knew that Walter's announcement affected me, too, but now the future held too many uncertainties.

"What I'm saying, Marjory, is that I want to be free sooner to begin building my claim. A claim that will allow me to provide for a wife. For you."

For me. He had worked out his obligations in order to marry. For longer than I cared to admit, I had hoped his feelings went that deep. Knowing they did heartened me. "Walter, that's wonderful."

He looked at me, his expression serious. "Is it?"

I wanted it to be. I wanted it so much. My throat closed around an ache I forced back. I had to think of Mother, of my family. "Yes. At least it would be, if I were free to accept. But how can I? You know Mother and the children need me. I'm not even sure when she will be well enough for me to leave her with them."

Walter glanced at the hill we were ascending and frowned. Unable to let got of the reins, he moved them both to one hand, and threw his leg over the seat, straddling it. "Come here," he commanded.

I scooted over, allowing him to cradle me in his arm. It felt safe to be held so. His embrace made me feel safe and wanted. His nearness fended off loneliness. Within his grasp, I knew I wanted the experience of giving, of taking, of sharing everything with the one who gave me hope and joy and the promise of laughter. Yet this wasn't the time for me. I could not begin my future at the expense of my family. And the knowing made it hurt all the more. Slowly, I let my breath escape, fighting tears.

"I want you to understand," Walter whispered into my hair. "Whatever your problems are, they'll become mine, too."

He stilled my attempted protest. "If you're willing to wait a few months for me, I'll be free to start a life of my own with you. And that includes your family. Whatever they need. We'll work it out together."

Walter. Sweet, wonderful Walter. Yet, dear God, how could I be free to marry until I knew Mother would recover? She might even remain too fragile ever to be left alone. I couldn't saddle him with three children and an invalid. Mother would hate it and eventually Walter would, too. "Walter," I said, trying to smile, "the thought of building a life with you is more than I ever dreamed of having, or of even wanting. But please, so much is unsettled for me. I can't be sure Mother's migraines will lessen once we reach the Oregon." I paused, pushing back despair. "Please let the future play itself out for now."

"But there's no . . ."

"Please, Walter. I cannot think otherwise right now. It's too hard. Let's at least wait the few months you've already asked for."

He squeezed my shoulders while rubbing my arm, considering, before he answered. "That isn't what I want, but I understand. God knows, you have enough to handle for now."

He bent down and kissed the top of my head. The charge of his feelings spiraled through me. Even with the future so uncertain, I snuggled into the intimacy, the protection, that he offered, and I allowed the sweet joy to cradle me for the moment.

When we finally pulled into camp late that night, Mother began to stir. She even acknowledged me with a weak smile before drifting off again. I didn't want to leave her, so Mrs. Meyers kindly offered to cook for all of us. Several times Mother came to herself, only to nod off once more. Finally, when Mrs. Meyers brought over some broth, Mother stirred. But she didn't open her eyes until Mrs. Meyers had left.

"Mother. Are you awake?" I asked.

"Hmmm. I guess so. What time of the day is it? I can't seem to remember."

"It's evening."

"Evening? But what . . . I know the sun was beating down and making us miserable only minutes ago." She looked worriedly around. "Something's wrong. What happened?"

"I really don't know, Mother. You were resting this afternoon when I heard noises, as of things being thrown around. When I got into the wagon, you were unconscious, lying half off the mattress, and your mouth was bleeding. You've been out ever since." She frowned, upset by my account.

"I remember the heat and the wagon pounding over this miserable trail. And yes, you were outside walking." She looked around, then at the canvas overhead. "The canvas . . . it was so bright. Quiet. Yes, it got quiet and kind of strange, as if I . . ." Her frown deepened, almost as if she were in pain. Her hand went to her head as she shook it in denial. Her gaze slid away, and she sighed. "We must have hit a rock, and it jolted me off the bedding, and I hit my head. I feel all right now, just very tired. I'm sure I'll feel better in the morning."

"I hope you're right." I glanced at her hands, checking for tremors. I noted that her eyes were troubled but she didn't seem confused, before coaxing Mother to drink some of Mrs. Meyers's broth. After finishing it, she wanted to go back to sleep, so I settled her down, then joined the Meyerses for a late supper. Mrs. Meyers was glad to see me, since my presence helped to distract the children's attention from Mother's prolonged absence. She rarely missed eating supper with them.

In Baker Valley, only days before reaching the Blue Mountains, we stopped early to take advantage of bunch grass and the welcome supply of wood and water. Mrs. Meyers mixed up some soda biscuits and baked them in her box stove. I boiled the few remaining dried vegetables left to us, and together we had a tempting meal. Mother had improved to the point that she could lean against the pillows and blankets we had propped against the tree and share our meal.

She continued to gain strength, yet often remained more solemn of spirit than she had been before that strange episode. When she was around the children, she told cheerful stories, but her attention often drifted, and when they left, she slept or remained withdrawn.

I drove our wagon through the Powder River Valley, since Mother was content either to rest or sleep. Because Walter said he needed to help his father, I continued to drive wherever he thought it safe as we passed through the foothills of the Blue Mountains.

At first I thought nothing of Walter's frequent absences. Then I began to wonder why he found it necessary to leave us so often. Ever since Baker Valley, after we'd climbed out of the canyon, I'd noticed his preoccupation. He rarely added to my com-

266

ments on the trail or our progress. I had said how wonderful it was finally to reach green grasses for the stock, and he had agreed that it shouldn't take too long to get beyond the mountains.

"Walter, is something on your mind?" I knew he hadn't been listening at all.

"No, why?" he asked, looking surprised.

"Because, your mind seems to be elsewhere."

He smiled. "Sorry. There are a few odds and ends that need my attention. Guess I'm putting them in order."

"Like what?" I asked.

He had just glanced at me and given an evasive answer about the time Mother wanted a sip of water.

Later, it also occurred to me that I hadn't seen anything of Tad since we left the Malheur. Even though the trail had been rough driving, I was surprised he hadn't once stopped by after supper. I mentioned it to Walter.

"Tad has sense enough to realize you no longer have the time to be entertained. After Fort Boise, the trail's kept him pretty busy, too, with Pa's teams. Poor lad's actually had to *work*."

I looked to see if Walter was teasing. I didn't think he was. "Say hello for me," I said. "And tell him I miss his company."

Walter gave me a sharp glance. "I'll tell him." He handed the reins back to me once we'd made it over the last ridge. "We're coming onto some even ground now. You'll do fine here. I'll be back before we circle up."

He jumped down, stumbling as he landed. When the wagon passed him, I noticed how tired he looked. I wondered if announcing his intention of leaving the store had caused trouble within his family. After climbing another ridge, we entered a small valley where the Grande Ronde River was a mere stream. Huckleberry bushes abounded, but to Mrs. Meyers's vexation all the berries were gone. Then we saw tall stands of awesome pine trees. None of us had ever seen their like before. The crisp air carried the sharp tang of pitch.

Then at last we faced the Blue Mountains. The cause of our worst worries since glimpsing their formidable bulk looming ahead when we left the Snake. At least it hadn't snowed, for which we all gave thanks.

At this point Walter again took to driving us. We traveled through a cold spell that left patches of mist settling in around us. Softly bumping along the needle-padded forest floor, the lonely creaking of our wagons echoed our insignificance under a cathedral of towering pines. When I looked up, rough columns of branchless tree trunks faded into a ceiling of hazy gray, leaving me disoriented and worried about losing our way.

By late afternoon, we stopped to clear away an immensely long, fallen tree. The forced delay gave us time to eat a belated cold luncheon. There was nothing save pine needles for our poor cattle to eat, and so they were left standing in their harnesses, drooping with exhaustion. They seemed able to ignore their hunger, content just to rest.

When Walter returned from his campsite, we picked our way again through the darkening forest. Awareness of his preoccupation grew with each muffled mile we covered. His moodiness closed in around me, as heavy as the misty dusk.

I could hardly bear my disappointment. First Mother had retreated behind a wall of melancholy, then Walter had withdrawn behind a wall of silence. He strove to camouflage his feelings, but I knew something was wrong. Was he upset because I'd put him off?

As we neared a place called Emigrant Springs, I could bear it no longer. "Walter, what is wrong? Are you having any trouble with Tad or your family?"

His head jerked up and he looked surprised. His brow furrowed. "Why do you ask that?"

"Because you seem preoccupied. And you're avoiding my question with one of your own. *Are* you having trouble?"

"We're heading for the roughest part of the trail, Marjory. Most men are preoccupied."

"I didn't ask about most men. I asked about you."

He hesitated, thinking. "Has Tad been complaining?"

Walter avoided looking at me as I asked, "Is that your answer?"

"Yes . . . I mean no."

His sigh spoke louder than his words.

"What I mean is, there is no problem. My family accepts my decision. Really."

I was deeply disappointed by his evasiveness. For the first time, I didn't believe something he'd said to me.

The next afternoon, I again tried to draw him out. I was desperate. If I couldn't talk to Walter about this, how could we ever hope to make a companionable life together?

"I hope you know you could discuss any problems or concerns with me. I wouldn't expect to advise you, but I would like to be of some comfort." I tried to catch his eye, and added, "As you have so often been to me." His attention remained riveted on the wagon ahead.

"I know," he finally answered. "And you are a great comfort. Really." He reached up, whipped his hat off and mopped his brow with his shirtsleeve. "But there is nothing that you can help me with at the moment." He paused in thought, then hastily added, "Except perhaps, to take over as often as possible for the next few days." Leaning forward, his elbows on his knees, the reins dangled from his hands. "Pa can use a little extra help whenever I'm free."

"Oh. Of course. I'm quite sure that by now I can do much more of the driving. Feel perfectly free at any time." I felt unreasonably hurt . . . and ashamed because of it.

"As a matter of fact," he continued, "when we reach the bottom of Cabbage Hill, beyond the pass, you can take over for a few days."

His refusal to explain himself increased my irritation. "Quite happy to," I remarked as I swung my feet around inside the wagon. I waited for some explanation for his change in attitude. There was none coming. "I think I'd better check on Mother." My anger turned to self-pity, which made his behavior even more unpalatable. The fact that he didn't seem to notice my unhappiness was the final straw, as he drew the team in for our night's stop at Emigrant Springs.

Eighteen

October 5, 1847 — morning
Dear Friend,
It was a hard, exhausting push to make it to Deadman's Pass. We circled up tightly, kept fires till dawn, and still I barely slept. I spent the night listening to wolves howling. Their lonely cries wore on me, lowering my spirits. Along with that, the occasional ear-splitting scream of a cougar left me ready to start shrieking myself.

It's now near dawn and I hear the campfires being laid and men leaving to gather their teams and cattle, so I take this minute for my complaints before I, too, begin another day.

I had the team ready by the time Walter arrived. He asked after Mother, and his genuine concern led me to hope that he was ready to talk. But once we were on the trail, he suggested I ride in the back with her.

"It'd probably be good to keep her distracted from her headaches by getting her to talk. Besides, it's pretty rough terrain here. She might need help."

Obviously, he was bent on keeping his own counsel by ignoring the fact that she slept a good part of the day and I could easily watch Mother from the front. *So much for talk,* I thought.

Trees and narrow pathways kept the children inside the Meyerses' wagon as we left for the crest of the pass. For a second day, the cold held us in its grip. If it hadn't been for the dampness that permeated everything, the chill would have been a relief from the unmerciful heat of a few days earlier. But as it was, we could only pray the snow would hold off for the next three weeks.

The mountain passes were treacherous to navigate. Although the underbrush was sparse, the crowded stands of tall pines, screened through a thick, hovering fog, were enough to make one shiver at the prospect of what lay hidden beyond.

Less than a mile down the trail, we saw a scraggy cow standing by the roadside, a frayed rope dangling from her halter. I watched it out the back as we drove past. The cow stood, head drooping, unheeding of the passing wagons. Before we'd gone far, a rider from up front passed us, no doubt looking to reclaim his wandering property. I watched him fade into the silent mist behind us.

As our trail curved back on itself, a piercing, agonized bawl rent the heavy silence beyond the barrier of trees. The team shied at the sudden cry. Our wagon lurched, but Walter steadied the horses. A moment later a cougar's scream sliced through the fog again. Then, beyond our wagons, silence returned.

The quiet tension left only the muffled sound of our wheels creaking over a bed of muddied needles until, from a distance, I heard the quick pace of a horse and rider returning. As he neared, Walter called out.

"Your cow?"

"Yeah. Damn cat," the rider hollered as he caught up to us.

"Tough. Try to get him?"

"Naw. Why waste a bullet? She'd already been downed."

The man, sorely aware of our need to hurry on, whacked his hat against his leg, scattering beads of water off the brim, then shoved it low over his forehead and continued onward.

The thought of such a grisly death chilled me. We had passed the exhausted stray only moments before. The predator must have been following us, stalking, waiting for something — or someone — to lag behind the others. The thought of being left alone in a place like this sent cold fear shooting up my spine. I scrambled over the seat to talk to Walter, my earlier hurts forgotten.

"Are they really out there, just waiting to catch one of us alone?" I asked.

"I doubt it. That cougar just got lucky. They're more likely to avoid the noise of a train."

"Are you sure?"

"Positive."

I looked ahead at the Meyerses' wagon, making sure Danny had not decided to walk. "I don't want any of the children out of the wagon until we leave these woods."

"Don't worry. Half of the time, there's no place to walk."

Once he'd reassured me, he slipped silently back into his own thoughts, closing me out as he had done since we left the canyon.

Even though we neared the nooning hour, shadows deepened all around us. The sun failed to penetrate the haze that drifted between bare tree trunks, leaving us in a shroud of gray.

I heard wagons slowing ahead, and we pulled to a stop. Our scout passed on word of a delay as he rode by.

"We'll lay over here for another cold nooning," Walter called back as he climbed down. "Mr. Colby's wheel needs changing. Stay put and I'll see if I can help. Better grab what you can to eat while I'm gone," he added.

The stop had roused Mother, and she sat up, smoothing her bedding and patting her plaited hair in place. "Marjory, ask the children to noon with us," she begged. "I haven't seen them since . . . for awhile."

Sounds of hammering to remove a resistant wheel gave our stalled wagons a busy sound. I jumped down, ran to the Meyerses' wagon, and explained that Mother wanted to see the children. Mr. Meyers carried Sarie as I took the boys back to our wagon. Having the children about, even for just a meal, brought life and color back to Mother's face. I hadn't seen her looking so well in days.

We had a good time chewing jerked buffalo and hard bread while sipping cool, sweet water. I worried that all three children would be too much for Mother, but the little ones were content to remain cradled in her arms while Danny recounted their latest experiences.

"Mrs. Meyers has a checkerboard and we play a game most every night." Danny looked at Mother with a sheepish grin. "I think she lets me win."

"Yeah. I win, too, all the time," Jamie chimed in.

"But she just keeps letting me win. No matter how bad I play. Mr. Meyers said first chance he got, he'd play me and I wouldn't get off so easy. He's nice," Danny continued.

"I play gun with Misser-My. I not get off easy, too." Jamie rolled from Mother's arm to sit forward, facing her in order to gain her full attention.

And he surely had gained our full attention, as we both looked at Danny for confirmation.

"Aw. He just means a stick that Mr. Meyers uses to show Jamie how to hold a rifle. They shoot pretend bears from the driver's box."

" 'Cept Sunday. God say you not shoot on Sunday."

Jamie settled back beside Mother, happily unaware of a worried frown that creased her brow. As for Danny, Jamie's interruptions had irked him, and he left Mother to the little ones, turning his attention to me.

Less than half an hour later, I noticed that Mother's expression had changed. She leaned against her propped-up pillow with a fixed smile, but her eyes were dull and her face had drained of color. Her hand massaged her temple.

"All right, children, it's time to get back to the Meyerses' wagon. We'll soon be leaving," I said, as casually as I could manage. "Danny, take Jamie, and I'll bring Sarie in a minute."

I helped the boys over the tailgate and watched them to the Meyerses' wagon before turning back to Mother.

"Is it bad?" I asked her.

"Not too terribly. It just hit so suddenly. Could I have another powder, Marjory?"

Her eyes closed as I fetched the doctor's medicine.

"Here, drink this." After her draught, I helped her lie flat. "If you're all right, I'll take Sarie back."

"I'm fine," she said, waiting for whatever relief was to come.

When I got Sarie to Mr. and Mrs. Meyers, it took me a minute to identify my growing unease as I reported Mother's relapse to Mrs. Meyers. Then it hit me.

"Where's Danny?" I asked.

Mrs. Meyers glanced up at my tone. "Why, he said he'd be just a minute. He was right here a second ago," she added, appearing puzzled by my concern.

I looked around, then at the box, and tapped Mr. Meyers's shoulder as he chewed some jerky. "Have you seen Danny?" I could hear the growing panic in my voice.

"No. Isn't he back with you?" One look at me and he added, "He can't be far away. Don't worry."

I ignored his calm, jumped down and turned toward sounds of the men working ahead. Several wagons up, I saw Walter emerge through the fog. "Walter," I cried out. "Have you seen Danny?"

He hastened toward me.

"Danny!" I shouted. I saw only the dreaded woods and thought of the cow. I started to dash toward the trees, but Walter caught my arm and spun me around.

"What do you think you're doing?" he growled.

"Danny's gone. The cougars, they'll . . ."

"Look," he said sharply; his voice cut through my hysteria. He pointed behind me.

Through my tears, I saw a figure coming through the trees. "Danny."

My brother hesitated, looking puzzled. Behind Walter, I heard Mr. Meyers. "There he is." And Mrs. Meyers poked her head out and asked what all the fuss was about. Walter still held my arm, but all I could think about was Danny. Danny, standing at the roadside just beyond our wagon.

I broke away from Walter and ran to my brother, who stared at me in confusion.

"What's the matter?" he asked.

I swooped him into my arms, hugging him tight. He relented only a moment, before breaking free from my grasp.

"What were you yelling at me for?"

"You weren't in the wagon. You must stay inside. Promise?"

"Okay, okay. But what'sa matter? The whole camp can hear you."

"Nothing's the matter now," I said, with a tearful laugh. "I just thought you'd gone off into the trees." Again, I shook off the haunting, bloody vision of that poor cow.

Danny drew himself up, glancing at the Meyerses and at Walter. His voice lowered to a hiss. "I did, dopey. I went out for a pee. Gosh. You didn't have to call out the cavalry."

"Danny," I said, aghast. "From now till we're out of here, you go between the wagons and never, ever, go without telling Mr. Meyers. Do you promise?"

Danny hunched his shoulders up to meet his hat brim, as if he hoped he could disappear entirely, and nodded.

"Thanks, Danny," I said, finally thinking to lower my voice.

Aware that I'd embarrassed my brother

enough for one afternoon, I managed a weak smile, apologized to the Meyerses for my panic, yet quietly emphasized my wish for caution. Mrs. Meyers received my comments with a stiff nod.

"Understand you're a bit overwrought, dear, but I ain't about to lose one of the children. Never have been known to be careless," she added with a sniff.

Again I apologized and then headed back to our wagon with Walter. I caught Walter's worried glance as we walked, but after assisting me into the wagon, he didn't bring up the incident again.

Before we headed down the barren western side of the Blue Mountains, we could see beyond the Columbia plateau. Like a great, ragged edging, separating heaven from earth, the formidable Cascades rode the horizon. They were beautiful — towering, white-capped mountains, such as I'd never seen before, very different from the sloping passes of the Rockies. But dread mingled with admiration. I shut out the thought of our train threading around and through those majestic cones of snow and forced myself to concentrate on the sight of the plateau below. Walter all but free-rolled our wagon down the slope of the Blues. At that point, I took the reins and Walter returned to his own affairs.

★ ★ ★

We traveled into valleys and through meadows during the next few days. Mother appreciated the less turbulent ride and the return to milder weather. She rested well, and insisted the children resume their visits. Her laughter and restored interest distracted me from thinking about Walter's pensive withdrawal.

I was surprised when Tad came to visit during a noon stop at a place called Well Springs.

"You've been quite a stranger to us," I said as he settled himself Indian fashion on the ground. I remained on my overturned box, where I could keep an ear out for Mother.

"No wonder," he said. "I've been all but lashed to our wagon. Two wagons to maintain keeps a man hopping. And, thanks to Walter, Pa ain't much of a hand lately."

"What does that mean?" I asked, surprised by his accusation.

"It means Pa ain't so young anymore. And Walter's high-handed announcement that he'd give us only two months when he'd promised more is no doubt what left Pa feeling poorly."

"Poorly, how?" I asked, with growing

concern.

"I don't know. His arm's sore and his chest hurts. So I'm left to do most of the hard work."

"Does he have a cold?"

"Naw."

"A bad heart?"

"He says no, but I suspect he's just protecting Walter, as usual." Tad leaned back on his hands, giving out a long sigh. "Oh, I don't know. I guess I'm just grumbling 'cause life seems to be crowding in on me. Seems a man oughta have some freedom before he takes on a lifetime of hard labor, wouldn't you think?"

"Uh-huh," I answered, barely listening to his complaints. Instead, I considered the possibility of Walter's father being ill. Had Walter said too much about going off on his own too soon? He'd feel terrible if he found his father suffered a heart complication after their talk. Poor Walter. And I'd been too hurt and self-pitying to think beyond my own concerns.

"Isn't Walter helping now, by spending more time driving the other wagon?" I asked.

"Yeah. Now that we're on easy ground."

I thought of our many needs. We'd kept Walter from helping his own father.

"Not that we can't do without him," Tad hurriedly added. "Pa can drive without much trouble. He really just needs to soak his arm at night, while I take care of everything else. Otherwise, we're doing fine."

He laughed, but it was a nervous laugh that I'd begun to recognize as being his cover for misspeaking.

"You know me," he said. "Complaining fills the tedious hours." He leaned forward again, picking at some weeds in front of him.

I saw Walter in the distance, hauling water back to his wagons from a deep spring. I felt guilty for having accepted the water he'd insisted on hauling for us earlier.

"You hear that we lost three wagons back at the Umatilla?" Tad asked. "They headed north to some mission after getting directions from those Indians here and about, who always seem to have something to trade."

"Yes," I answered, reluctantly looking away from Walter. "Walter wanted us to go to the doctor's mission too, but then he heard from the Indians passing by earlier that there were cases of measles there."

"Must not have been too bad. The others went," Tad said.

"Just the same, I'm glad we didn't go."

"Yeah. I suppose Walter was right." He let out another resigned sigh, stood and brushed himself off.

"You know," he said, "I think I'd better find me a way of getting to like honest labor, as Walter calls it. It appears I'm going to be getting well acquainted with it, like it or not." He grinned. "Think I'll be just as fetchin' to the girls, wearing an apron and carrying a figuring pencil behind my ear?"

I looked up at him, trying to focus on Tad rather than on my worries about Walter.

"I think you'll have the girls lining up clear into the streets, just to have you figure their charges for them."

Cocking his hat at a jaunty angle, he threw me a sassy look. "A gal as pretty as you should know her own kind. 'Pears I've found the perfect way to weather the beginning of a long career behind a counter."

I couldn't help but smile, but once he'd left, my thoughts returned to Walter.

I had served up my troubles to Walter as if they deserved blue ribbons. *Solve mine first.* Never did I stop to take notice of any problems he might have. If he was distracted, I sulked because his entire attention wasn't focused on me.

It would be hard to trust a woman who demanded his energy and sympathy while showing no understanding for his problems. It wasn't a pretty reflection to face in my mirror. Selfishness pinches the face, my grandmother used to say, and suddenly remembering Grandmother and the years before her passing left me with a pang of homesickness. But it quickly passed. And as if to fill the void came resolution.

I will do better, I promised myself, *by both Mother and Walter.*

Nineteen

October 14, 1847
Dear Friend,
After crossing the fearsome Deschutes River, we are finally in Oregon territory. We will make the Columbia by tomorrow, then raft down to the Sandy River and on to the Willamette Valley. I can't believe we're so close to journey's end. I know Mother will improve quickly once we're there and settled.

I had hoped to talk to Walter alone, but as yet no opportunity has arisen. In truth, I wonder what talking can accomplish. After apologizing for my self-centeredness, what then? I continue to have responsibilities and, now more than ever, so does Walter. He cannot leave his family and allow his father to risk his health.

Perhaps when the opportunity arrives, I'll know what to say.

When we pulled out for The Dalles, Walter rode on ahead to trade off two of our horses. They were spent and couldn't go much farther. One had favored his left foreleg since Four Man Canyon. We finally tied him behind the wagon with Ginger, who was almost as bad. Pulling without two horses in reserve was a hardship. Poor Ginger and Lightning; they'd brought us so far with the last of their strength, only to be cast aside near trail's end. Even Walter praised their stamina.

He expected to make a good trade at The Dalles, hearing that some drivers left their teams and wagons behind when Indians were hired to take the pioneers past the rapids and ferry the rest of their belongings down to the Fort Vancouver settlement.

Most of the teams were near exhaustion when we finally made camp six miles before reaching The Dalles. By then the teams were not alone in needing rest and good food. We, too, were ready for a change of diet. Earlier, during our noon stop, I had purchased a salmon and a few potatoes from a friendly Cayuse.

As I took the fish from the fire, Walter returned with a horse and mule. He dismounted, nodding toward the team behind him.

"It was the best I could do," he said, shrugging.

He tied up the animals and accepted my

offer to sup with us.

"The mule is in good shape, but I'm afraid the horse is hardly better than what we traded," he said.

"At least neither is limping," I replied. "And look on the bright side. Our team is so played out, they aren't likely to reject the new members."

Walter frowned. "I had hoped for better."

I gestured toward our fire. "Tonight, your luck has changed. Look. Fresh fish. It's a salmon, and I'm told it's very good."

He quickly succumbed to the enticing aroma, and demolished his portion. After a second cup of coffee, he put his tin down and stood, stretching, then motioned for me to step away from camp.

At last he wanted to talk. I was all the more touched because he looked so weary. A dark stubble shadowed his face, and I had noticed an unusual droop to his shoulders while he'd bent over his food. And still he wanted to talk before turning in. I should have known that if he had time to think things out, he'd share his concerns with me. Who better than I could understand worries over a parent's health?

We walked a ways before he invited me to sit on the ground. Then he joined me. After a meal of fresh meat and being with Walter, life was good again. The evening crispness settled over the soft grasslands of the valley, and I could almost smell the river, fresh and clean, a few miles off.

Walter removed his hat, raking one hand along the side of his head while he drew up his knees. He leaned forward, elbows braced against knees, as he twirled his hat on one finger. I glanced at him and noticed a cowlick of hair standing straight up. I had to fight an urge to smooth it down, sensing the intimate gesture unwise while this emotional distance remained between us.

"Marjory, I've been talking to the Captain."

I combed my fingers through the grass beside me, trying to refocus my attention from his hair to this unexpected topic.

"He told me about a new trail that opened up last year," Walter continued. "It's become the choice of many drivers since it opened."

Disappointment washed over me. I looked up to find him watching me. "New trail?" I asked, letting a fist full of plucked grass scatter in the breeze as I lifted my hand to watch them fall.

"Yes," he replied. He scooted around to face me. "It'd save us the dangers of going down the Columbia."

"But surely rafting would be easier than trudging across more trail, wouldn't it?"

"Not really. That river is treacherous. You also have to take your wagon apart, stack it onto a raft and pray you arrive right side up. Meanwhile, I'd shuttle the team along the narrow banks to join you, and re-assemble the wagons before continuing on."

"And what about this new route?"

He hesitated, returning his hat to his head and slipping a dried weed between his teeth. "I admit that I don't know all that much about it. But a lot of wagons are beginning to use it. In fact, I talked to some folks at The Dalles, who plan to start for it this afternoon."

I hesitated. I'd pictured a raft being so much easier for Mother.

"I think it's the best option, Marjory. I've spoken to my father and to the scout. He's willing to lead our wagons over, and four other families want to join us."

"Rafting still sounds faster to me," I said, hating to give in to the promise of more rough trails for Mother. "Why isn't everyone taking the new trail, if it's so good?"

"Because the Barlow toll road is so new, even the Captain has never been on it. Going by river sounds faster to many folks, and they don't realize the dangers involved. But every year, wagons and lives are lost to the rapid current and angry falls. The Captain agrees it's a better option for us." He hesitated, then asked, "What do you say?"

It was hard to accept the idea of more travel by wagons, but I valued his judgment. Besides, Mother hated the water.

"All right, Walter. Whatever you think best."

I was disappointed about this change in plans, but found it even harder to keep personal worries out of my thoughts. Didn't Walter notice the distance growing between us, or didn't he care? I glanced his way and was startled. Far from looking uncaring or even pleased by my acceptance of his plan, he seemed apprehensive, even sad. His shoulders sagged as he stared into the twilight. Then he gathered himself up, dusted his britches and helped me to my feet.

"I'm glad you agree," he said.

He walked me back to camp and said goodnight as he would to a stranger. I stood there looking after him, puzzled, wanting to call him back. After his efforts to improve our stock and his genuine concern for Mother's health, I couldn't understand his reactions to me this past week.

★ ★ ★

It was barely dawn when we bade farewell to the train we had traveled with for so long, and our seven wagons turned south while the Captain led the others north toward the Columbia River. It felt strange, even lonely, to move along a trail that was little more than a path, listening to the sounds of a train now reduced to less than half our original wagons. I missed the clattering, squeaking noises of our former numbers. At least there was comfort in being sandwiched between the Wilkinses' wagons ahead and the Meyerses' wagon following behind.

Mother no longer asked about our progress, accepting day-to-day happenings as they occurred. I decided not to bring up our change in plans until she asked. Her headaches, which had increased in frequency and in severity, took most of her attention.

After several days of travel, we double-teamed each wagon to cross a hilly stretch of land. When we at last reached the toll gate, I gave Walter our share of the toll, five dollars and fifty cents. It seemed little enough, since I'd expected the last part of our trip to cost much more, but then perhaps heavier expenses were still to come. Finally we had the luxury of stopping in a lush meadow fringed with red cedar and a clear creek.

The rest gave our animals a much-needed boost.

I assured Walter that Danny and I could take care of the team, so he hurried off to his father's wagons. The children came to say goodnight to Mother, who no longer left her bed more than was necessary. I had a quick cup of coffee with Mrs. Meyers when I brought them back for the night.

"You look so tired, Marjory," she said, handing me a tin. "It ain't right for a girl your age to have such responsibilities."

"I'm all right." I clutched the cup, inhaling the rising aroma.

"Of course, you're doing just fine, but it still ain't right. I hope you know the mister and me will do anything we can to help out. And it ain't no burden neither. Why we just love those younguns."

"That's very kind of you," I said tonelessly, feeling wearier by the minute.

"T'aint kindness. It's as I said. We love it. And you and your ma ain't to worry. The little ones is gettin' along just fine with us."

She looked as if she were about to say more, but after glancing my way, she took my cup and spoke in a more comforting tone. "Girl, you look tuckered. Go on back and try to rest comfortable. The Lord has a way of working things out, so don't you go a wasting your energies trying to do His business for Him." She smiled. "You're doing all a body could ask. I know your ma is proud of you. Now, go get some rest."

I thanked her again for her kindness, this time with more sincerity. She did mean well, and I had much to be grateful for.

Mother's sleep seemed untroubled, so I went back to our fire to rest my nerves before turning in. But too many concerns challenged my peace: Mother's ups and downs, the children's absence, our change in route, and Walter's distance. Round and round, first this problem then that, one followed upon another until I about lost the ability to think at all.

Consumed by my own struggles, I didn't hear Walter come up until he spoke.

"Up kind of late, aren't you?"

"Oh!" I jumped, almost choking as my breath caught.

"Sorry. Thought you heard me coming."

"Well, I didn't," I said, annoyed and trying to cover my fright.

"What were you so intent on?" he asked, while plopping down where he could face me.

I tried to sound casual. "Today, tomorrow, lots of things, I guess."

"Are you worried about taking this trail?"

"No, not really. I trust your judgment."

He frowned while watching the fire. "I hope you're right to do so. I had certainly hoped for an easier road than this."

"Now *you* sound worried," I said, forcing a smile. He didn't respond right away.

"Even if the river had been easier," he said, "this is a busy time at The Dalles. I didn't think your Mother should wait so long to reach Oregon City."

He sounded troubled, so I tried to encourage him. "I'm sure that if she'd had a choice, she would have chosen to walk over hot coals rather than to raft down a river. Besides, getting to a settlement early is what I want, too. I know things will be better then." I found myself smiling into the darkness. "In fact, Mother and I already have much to be thankful for. While she felt better, we had more fun and talked more than we had in a long time. I can't tell you what that means to me."

I hoped my reassurance would make him feel easier. Perhaps it would help us to discuss personal issues between ourselves. After several moments, I broke into Walter's thoughtful silence. "How's your father doing, Walter?"

"Pa? He's fine. Why?"

"When I talked to Tad, he said your

father didn't feel well."

"Tad! Huh. He'd have it that Pa should be put to bed, if it meant I'd stay and give Tad all the free time he wanted."

"Isn't your father ill at all?"

"Oh, he has a bad arm. Rheumatics. Started bothering him while we were working our way out of Burnt Canyon. The dampness over the Blues didn't help either. But he's better now."

Confused by Tad's accusations and Walter's offhandedness, I didn't know what to think. Was Walter trying to shield me from worry or had Tad exaggerated? Either seemed possible. And yet if Walter wasn't underplaying his father's condition, would he have spent so much time driving for his father? It was time we had a frank discussion.

"Walter, please tell me what has been bothering you lately."

"Bothering me? How do you mean?" he asked.

I resented this evasion, but kept my tone level. "I mean that you've been distant, as though you had something on your mind, or as if you were worried about something. What is it?"

"I've told you before, nothing that half the men on the train aren't worrying over.

The trail conditions, the weather, keeping our wagons together. That's it." He shrugged and moved as if to get up.

"Walter." My frustration sounded in my voice and he hesitated. "Please don't pretend you don't know what I mean. One day you ask me to wait for you, the next, you're avoiding me, and our conversations have the depth of a dry creek bed. Please talk to me."

He sat fidgeting with his hat, avoiding my eyes. Several times he looked as if he were about to speak, but then retreated behind the business of mutilating his hat. I waited, hoping for some honesty. There shouldn't be anything we couldn't talk over. After several minutes, he dented the crown of his hat, settled it on his head and stood. "Marjory, it's late. And I know we're both tired. If I've done anything to hurt your feelings, I'm sorry. Believe me, please. Nothing has changed." He reached out for me, but I turned away to spread the hot coals and put out the fire. Anger and disappointment warred within me. But as I turned to face him again, loneliness pushed to the forefront.

"Marjory, you know how I feel. Nothing is more important to me than you." He forced a tired smile. "Nothing, that is, except a little sleep. You'd better get some, too." He yawned. "Heard the next few days ahead are a little rough."

He caught my arm and pulled me toward him. Wrapping his arms about me, he rested his chin on top of my hair. With a tired sigh, he moved back, brushing my lips with a kiss as he whispered, "Pleasant dreams, Marjory."

Torn between responding to his gestures and resisting being put off, I did nothing. He walked off into the shadows of dying campfires that formed a flickering circle. Heavy of heart, I turned in without a thought for my daily journal entry.

By the time we reached Barlow's Pass, we'd gone through timber I never knew existed. Huge giants, wide enough to hide a wagon, surrounded us. We had surely come to a new land.

In some places we forged along a narrow pathway etched among towering trees that cut off all sight of the sky. The lofty dome of green above us kept the forest dark, damp and mysterious. Often our floor was spongy, or worse, we'd sink into mud holes, first one wheel then, bang, the next. Up steep hills we went, then down slippery rock paths, winding, twisting, up and over the most miserable of trails. We drove over stumps chopped off just low enough to allow our wagons to pass. Fallen trees had to be cut through or, where possible, gone around.

Of all these trials, the worst was the occasional fearful sound from unseen wildlife living within this dark and eerie mountainside. I took courage from the creaking, plodding sounds of our wagons, knowing that Danny would not venture out alone again. Walter, once more at the reins, also did much to improve my spirits.

I sat close to Mother, trying to keep her from bouncing about in her sleep. I inhaled the musty yet pleasant smells of a world plunged into semi-darkness through the opened canvas in back. The arid, dust-choked trails of earlier days were forgotten amid the cleansing pungency of fir, cedar and moss that permeated our wagon.

We camped in a small glade with mountain-fed water, but our animals found nothing to forage on in the forests. They refused to eat the needled branches we offered. There was nothing for them save some flour and what little amounts of pick brush we could find.

As our fire died down, Tad stopped by. "Been checkin' your mare. Walter's worried about her shoe."

"Is it holding?"

"Yup. Got any coffee left?"

I got out a tin and drained the pot.

"Thanks." He sat hunched over the cup, letting the steam rise to his face. "Pa's got Walter figurin' out what savings is left for the new store. I'm not much for figures, but Pa, he's pleased as punch 'bout the money he saved by taking this new route. 'Course, I can't argue. Forty-five dollars a wagon saved against ferrying costs can't be ignored." Tad frowned as he set his cup on the log beside him. "Good ol' Walt. Saves the day again."

Tad's complaints were becoming a ritual. Barely registering his grumbling, I allowed his monologue to divert my mind from my own troubles.

"Truth is," he continued without pause, "I was looking forward to the raft trip." With that, he absently lifted his steaming cup to his lips.

"Arghh!" Throwing the cup down, he shot up, holding his mouth as he danced about. "Ye gads, woman. Ow-ooh! I ain't no egg that needs poachin'." He sucked cool air in and puffed out his cheeks.

I jumped up. "Oh, Tad. I'm so sorry."

He glared at me, then swiped his chin

with his shirtsleeve and broke into a sheepish grin. "You nearly scalded me to death."

I laughed with relief at his recovery. "When you beg the last of the coffee that's been on the fire all evening, it's bound to be warm."

Once again I found that Tad left me in a better mood than he'd found me. I watched him saunter off, muttering about my blasted coffee and asking himself what it would take to qualify as *hot*.

The next morning we labored up a miserable hill. Mother had me concerned. She was very pale and her headache was constant now, the powders only dimming the pain.

After her last dose, she rallied, making an effort to talk past her discomfort.

"Marjory?"

"Yes. I'm here."

"The children. Are they all right?"

"Yes, Mother. They're playing in the wagon ahead of us."

Her lips curved, attempting a smile. After a moment, she roused herself again.

"Marjory, your father and I did love each other. That's important in a marriage." Her eyes closed, then opened, seeking mine again. "Plan carefully, child. I want you to be happy."

Distressed, I tried to respond to her concerns. "I will. I'm happy now, with you and the children." She frowned, but I didn't know what I'd done to make her do it. Desperately, I struggled to think of something to comfort her. "We'll all be okay, Mama. Honest."

"I know." She settled into a quiet rest for some time. When she woke, her eyes looked clearer. "Where are we now, Marjory?"

"We'll be stopping soon to eat. Are you hungry?"

She ignored my question. "Good. Have the children come spend the noon hour with me." She looked up at me. "You look tired. Are you getting enough rest?"

"Of course. I haven't been driving for days. Walter has been doing everything."

At first my words seemed to confuse her, then a wide smile lightened her features. "He's a good man. I like him." She caught my gaze; her eyes were clear and intent, and her tone turned serious. "You do, too, don't you?"

Denial died on my lips. Her concern left no room for dissembling. "Yes. Yes, I do like him."

"Does he feel the same?"

I hesitated, but her look held me. "I think so."

"Good." Her head sank deeper into the pillow and her expression became peaceful. "You . . . two do well together."

There was no need to respond, as a deep sleep overcame her. I was relieved, as I had no heart to tell her it wasn't that easy. I couldn't be responsible for putting Walter's dream beyond reach, or even delaying it. Nor could I ask him to choose my needs over his father's. I could only hope to have time. Time to get Mother well and settled. Time for Walter to help his father before working his own land.

The trail eased some, but Mother's sleep became agitated. She started to moan. I hadn't seen her like this before. I was about to call Walter when the wagons came to a stop. I heard Tad ride up and speak with Walter. Then Walter called back to say a wagon had stopped to replace an ox gone lame.

I told Walter about Mother. He came back with me and sat by her mattress. I was surprised that she didn't quiet once the wagon had stopped. Instead, her agitation grew and she began to whimper. Thinking it to be a bad dream, I shook her. "Mother wake up. Mother. It's me, Marjory."

She finally looked up in my direction, but not as though she saw me. Then she grasped her head, again moaning.

"Mother, are you all right?" My voice rose in concern. "Mother?"

She tried to focus on me. "Don't. Please. My head . . . hurts so."

"I'll mix her a powder," Walter said.

"Do you know what to do?"

"Yes." He took a tin from our medicine box, and went out to our water barrel. After a few moments, he returned. "Here. Give her this."

As I took the cup, he said, "Tad stopped by. I have to go, but don't worry. Just stay with your mother. All right?"

I nodded, though his words barely registered. I had all I could do to get Mother to drink her powder. I barely noticed Walter's leaving until he was gone. Mother took longer than usual to calm after the medicine. I'd heard how bad migraines could get, but I worried over this latest turn. I wished Walter hadn't left. Fifteen minutes later, he still hadn't returned, but Mother seemed less disturbed.

Then the wagon lurched under his weight as I felt him climb aboard. I looked up front to speak, only to stare dumbly into the face of our train's scout.

"Didna' mean to sceer you any, Ma'am. Young Wilkins asked me to take a spell at drivin'."

"Why? Where is he?" Immediately, I wondered if his father had taken ill.

The scout worked his jaw, chewing in that disgusting way he had, then turned his head to spit. He looked over at me and said, "Had some business with a feller up yonder." He nodded forward. "On the train a few hours before us."

I sat staring at him, dumbfounded. "There's another train on this trail? How do you know?"

"Wilkins talked to 'em while at The Dalles. Knowed when they was leaving. I been a' seeing their signs, too. Good at signs, I is. They ain't too far up thar . . ."

"Is he going alone? Out there?" I looked ahead into the shadowy forest. The horror of his getting lost shut out all fears of my being left alone.

"He's got my map. He'll be fine. He kin cut 'cross yonder, an' backtrack till they meets up."

"But why would Walter need to meet with them? With strangers?" I asked, trying to keep my tone under control. *And why now?* How could Walter leave with Mother taking a turn for the worse?

The scout shrugged, took up the reins, and hollered back to me. "Don't know much about it, Ma'am. Best ask when he returns. We's gotta move out now."

I heard the other wagons start up as he clucked at the team, and we pulled away. I checked on Mother and then moved forward, still full of troubling questions.

"Why didn't Walter come back with you to tell me he was going?"

"No need. I told 'im I'd s'plain. Ain't no time fer dallyin'."

Up ahead I saw a small clearing where the other wagons pulled off the trail as far as possible. Our driver kept going and I held my breath, praying we'd clear between trees and wagons. Without even slowing, he gained the lead. I looked back to see the others falling in behind. Now the Meyerses' wagon was last, adding to my discomfort.

I returned to Mother, feeling an overwhelming loneliness, wishing again for Walter's reassurance. Mother's spell had frightened me badly. Walter had seen that. Yet he'd left abruptly. Why?

I knew, other than her powders, not much more could be done until we got Mother off this miserable road and into a proper bed. *But to have left without a word.* I turned away from my thoughts. It must have been his father, I told myself. Poor Walter.

Recalling my earlier vow to do better by Walter, I admitted I couldn't claim much success. Instead of doubts, Walter had a right to expect my support. I leaned back against the trunk to steady myself as we traveled over the bumpy road.

After some time, our wagon slowed. "I'll be back soon, Mother," I whispered, in case she wasn't actually asleep. Hoping to see Walter riding back, I climbed up front just in time to miss by inches a wad of tobacco juice as it shot past me. I flinched, casting the scout a frown.

He grinned as he tolerantly explained, "Miss, if they be one talent most folks knows me fer, it's that of being a . . . durned good sure-spitter. Don't ever miss where I aims to, never fear."

I set my jaw and looked ahead into a bright western sun, irritated at not seeing Walter and disgusted by the scout's manners. I was ready to slip back into the wagon when a brightness caught my attention. It was as if the forests ahead had moved aside to clear the way before us.

We drew to a stop. No one made a move to pull off the road as the scout swung down from our wagon. I quickly followed him. We walked ahead of the horses. The other drivers got down and followed, too.

As our scout stopped short, I almost ran into him and gasped at finding myself standing at what appeared to be the edge of the earth. Directly before us, the road dropped into a chasm of rocks and mud at a pitch so steep, I could see no possible way of descending. My heart dropped, as if I myself had been flung ruthlessly to the bottom of the abyss before me.

"Whooee," whistled the scout. "Now that there's a plumb long ways down." He bent and tossed a small rock over the edge. It didn't hit until almost a third of the way down. No one said another word for some moments.

I stood there beside a person as near to being a stranger as I'd find on the train, facing sure disaster for my family. I felt more alone than I'd ever been before.

A thousand rivers would have been better than this.

Twenty

October 24, 1847
Dear Friend,
Dear God. Be with us, please. This train must move on, even though the chute is fiercely steep. If only I could talk to Mother about our descent, to prepare her. Maybe our fear is no greater than that of the others, but our risks surely are. They see only the task before them. I see only the danger for Mother. And I can do nothing but wait.

I set my journal aside, watching Mother, wishing she'd open her eyes, if only for a minute. Listening to the men chopping down drag trees and discarding deck boards to lighten their wagons made me feel even worse. There was no one to speak out for us, no one committed to our safety. Even good folks had to attend to their own needs first. Papa would have done the same.

When I'd stood at the top of the abyss with our scout, looking at sure disaster for my mother, I'd asked him what we could do. He had shrugged, aimed and spat before drawling, "Git down it, I reckon."

The only solace left me was prayer, so I prayed. Then I determined to do what I could to prepare for the inevitable. As I looked for the best method of securing loose objects, Tad came by and called to me.

I made my way to the back. "What?"

"I don't want to disturb your ma. Come out here."

I crawled over the tailgate and jumped down. Tad stood with several mattresses and some rope in his arms. I could feel his eagerness for the challenge.

For just a moment, I hated him for that. Then reason returned, and I was ready to listen.

"While the others are cutting drag trees, I've come to help."

"To help me cut a drag tree?" I asked.

"Of course not. The others are doing that. But I have plenty of rope for tying the end of the trunk to your axle when they're ready," he said cheerfully.

"Thanks, but I wish we didn't have to rely on a tree dragging behind us to keep us from hurtling to the bottom. What if the branches only skim over the shale on a hill this steep?"

Tad just grinned. "Ever try dragging a pine tree by the chopped-off end? Those branches dig into everything they scrape against. It'll slow you down, don't worry.

But the scout and I have talked about how to make this as easy as possible on your ma. He says suspending her bed from the bows overhead won't work on such a steep incline." Tad dropped his burden near our wagon. "So, first we need to pack all your heavy stuff forward and tie it down."

He walked up front and climbed in over the box, with me following.

"I'll move stuff up front, and you can take down everything hanging from overhead," he said. "We don't want anything falling."

I removed Papa's rifle and smaller items tied to the bows, wishing it was Walter rather than Tad trying to help us. "Do you know why your brother left the train so suddenly?"

" 'Cause he went chasing after some train up ahead. Oh, gosh. Didn't I tell you?"

I straightened, almost dropping the rifle. "Didn't you tell me what? I haven't seen you since he left."

"Really? I'm sorry. Thought sure I had." He was struggling to secure the trunk in place.

"Well? What were you supposed to tell me?" I gripped the butt of the rifle, and the tip of its barrel dug into the floor as I leaned heavily on it.

Tad tugged on the rope, holding back the

barrels and sacks of food supplies and household items behind the trunk. "He was in such an all-fired hurry. Didn't get all of it. Something about having to catch someone up ahead. Matter of life and death." Stopping short as he looked up, he hurried on. "But don't you worry, now. He'll be back. Real soon," Tad said reassuringly.

My knees felt weak and my emotions tumbled about, one over the other. He had left me word, but he did ride off, and I was still left with a question. Why? Slowly, while storing the rifle away with care, I tried to make sense of it. Walter had left before we reached the chute. The scout said he'd taken a short cut through the woods to meet this mysterious train, so he couldn't have seen what lay ahead for Mother.

Just then, Tad took a corner of Mother's mattress. "All right. Everything looks well tied down, so let's slide your Mother's mattress toward the tailgate for a minute."

That brought me around. I rushed to help, making sure his energies were not spent at Mother's expense. But when it came to Mother, he demonstrated the greatest care. I could almost forgive his careless memory. When we tugged her mattress toward the tailgate, her pillow caught, pulling it free of the bedding, and causing her head to jar against the mattress. Thankfully it did not disturb her sleep. Tad hauled in the padding he had left outside and began overlapping one mattress against the other, until the trunk and boxes were padded partway up from the bottom.

"I am sorry, Marjory, for forgetting Walt's message," Tad said, as he struggled with the mattresses. "It's just that he's always telling me something or other and I just don't listen half the time. Can't figure the big hurry anyway. Surely we'd meet up with this doctor at a more convenient place. They gotta rest up, too."

I stopped and swung around to face him. "Doctor? What doctor?"

"Huh?" He looked up from his work. "Didn't I mention that?"

"No, you did not. Just exactly what did he say about a doctor?"

"Nothing, really. Just mentioned that they had one on the train he was chasing after. Really."

I glared at him.

"Honest. That's all he said. But you gotta realize, Marjory, he always has some bee in his bonnet."

I watched Tad return to padding the floor, trying to fit this last shred of information into the tangle of doubt that Walter's absence created. I knew Walter worried about Mother, but she'd already seen a doctor. So, if he didn't go for Mother's sake, who did need a doctor? Walter's father? But surely Tad would know about that. However, Tad was a genius at blocking out facts that he considered inconvenient.

Tad adjusted the extra mattresses that padded the floorboards where Mother would lie.

"There. Now maybe we better wake her and get her settled."

Only then did I picture the actual journey. "She's going to ride all the way down inside the wagon?"

"Marjory, there isn't any way that she can climb down on her own. She's too weak. So we're taking extra precautions for her. She'll be all right. Honest."

I knelt down and shook her gently, trying to wake her. "Mother? Mother?" I called louder. At the very least, she should know what we were doing. But she didn't respond.

"Mother!" I shouted. "Please." Her head rolled back and forth as she moaned, and I had to face the fact that she wasn't merely sleeping. "She . . . she won't wake up."

For the first time since we'd stopped at Laurel Hill, a look of concern crossed Tad's face. "Wait here. I'll fetch somebody."

Minutes after scrambling out of the wagon, I heard him returning with Mrs. Meyers. She climbed in and knelt beside Mother. After trying to wake her, and listening to her breathing, Mrs. Meyers faced me.

"I'm sorry, dear. I fear she might be in a coma."

Coma. I pushed the word away, trying to think of some other way to get her down the hill.

There wasn't any.

Mrs. Meyers reached out and patted my hand. "There's nothing you can do. And maybe it's the Lord's way of sparing your ma the fear of being let down the chute that-a-way."

She put her arm around me. "It's for the best, dear."

She and Tad bent to finish his task. They moved Mother's mattress onto the cushioned bed he'd made.

"Here. Let's brace her, so. It'll help her on the way down." He angled her to lean slightly back against the trunk.

Then they lashed her, blankets and all, against the anchored chest and boxes, so she couldn't roll about. She lay in a prison of bedding, unaware of what was to come.

And I couldn't tell her. I couldn't explain why it was necessary to bind her so tightly.

Tad helped Mrs. Meyers over the tailgate and turned back for me. I looked at him, thinking about Mother. About her waking halfway down, alone, not understanding why or what was happening. Hearing the noise of scraping hooves, sliding rocks and crashing limbs as the team tried to break their plunge. Only able to imagine what was happening. "No," I said, as he reached up for me. "I'm staying with Mother. I can't leave her." For a moment they looked up at me in shocked silence.

"She's alone. I can't let her wake up alone." A strong pulse throbbed inside my ears. I clutched the top edge of the tailgate. "She needs me."

"But dear, think what you're doing," Mrs. Meyers pleaded.

She didn't understand. How could she? It was more than my fear of Mother waking. There was guilt. Guilt over my impatience and hostility, for judging her when she was ill, for . . . for not sharing Papa. This time I could be there for her.

I couldn't explain, but I wouldn't, I couldn't, leave Mother. Tad looked to Mrs. Meyers, perplexed, as if this situation were out of his depth. Before I could reassure him, I spotted Danny watching us, standing just beyond the wagon behind ours, standing alone, his hands jammed into his pockets. I didn't think he could hear us, but he must have sensed a drama was going on that somehow involved him. His eyes were wide, intent on our actions, and I realized how much my decision did involve him. Danny, Jamie and Sarie. Three young children, more dependent on my actions than they could ever guess.

Are the children all right? Mother had asked me. Her concern had been for the children, even in her pain. She hadn't wasted energies on apologies or vindication. Her thoughts were first and foremost for her children. For me.

My thoughts had centered on guilt.

Tad and Mrs. Meyers watched me anxiously. Tears clouded my vision, yet I saw Mother waking, hurting, frightened and alone in a runaway wagon. And I saw Danny, also alone, waiting.

"All right," I sobbed. Blindly reaching for Tad, I climbed over the gate and he swung me down from the wagon.

Clumsily, he patted my shoulder. "The scout said she'll be safe. We'll ease the wagon down gently as we can. Promise."

The absurdity of his promise stung me. I

walked over to Danny, numb, trying to keep my mind centered on first things first. He looked at me, wordlessly clutched my hand, and together we walked to the edge of the chute to wait.

The big Laurel. How innocent it sounded. Like a large flower, adorning some fancy table setting. I looked down at the boulders and sheets of jagged shale covering the drop before us. A spring muddied what ground could be seen, adding to the danger. How could our teams ever negotiate this bed of loose rocks? It was a waiting landslide, ready to sweep the unwary off their feet to the unforgiving bottom below.

I watched as the men tied a thirty-foot drag tree to our axle. One of the younger women with her two youngsters picked her way down the edge of the hillside.

I ran back to Mrs. Meyers.

"Can you bring the boys, if I take Sarie? I have to be there when Mother reaches the bottom."

Before she could answer, Danny objected. "I want to go with you."

I knelt down to face him. "Danny. I need you to help Mrs. Meyers with Jamie. She can't do it alone. Please!"

He hesitated, then slowly nodded agreement. I turned back to Mrs. Meyers.

"Go on," she said. "I'll manage with Danny's help."

I scooped Sarie up and ran to follow the other woman. Clasping Sarie tightly to me, I crawled over logs and slid, squatting on my heels, sidestepped boulders, waded through mud holes and slipped on loose shale. Sometimes my progress was painfully slow, with the weight of Sarie pulling against my arms, and at other times I held tight and tried to keep my feet under me as I plunged down the lesser slopes. Sarie alternated between enjoying the game and screaming for me to stop.

After covering about ten rods, I caught up to Mrs. Johnson, who had an even harder struggle with two children, both under five.

"Is yours the first wagon to be lowered?" she asked.

I looked back. They hadn't begun yet. "Yes," I answered, catching my breath.

We rested a moment, and then renewed our trek. Off to our left, we came across the remains of a wagon rotting in a hollow. It lay dashed against the rocks. Boards, wheels and the broken head of a hobbyhorse with one large, black eye staring skyward littered its own lonely gravesite. Pieces of canvas, caught in a scrub, swayed listlessly in the breeze.

Neither of us commented, turning our heads away as if we'd come upon a scene of indecency.

From above, men's voices, coaxing and threatening the team, met with the frantic whinnies from horses resisting the madness being demanded of them. I could see the poor beasts pulling back and trying to avoid the path. But they had no choice; all that was left was to frantically pick their way down, struggling to hold their burden back as it threatened to overrun them.

We hurried, climbing down over sixty rods before coming to a muddy bottom. Our wagon behind us careened over rocks and slid through mud, the weight pushing against the team, nearly forcing them to their knees, but the scout scrambled alongside, steadying, encouraging and guiding the terrified animals. Occasionally, a foothold was found for wagon and team to pause and recuperate. Then they plunged forward, their merciless descent slowed by the splayed branches of the drag tree and the brute strength of the horses.

I watched the bowed canvas lurching erratically from side to side, knowing that Mother would be able to endure her pain only if she remained in a coma.

It seemed an eternity, but finally the team

reached bottom, pulling out of the way, their sides heaving, eyes wide with fright, and sweat running in ragged rivulets down their backs. I handed Sarie to Mrs. Johnson and ran the short distance to our wagon. The scout tried to get inside first, but was slowed by the horses, and I scrambled over the tailgate.

Landing on my hands and knees, I looked over to Mother. Her eyes stared back at me, wide, blank, unseeing, like those of the broken hobbyhorse in the hollow. Like Papa.

But that couldn't be. She was sleeping, only sleeping. I looked about frantically. She was still lashed in. Secure, safe from anything harmful. The wagon was undamaged. All had remained anchored.

Perhaps she was in shock. Or was having one of her misty spells. Yes, it had to be that. It couldn't be like Papa. Not like . . . But her eyes, I couldn't refute her eyes.

I crawled over and sank down beside her, laying my head against her breast. There was no rise or fall, no resistance, only limp indifference.

"Mama, no! Not you, too. Please, God!" I hadn't even told her how sorry I was. I hadn't understood. "I'm so sorry, Mama," I whispered into the stillness.

Slowly, I became aware of our scout. He patted me, gently tugging. "Please, Miss. There be nothin' ya kin do."

I thought of the last time Mother and I had talked. And I remembered. *The children.* I looked at her as if she could speak. "What will we do, Mother?"

"Miss. C'mon now. Ye'll be makin' yerself sick."

I clung tighter. *We can't lose you, too.*

"She's gone, I tell ya. Come away now, Miss."

His hands gently pulled at my arms from behind, easing me to my feet. I didn't want to leave her and glanced back, praying it wasn't true. And for one single second, it wasn't. She stood tall against a mist of white, wet hair cascading down her back, grabbing at our makeshift sheet as it teetered, threatening to fall. I could hear her gentle laugh. For a moment, I felt her nearness. Her smile. Her forgiveness. Then the emptiness returned.

The scout moved me to the back of the wagon and urged me to sit, leaning me against the tailgate; the tailgate where I had first seen the stillness come over Papa. I felt a blanket being lowered over me. I didn't want it, but I didn't protest. What did it matter? It wouldn't warm the coldness that began to crawl up my limbs. And I didn't want it to. I welcomed a lack of feeling. I sank into it.

But he wouldn't leave me to it. He patted and soothed me and looked out the back for someone to help him. It was that gesture, that anxious look of his, that struck a chord. I knew, then. My time was up. Others needed to get down the hill. We needed to get back to the trail. To move on. I heard him hail someone and felt his weight leave the wagon as he jumped down. Yes, leave, I thought. Go back to the trail and leave me be. For me, there was no hurry. There was nowhere to go now.

The worst had happened. Mother had died alone. Slowly, a question formed and I couldn't get away from it. What had happened? Had she awakened to find herself restrained while the wagon careened downhill? Did she think she'd been tied and left behind, helpless? What must she have felt? That I'd left her behind and had jumped for safety?

My mind battered against the wall of questions, but they were unanswerable. I could never share Mother's last few moments. Forgiven or not, I'd been left behind, and she'd gone on. I gave way to tears, and the tears gave way to the silence of grief.

Then Mrs. Johnson joined me. She was alone. And the comforting began again. I tried to remain beyond the words. I wanted to stay in the emptiness of solitude.

It was the sounds of wagons struggling down the chute that finally made me sit up. Thunderous screeching and banging came from wagons descending behind us. The shouts of drivers guiding, exhorting the teams, could be heard above the din as two more wagons made it down, moving on to make room for the next. I pushed my hair away from my face. A remnant of emptiness remained as I turned back to Mother. A blanket had been placed over her.

But that wasn't right, I thought. *She isn't ready yet.*

Calmly, I lifted the blanket. The pain would return, but it was not with me at the moment. I had learned what needed to be done. I laid out her dress and Mrs. Johnson helped me. I fixed her hair and crossed her arms. I would have closed her eyes, but it was too late. Instead, I dampened a rag with her cologne and washed her face, then draped my handkerchief across her. Now she was ready. I tucked the blanket back around her.

Within minutes the scout returned, calling Mrs. Johnson to the back of the wagon. As they talked, the word "children" penetrated my seclusion as nothing else could have.

"Sarie." I hurriedly joined Mrs. Johnson. "Where is Sarie?"

"Right over there," Mrs. Johnson said. "Scout took the children to the ladies who followed us down. He thought to give us some time to see to your mother."

"Thank you," I mumbled as I scrambled out the back of the wagon. I ran to the woman holding Sarie. She was waiting in a small group who had watched their wagons make the descent. "Sarie," I called out. "Come on, sweetie." I reached for her and she lunged into my arms. Once again chubby cheeks covered by warm tears nuzzled against my neck, pulling me back from the edge of self-pity.

By now three wagons had made it down. The muddy hollow buzzed with activity, but I didn't feel a part of any of it. I watched the first Wilkins wagon lumber down the treacherous terrain as though I had never heard of the Wilkins family. I clung instead to Sarie.

"Are ya all right, now, Miss? Miss?"

The scout had come up behind me. "Yes. I'm quite all right." I rested my cheek on Sarie's head.

"Mrs. Meyers and Mrs. Wilkins are on their way down with the little 'uns. They'll come to ya shortly."

Jamie. Danny. How can I tell them? My mind stepped around the question.

Tad's wagon reached bottom before the women did. I saw him coming toward me, but I concentrated on the last wagons yet to come.

"Marjory, I just heard. I'm so sorry. You've had such horrible things happen to you. Can I do anything? Anything at all?"

Mr. Wilkins's wagon positioned itself. It would be next. I looked at Tad. "No, there's nothing." A sense of waiting took a strong hold on me.

"Are you all right?" Tad asked.

I didn't watch the wagon as it started down. "Yes, I'm fine, Tad."

His expression was doubtful, but I didn't care. Sarie became restless, but I held her closer. Tad gave up trying to keep me engaged in conversation and, when he spotted his mother and Mrs. Meyers, he excused himself.

Mrs. Meyers left the boys with Mrs. Wilkins and met Tad. That was good. I needed time before telling Danny. I could see her taking in the news, shaking her head, tsk, tsking. But I was grateful she'd diverted the boys' attention by letting them watch the action with Mrs. Wilkins. Danny started to come my way when he spotted me, but Mrs. Wilkins called him back, pulling some jerky from her pocket. He hesitated. When I signaled for him to stay, he turned back.

Finally there was one more wagon to come. Then it would be time.

It took a while for the last wagon to start down. Mrs. Meyers had joined me and hovered about, fussing. I didn't want her concern or her pity. I just wanted to see to Mother.

But Mrs. Meyers insisted I go with her to the fire pit that had been started. Just for a cup of hot coffee, she said. I went. After drinking the coffee I felt calmer, but still I could think of little else than seeing to Mother. But Mrs. Meyers had other priorities. She wanted to know about the children. Should she wait for me to tell them? What would I say? Could she help? I didn't know how I could tell the children. The prospect was as painful as losing Mother had been. But it was no use; they had to come first and I knew I had to be the one to tell them. Laying Mother to rest would come in its own good time.

Mrs. Meyers's questions had to be dealt with, before she decided to tell the children about their mother's death herself. Sarie had fallen asleep in my arms. I closed my eyes. What would I tell them? And when? I took a deep breath and met Mrs. Meyers's anxious gaze.

"I'll tell Danny, so he can attend Mother's service. When your wagon is down, I'd like you to keep Jamie and Sarie inside." I rubbed Sarie's leg as she slept. "I'll talk to Jamie, telling him a little, but he couldn't understand about Papa and I'd rather he didn't have to go through another funeral."

Mrs. Meyers looked surprised. "Yes. I believe you're right. That does seem best."

The funeral was different from Papa's. The ground was wet, the trench deeper. Rocks were piled nearby. Our scout, though genuine of spirit, had little to say. "Her younguns will miss her, Lord. But she'll be best off with you and yours. Amen."

Danny stood with me. He was quiet and pale. Later, I must spend time reassuring him, I thought. I didn't want him to feel alone. He squeezed my hand and stood on tiptoe to whisper, "Where is Walter?"

I almost gave way. Did everyone Danny cared about have to leave him behind? "I'm not sure, Danny. We'll ask Tad later."

He clung to my hand and stayed beside me everywhere I went.

After the service, Tad caught up to us as we walked to our wagon. "We're going farther on to find a camping spot. Ma wants you to sup with us when we stop. You and the children. Is that all right?"

I came up with the first excuse I could think of. "I don't want to disturb your father. We'll be fine."

"Why should you disturb Pa?"

"Isn't that why Walter went up ahead? For a doctor?"

"I don't know why he went. Maybe he just couldn't wait to make a claim. Whatever it was, it wasn't for Pa. His rheumatism is a lot better now. Has been for days."

I felt something slip inside. It hurt — hurt somewhere deep — but I would not allow myself to think of Walter now. What did his reasons matter? He'd left. I had the children to think of. "Thank your mother for me, Tad. But I'd rather be alone with the children for now."

We had already lined up the wagons to resume our travels when I heard Mrs. Meyers asking the scout to wait for her. He had taken over driving our wagon and resented delays, but she insisted on joining me. I didn't want to visit, but I made room for her to sit down.

"The little ones fell asleep during the funeral, Marjory. They were exhausted." She looked at Danny, who sat very near me. "Dear, would you go to my wagon to wait for them to wake? I'll visit with your sister and you can tell us when they're up."

I resented her request, wanting to keep Danny with me, but it was easier to give in since I wasn't sure why she had come. I gave him a reassuring nod. "I'll be right here."

He jumped down and trudged over to the Meyerses' wagon.

"We'll camp soon. The mister says it's not far to grass."

I nodded.

"Dear, I hope you know how fond we are of you. And the children, too, of course."

"Yes. You've been a godsend." A godsend, I thought, but not now. Please, not now. I was tired. I wanted — needed — time alone.

Her face softened with a smile, but then she turned serious again. Her bonnet slipped to hang down her back as the wagon started with a lurch.

"It seems cruel to speak to you so soon after your loss. I mean, if we weren't so close to our destination . . . Well, you'll be needin' time to think on it." Her hands tortured a corner of her apron.

"Think on what, Mrs. Meyers?" I covered a yawn. *If I could only sleep for awhile.*

"Poor thing. You've been so brave. Especially for one so young. Your whole life is ahead of you. You should have proper opportunity to live it."

"I will," I said dully.

She sighed. "It'll be pretty hard, if you have to raise three little ones with no help. You'll do your best, but will it really be right for the children?"

"What do you mean?"

She shifted nervously. Now, pleating her apron with her fingers, I could see her struggling for the right words. *Why can't this wait?* I wondered. *At least until camp. I'll be able to think better then.*

"Marjory, a girl of fifteen . . ."

"I'm almost sixteen."

"Of course, dear. But you'll still have it hard, finding work to support four people. And who will care for the children while you work? Wait!" She raised her hand to stave off my protest. "Let me finish. If you marry, it would be better for you, but wouldn't the children be an unfair burden for a young man just starting out? And wouldn't they eventually feel it?"

"What are you trying to say?"

She sighed, ready to plunge forward. "We . . . the mister and me, we always wanted children. We're getting on in years, now, you see. A farm needs children. To someday take over."

She hurried on. "Not that that's why we're approaching you. Not at all. We love the children. More than you could guess." Returning her attention to her hands, she continued, "And we can well support them."

The wagon pulsed with unspoken emotion as we rolled along the trail. The deafening silence lasted for several minutes. Then she met my gaze, unflinching, determined. I found myself stiffening.

She sighed. "I know how cruel this must seem to you. With your latest loss and all. But, you see, now would be best for the children. I mean, to make other changes in their lives," she said in a flurry. "It would be so much easier in the long run, to make a complete break here, now, with only two days till we leave the train."

I sat rigid, stunned by her words.

"I'm sorry, child. This is hard. I really am sorry. But don't you see? We're hoping our offer will be good for all of us. I don't say it ain't hard to think of, but you must. You got no means to care for the little ones. You'll be hard pressed to find your own way."

A coil tightened in my stomach. "What you're saying is . . ."

She knelt down before me, folding my hands in hers. "Child, child, I'm saying the good Lord is providing an answer to a very painful situation. You have lost both your parents. We have wanted a family for these many years. Someone to love, to turn our land over to in the years ahead."

I sat there gaping at her. I had to stop her words. I had to have time to think. But still I sat, dumbstruck. Her words began to hurt. They pounded at me. And Mrs. Meyers kept on, talking . . . talking.

"Also, the children have come to know us. To care for us, I believe. Don't you see? It's almost as if God has pointed the way for you."

I drew back against the words as I huddled against the stacked bedding.

"It seems cruel not to offer you a place, too. I know that. We thought long and hard on it. But don't you see? It wouldn't work. The children could never accept us as family, if they had you to turn to. They'd be forever torn."

She leaned forward, her gnarled hands touching me. "You do see that, don't you?"

Her voice grated on my nerves. I felt as if I might break, and still I sat there wondering at my lack of reaction. I just wanted her voice to stop.

"We'd provide for their future. Everything we have would go to them . . ."

"Please," I interrupted. "Not now. Not tonight. After supper, we'll talk then. If you could send Danny over when we stop, I'll talk with him. Then we can discuss it."

Relief washed over her pinched face. "Yes. That would be good. Come eat supper with us first. Then we'll talk." She scrambled towards the driver, turning just before asking him to let her down. "Hard as it seems, Marjory, we must do what's best for the children."

She must have seen me flinch.

"We'll talk later, child. Bless you."

What's best for the children. Her words echoed in the stillness. *What's best for the children.*

Twenty-One

October 24, 1847
Dear Friend,

Perhaps writing will help me sort things through the decisions I have to make. It's so hard. I wish I could talk with Mother just once more. Her death leaves an emptiness in me and, even worse, a fear. A fear that gnaws at my decisions and feeds my doubt. Yet I can't give in, for the children are depending on me. I must think of what is best for the children.

Lord, help me see clearly. Tell me how we should go.

I've given much consideration to Mrs. Meyers's offer. She is quite right. I don't know how I can support the four of us. We have some money. Maybe even enough for the whole winter, if I'm careful. But what then? If I do find work, how could I leave Sarie and Jamie all day with Danny? He's only eight.

Yet, how can we separate?

I know the children would be well cared for by the Meyerses. They could give them security and even build for their future.

Mother. What would you have me do?

That evening as I waited for us to stop and make camp, I sorted through everything again: all my reasons to keep our family together and the truth of what Mrs. Meyers had said. I was well aware of how unforgiving the frontier could be, if I chose unwisely. There were no societies in the Oregon looking out for orphans, or established church organizations to help the destitute. Father had warned me that each family had to eke out its own survival.

I thought about Mother's love for us and about Danny's anxiety over losing Papa, and now Mother. I thought, too, of the Meyerses. Of Mrs. Meyers. She was kindhearted, but she was older, less understanding. Still, she was well intentioned and established.

I was family, but . . . My thoughts went around in circles, and I was no closer to an answer when we stopped for the night.

Danny helped the scout water our team. At last he came running to our wagon, and still I didn't know what to do. It would soon be time to go to the Meyerses' wagon for

338

supper. I had to make a decision.

"Danny," I said, when he returned, climbing over the box. "I want to talk to you about what we'll do now that Mother's gone."

He sat beside me, quiet, looking at his feet.

"Without Mother, it will be very hard for us to make a living on our own, Danny. I want us to remain together, but it might not be possible." I glanced at him, but he didn't look up. "The Meyerses have grown very fond of us all, but since I'm grown, they have offered to raise Sarie, Jamie and you. They'd like to do for you just as Mama and Papa would have done."

He remained silent.

"Danny? What do you think?"

His shoe scuffed at a floor brace. After some minutes, he mumbled something.

"What? I didn't hear you, Danny. What did you say?"

His arms stiffened as he gripped the seat and he lifted his eyes to mine. They shone bright through the night's shadows. "Why did Mama have to leave us, too?"

His voice was stiff with anger. I was surprised at the forcefulness of his feelings, feelings that I well understood. I had asked the same question. I paused to collect myself. *Please God,* I prayed silently, *help me to ease his pain.* "I can't answer that, Danny. But I know that she didn't want to leave us." I thought about Mother's simple faith. *God is Love.* "I can't believe it was something that God caused or even wanted to happen. I believe He wants the best for us . . ."

Danny didn't wait for me to finish before lashing out. "Why didn't He stop at least one of them from dying? If He really loves us, why didn't He?" Then he slumped back down on the bench. "He could have. He could have *easy,* if He'd wanted to." He looked as if he was working hard to keep from crying.

I had to make him understand. But what could I say? Then I remembered Golgotha. "I feel a lot like you do, Danny."

I could see his struggle between anger and acceptance.

"But we're not alone. Jesus asked God the same thing. *Why? Why did thou forsake me?* Remember?" I wasn't too sure where I was going, but I pushed on. If I stuck to the truth, God would help.

"Did God forsake Jesus?" I asked.

Danny shrugged. "No." He thought for a moment, then looked at me, defiance putting an edge to his voice. "But Jesus was supposed to die. Mama and Papa weren't. They had *us* to take care of."

"That's true. But God doesn't pick some to live and some to die. He gives us the freedom of choice and then stands by us, always there to give comfort when things go bad for us. Do you remember how Mother always told us not to be afraid, like when your little friend died from measles?"

"Yes," he answered reluctantly.

"Remember how she said that he wasn't alone, that God would be with him if he got better or even if he didn't?"

"Yes."

"Well, He is always there, to encourage, to forgive and to love us. That's what He did when He received our parents after Papa's accident and Mother's illness. He received them with love. And when bad things happen to us, He is there for us, too."

There was less starch to Danny's profile and I waited for his reaction. I waited for quite awhile. At last, he relented and turned toward me.

"What was wrong with Mama, Marjory?"

"I don't really know. Her headaches made her weak and something went very wrong. I just don't know what."

"Oh." After another moment, he looked up at me again. "But she still loved us and really would have stayed if she could have?"

"Yes, Danny. Yes. I know Mama loved us, above everything. Her thoughts were always for us, even when she was very ill." I felt her love wash over me, and suddenly I knew there was only one answer I could give the Meyerses.

I must keep us together.

God forgive me if I'm wrong. I could not break up the last of our family; it was all the children had ever known. Somehow I'd make the remainder of Papa's savings last until I found a way.

I helped Mrs. Meyers with the last of the supper preparations, avoiding the subject that preyed on both our minds. The air was heavy with the promise of rain. During the meal we sat in a circle around the fire in virtual silence, and only when we all knew it was time for me either to take the children or agree to leave them, did I speak.

"Mrs. Meyers, you have been good to our family," I began. The words flowed, even though I hardly knew what I was about to say. I wanted to give my answer, take the children and go. "I can't express my gratitude enough." Her knuckles whitened as she waited on my every word. "I'm sorry, but we must stay together. Please try to understand."

Mrs. Meyers's face seemed to crumple. Mr. Meyers moved to stand beside her, slipping his hand under her elbow while addressing me. I focused on keeping my knees steady.

"We understand." His voice remained kindly yet firm, as he patted his wife's hand reassuringly. "We knowed it's your decision to make. Our offer were made so's you'd have a choice." His arm drew tighter around his wife, cradling her, supporting her. She straightened.

"Ain't that right?" he said, seeking her eyes.

I saw their shared grief, and I felt vulnerable and alone.

Mrs. Meyers forced agreement past a voice broken by pain. "Yes . . . we hoped . . . but 'twas your decision to make."

Yes, my decision. Made alone, on my own. And if I was wrong . . . "They have lost both mother and father. They can't lose me, too. It wouldn't be right. We have to stay together."

The Meyerses had done nothing but good by me. I wanted to make them understand, but the decision was made and I needed to get our family back to our own wagon.

Mrs. Meyers watched Danny, now tying Jamie's shoelace. "I can't agree with you, yet don't think hard of me. It's easier to be generous when you're young. When you can find one way or 'nother to keep trying for what's important to you. But we ain't gonna have no other chances of raising younguns. We were settled on that, till . . . It just don't seem fair." Her voice rose as she spoke. "You ain't even started your life yet. It's all ahead for you. What can you possibly offer them?" She covered her face with her apron.

I knew her pain, but I couldn't help her. "You have everything to offer them," I agreed. "Everything, except their past. Only I can keep that alive for them. They need to remember Mother and Papa, through me. I'm sorry."

She said nothing more. Mr. Meyers helped me to gather the children's things. As I held Sarie, I tried to thank the Meyerses for all they'd done, but saw it was best to leave that for later.

Jamie and Sarie didn't realize their change in beds meant another tremendous change in their lives. Danny did.

By the time we returned to our wagon, Sarie and Jamie were tired enough to hunker down in their covers with few questions. I prattled on about reaching our destination very soon, until their eyes drooped and their questions dwindled.

When they drifted off, Danny and I crawled into bed, too. Exhaustion pressed in on me, and I had little energy left. I listened to the gentle sounds of camp life winding down, when a whisper broke through the darkness.

"Marjory?"

"Yes?"

"I'm glad we're staying together. It'll be all right. I know it will. Just wait till Walter gets back. He'll help with the team again. You'll see."

A fresh sadness swept over me, and I tried to keep my voice from breaking as I bade Danny goodnight.

I tossed without sleeping, even though I was exhausted. Rain began pelting the canvas. The uneven splattering overhead refused to lull me into dreamless sleep. Instead, I at last gave in and rummaged through Mother's medicine bag to find the familiar bottle of laudanum that she used during times of fevers and the like. Carefully, I unscrewed the lid and sipped a dose.

Some time later, I roused to the noisy clatter of riders pulling into camp, but was too drowsy to be concerned. Still later, I was dimly aware of hearing my name breaking above the pounding cloudburst.

Yet, by the next morning, the tangy freshness of a rain-swept day made me wonder if I hadn't dreamed the disturbances. That is, until I saw Walter purposefully making his way to our wagon, even before breakfast fires were underway. He hesitated as he reached me.

"Marjory. I tried to wake you when I got in last night, but couldn't. We must talk now. Please. Ma is making breakfast for the children. Will you walk to the river with me?"

I had wanted dearly to talk yesterday. When he'd left me alone, when I had needed him most. But now, I'd tucked all emotion away. It seemed easier that way.

"We are so near the end of the trail. Can't we wait until then?"

"That's just why we can't. Please, Marjory."

I didn't have the heart to speak of my feelings, or the will to refuse him.

He spotted his mother coming and waved at her, then took my arm, ushering me toward the river. We stopped near a tree, and he waited for me to sit. He paced while I leaned against the rough bark. Finally he lowered himself, sitting so as to face me.

"Yesterday I knew I had to go for the doctor. The train that had left a half a day ahead of us had a medical man with them."

"Why didn't you tell me you were going?" I asked.

"I did. I had to hurry to catch them as soon as possible, so I told Tad to let you know there was a doctor ahead that I thought could help make things easier for your mother."

"You told Tad that the doctor was for my mother?"

"Sure. Who else would need one?" he asked.

"I thought your father might have taken ill."

"My father? Why did you think that?"

"Earlier, Tad was worried . . ."

"Tad! Tad doesn't know how to worry. I'm sorry this was such a mess. You must have wondered about a lot of things. To be honest, I had been feeling guilty enough about this disastrous trail. It was so much worse than I'd been led to expect."

I stared at him. "I could hardly blame you for that."

"I had thought it would be better than the rapids. I blame myself for what happened to your mother."

"But why should you blame yourself for Mother's death?" I asked, surprised by his comment. I had been the one to leave her alone in the wagon during that dreadful descent.

"You don't understand. I knew about your mother's illness from the doctor at the fort. You see, he thought it was more than the migraine. He thought . . . well, that she had something growing in her head."

"Something growing?" I gasped, not understanding.

"Yes. He thought it could be a tumor."

I was stunned. "Why didn't he *tell* me?"

"There wasn't any way for him to be sure or to know how bad it was. He thought it could be something that came and went for months or even years." Again Walter looked away. "But he did think the trip would likely aggravate it."

"And he told you instead of me. Why didn't *you* tell me?" I shouted, struggling to get to my feet. But Walter restrained me.

"Please. Let me explain," he urged.

"Explain! Explain what? Why he didn't warn us? Or, at the least, why you didn't? How could you do such a thing!"

"There was nothing you could do. You had nowhere to go but forward. He even thought little could have been done in a hospital back home. This growth could continue, or it could cause a blood vessel to burst. Especially under the strain of traveling. There was no way of knowing. There was nothing you could have done under the circumstances."

I struggled with his words, trying to piece them together, to understand what they meant.

"How long did he think she'd had this . . . this problem?"

"At the least, months before you left home."

My guilt came rushing back. I sank back against the tree. Poor Mother. No wonder she dreaded the trip. And we never once asked why she was feeling poorly. Why she felt uneasy, why she had headaches. We just assumed. Papa and I were too busy, too pleased with ourselves and our adventure to notice.

She'd struggled over tortuous miles, fighting the pain and nausea all the way. The mountains had been bad enough, but the last canyon had been unbearable. And then this last hill . . . Suddenly my mind latched onto the decision made at The Dalles.

"You chose this miserable trail for Mother over a river?" My shock and fear as I had looked down the Big Laurel rushed back. *Had* she awakened, alone, abandoned, fearful? Finding herself tied down, feeling the steep pitch of the wagon, hearing the panicked animals? What had she thought? I closed my eyes against the images that I couldn't shut out.

I was so angry, I trembled with it. Anger and betrayal fed feelings of self-disgust, until I felt fouled by my own cowardly selfishness. I'd been afraid. I'd left her alone. My anger searched for a target. Why had we chosen the trail? *Why?*

Then I remembered something. Something my mind latched onto and couldn't let go of. A fragment of Tad's earlier comment came back to me, something about Walter having saved his father money. A lot of money!

Fifty dollars a wagon — five months' wages — slammed its way into my mind. "Oh, dear God," I cried, looking at Walter as if he'd grown a serpent's head. "Was it because of the river, or was it because of the money?" I hurled this last accusation at him as I broke free and stood, almost knocking him over. His surprised exclamation rang in my ears as I ran back to camp.

"Money? What money?"

I had no room in my heart to form an answer. My fury had at last found release.

Twenty-Two

October 25, 1847
Dear Friend,

I am past anger and beyond grief.

Walter sits up front, his back rigid, prideful, as though he was the one betrayed.

Once I calmed down, I hoped he would deny my charge of choosing this trail for mercenary reasons, because his lack of denial makes it harder for me to tell him that I could never truly believe such a thing of him. Yet, I now realize that, though my anger was confused and misdirected, I did have serious cause for my reaction, a cause that cannot be overlooked.

All morning, we drove through miserable mud. After writing in my journal, I had nothing to do but wait for Jamie and Sarie to awaken. Mrs. Wilkins had invited Danny to ride with Tad, tempting him with the opportunity to help drive a team of oxen. I had agreed to allow this because my encounter with Walter had left me drained, and I knew Tad's company would be much better for

Danny than mine.

I'd barely stored our gear away, setting aside the stewed peaches that Mrs. Wilkins had fixed for the children's breakfast, before the train was ready to break camp. Having made sure the team was ready to go, I settled myself in the wagon beside my sleeping brother and sister.

I hadn't been sure who would drive us: Walter, now that he was back, or the scout. Certainly the road was beyond my capability. Then, just before the wagons began to pull out, Walter had climbed up front and urged our team onto the muddy trail.

Within the hour, the children woke up and greedily feasted on the fruit, hard bread and watered coffee I had saved for them.

We passed the early hours of travel slipping and sliding, until at last the road became drier. I found Sarie easy enough to amuse, but Jamie became fretful once he realized Mother was not in her bed where he'd expected to find her. Last night I'd been glad for the darkness and their exhaustion. They'd been too tired to notice her absence. When they awoke, they fell willingly into their morning routine until it occurred to Jamie that this morning was different. When he was in our wagon, he played with Mama. And Mama was not here. It was foolish to think I could keep him busy enough that he wouldn't notice.

Once he did, he would not be distracted.

He demanded that Mama should come show him the shineys, refusing to accept any of her trinkets from me. I could avoid it no longer; it was time for me to talk to him. I had to somehow explain to a child barely four that not only had he lost his father, but now his mother was gone, too. The sum total of his little world, as he knew it, was gone.

I shut out my own sense of loss, carefully schooling my emotions. I thought about how to tell him. I remembered the times Mother had got us to accept nasty tonics: a little at a time, taken with lots of sweets.

Jamie still waited for me to produce Mother. Mother gave him the shineys, not me. His mouth was set and his eyes took on a mulish cast. I picked out Mother's brooch, with its glittering stones, and offered it to Jamie.

"Jamie. Come sit on my lap," I pleaded.

"No!" He frowned. "*Mama's* lap."

I moved to where he had backed up, scrunched down in a corner. My heart twisted sharply, and I took him in my arms. "Jamie, do you remember when Mama told you that Papa had gone to see Jesus in Heaven?"

"No," he said sulkily. He struggled to get down from my lap, pushing the brooch away. "I want Mama!" I tried to coax him into remaining with me, but when I slipped his favorite stuffed dog onto his lap, he threw it across the wagon.

"Jamie, please." His eyes grew apprehensive. I held him tight. "Jamie, Mama isn't here. She's gone to see Papa."

He relented long enough to accept a comforting nuzzle. But then he struggled, desperately resisting compromise. "Mama," he called out, again trying to get down. Sarie banged a spoon against her tin enthusiastically.

"Mama wants me to take care of you, Jamie," I said, ignoring the noise. He glanced at Mother's folded stack of blankets, then looked back to me with a worried glower and started to whine. I searched my brain for a distraction, wondering just how much more I should say. "Jamie, Mama wants you to be a good boy for me. Will you do that?"

"No. I want Mama!" He wriggled free of my grasp. Sarie's carefree noise seemed to ease his tension. I know the accumulating changes in his life must be frightening him, that my own sadness must alarm him, yet Sarie's loud play restored some familiarity to his morning. I saw the threat of hysteria give way to a declaration of rebellion.

As I searched for something to distract him before I lost ground, Walter turned around. He held up the reins to Jamie.

"Jamie. Wanna sit with me and drive the horses?"

Jamie looked at Walter, torn between suspicion and temptation. He'd often begged to sit in the box to *drive,* and had fretted because only Danny had been allowed. I could not contain my relief.

Walter glanced at me. "Don't worry. It'll be safe enough."

"Thank you," I said stiffly.

When we pulled in for the evening, Walter tended the horses and left, even before I had a proper fire going. Danny returned from his ride with Tad. Helping to drive a team of oxen was the best distraction possible for Danny. He even looked more relaxed, though still somewhat subdued.

I put some dried peaches in water to boil, when Mr. Meyers arrived with rice his wife had fixed during our noon stop.

"She figured you had enough on your hands your first night," Mr. Meyers explained. "Would've asked you to supper, but figured you'd prefer to keep the children t'home. Best for all concerned, as things is."

He held the pot out, as if in a hurry to complete his mission. " 'Sides, we'll be off the hillside and near the Foster farm by late tomorrow. We're cuttin' off south then. So it's best to have things as they is."

I reached for his kettle, catching his eye as he handed it over. "Thank you, Mr. Meyers. Thank you both for your many kindnesses."

He resettled his hat, looking embarrassed. "Welcome," he muttered, and quickly made for his wagon. Perhaps, I thought, I could say a proper goodbye before they left us.

It had been a long, confusing day, and by the time all three fatigued children were in bed, I sat out for one more cup of coffee. I, too, felt drained.

Occasional sparks from our campfire shot into the air, drifting lazily to meet the brilliant star-speckled blackness overhead. Even blacker columns rose skyward, encircling camp, as if the tall, indiscernible trees surrounding us acted as a chimney for our fires. I watched the last ember rise, fade and die, becoming lost in the sharp chill of fall's warning breath to the foothills that we'd soon leave behind us.

My spirits were low. But I knew I had to use my energies to plan our first move once we reached Oregon City, only a few days away.

While my mind pondered sluggishly over the chores yet to be done, I heard a twig snap. My heart sank as I looked up. I would know that figure even on the darkest of nights. There was no time to make a discreet exit, and the last ounce of my courage drained away at the prospect of another confrontation with Walter.

He strode into camp and stood before me. I remained leaning forward, hugging my knees, resting my chin against them, as I watched the coffee slosh about the cup I held before me. I could see his feet and waited for what seemed a lifetime before he spoke.

"I had a talk with Tad," he announced, as though that should have some special meaning for me.

My eyes remained fixed on the swirls of brown liquid in my tin.

"It took awhile to drag it out of him, but I think we figured out where you got your suspicions."

When I still made no comment, he went on. "This accusation concerning money. Were you referring to what Tad said about Pa's relief at saving ferrying expenses? Did you believe that money had *anything* to do with my wanting you to take this trail?"

A deep tiredness fell upon me. "No," I whispered.

"No? Wasn't that what you accused me of last night?"

I had no energy for explanations now. I was tired and knew the real problem ran too deep to do anything about at this point. "Yes, but I didn't really mean that. I was confused. And I'm so tired tonight." After a long moment where all I heard was the snap of an occasional spark, I heard his sigh. A long, tired sigh that wrapped around my name.

"Marjory." He dropped down beside me, not close enough to touch. "I know you're exhausted, and I can appreciate the pain of losing your mother. It's only that if we don't talk this out now, we may never have as good an opportunity again. Once we get to Oregon City . . . please, Marjory. You've always been honest. Talk to me now."

I looked over at him. "Honest. Yes. But have you been as honest with me? How could you not have told me, Walter?"

He drew up his legs and leaned back against his arms. "You mean about what the doctor had told me?"

"Of course. How could you have kept that from me? I might have made different decisions, if I'd known."

"But the doctor said it couldn't do you any good to know. There was nothing to be done. He couldn't tell how big the tumor was or how fast it might progress. Your father was gone, and there was nothing to be done for your mother, and he thought telling her would only add to her burdens, since she had no choice but to continue on the trail. So, he told me."

"That's just it, Walter. He told you, and yet you didn't say a word to me. The doctor didn't know me. He might wonder what I'd do. But, you! You talked as if we'd marry. Was I not to be your partner in our life together? Was I supposed to be sheltered from bad news, like some witless debutante?" I went back to staring at my coffee. "Don't you see? Instead of giving me the opportunity to explore what options Mother might choose, or at the least, to ask questions that I can never ask now, or to tell her things that I needed to say, you made those decisions for me. It was my mother, my family, and they were my decisions."

I hurled the last accusation at him like a knife. I could almost hear the impact. For long moments, there was nothing but silence. But for the first time since he had told me, I could draw a deep breath of air. Defining and declaring my expectations of him was freeing somehow. How he chose to react was up to him. I knew now what I wanted for myself and for my family. It wouldn't come easy, but I would get there, even alone. My mind traveled through discoveries unfurling before me, until Walter's sigh startled me.

"Oh, God, Marjory. I didn't see it from your perspective. I'm so sorry." He glanced at me, his eyes full of misery, before looking away. "I did want to tell you. So many times. I even began to avoid spending too much time with you, for fear I'd slip. But I hated that you already had so much on your shoulders. By the time we'd reached Fort Boise, you looked ready to drop. I was afraid the news about your mother would be the last straw. And then I saw your relationship with her changing. You looked happy. I didn't want to change that. I couldn't bear turning it all to ashes. But I was wrong." He scooted around to face me, reaching out, grasping my hands. His grip tightened as his intensity grew. "It was stupid of me. Can you forgive me?"

I looked at him, wondering. I didn't want to be protected. I had begun to wonder if things would have been different if Mother hadn't protected Papa quite so much.

Events happened so fast; he never saw the consequences of his adventures. Or if he did, Mother let him ignore them. I loved Papa, and I loved Mother, but I did not want to protect or to be protected by my life's partner. Walter drew my hands to him, demanding my attention.

"I didn't keep anything from you because I didn't respect you, please believe that. I was wrong to shelter you and hinder your choices."

He touched my chin, forcing me to look at him.

"And I swear, I'll never do anything like that again."

He meant it. I knew in my heart he meant every word he said. If we could cross such a chasm through trust, I knew we could cross into the future through faith. I smiled through tears of thankfulness and love. "I believe you. And that's all I ask, Walter. That we trust each other."

I broke free of his grip and threw my arms around him, knocking him over. Down we both went, hitting the ground and rolling over on our sides as I clung to his neck.

We stared at each other, exchanging wordless reassurances and silent pledges. Walter lifted himself on one elbow and leaned over me. I felt the pounding of his heart and smelled his honest sweat and the freshness of witch hazel astringent.

Our lips met, tentatively, gently, then separated. He searched my face before kissing me again. The sweet taste of his love swept away all the bitter traces of loneliness, doubt and fear. Loving, being loved, belonging — all those feelings took on new meanings. Before I could resist, he pushed himself away, shaking his head. A slow smile spread across his face until it lit his eyes, as a hint of smug satisfaction challenged me.

"I'd say this is an appropriate time for you to agree to marry me," he said.

"Marry you when?" I asked, my ecstatic relief suddenly confronted by the proximity of commitment.

His smile broadened. "Well, I *could* wait to ask Danny for permission to set a date, but that seems a poor idea, for two reasons. First," he said, giving me a tight squeeze, "I suspect we'd best declare for each other publicly, to give our families time to adjust. And second, it might set a bad precedent to ask permission to wed from a child I fully expect to parent until he reaches maturity."

I closed my eyes. So many changes. The future came rushing toward me, pushing against insights not yet cured by time.

"Walter." I took a deep breath. "Walter, you know I want us to marry. But now I have even more responsibility, and there is your father to consider."

Walter got to his feet and pulled me up. We stood close, facing each other. "You've mentioned my father before. What about him?"

"When Tad mentioned your father's illness, he also brought up your promise to give them some time. Tad is one matter, but I will not come between you and your father."

He grinned and tapped my nose. "You wouldn't be the same girl I've just proposed to, if you did." He shook his head, amused. "I had originally thought you and your mother could winter in Oregon City, while I spent a few months helping Pa, then building a cabin by spring. But things are different now."

He drew me into his arms again and held me tight. I felt his compassion, and I drew heavily on it to warm and strengthen me. He rested his chin on my hair and rubbed the back of my neck.

"What about this idea? You and the children could use the two months that I have promised my father to adjust to your own loss. We'll find you a place in town, near my family. After the two months, we can marry and find our land together."

I started to protest. He cut me off. "Think of the people on our train. They have to build as they go. It's not easy, but I've seen your courage. Even Tad has been affected by it. You've actually shamed him into growing up."

"I doubt he'll lose that boyish charm of his, but I'm glad he's ready to settle down," I said, laughing.

At last I felt security settle in around me. Walter, the children, the future, all anchored by trusting love — this was the new beginning. It came to me now, like a gift. A gift from ashes, far beyond what I'd asked for. I thought of Papa. God's blessings did come, not always to fulfill requests, but to fulfill needs.

The trail ahead now seemed welcoming. We were only days from Oregon City. Walter would help his father and I would concentrate on helping Danny and the children accept our new life. Time could be our friend now.

Locked in Walter's arms, a pleasant thought occurred to me as I considered the future. I leaned back far enough to catch his eye. "After only two months, I'll still have some of Papa's money left for a proper dowry. So, don't think your bride comes to you empty-handed."

He squeezed me back under his chin and I heard the low rumble of his chuckle. "Now, you don't think I overlooked that little fact, do you? Just why do you think I asked you to marry me?"

My trust had been fully restored. "Because you love me," I replied, smugly self-confident.

This time his hug signaled more than reassurance. "As our scout would say, 'You're sure-spittin' right about that,' my girl." His embrace tightened, as if he recalled what had almost been lost. "You're sure right about that."

And I knew I was.

About the Author

Sharon Lee Thomas was born and raised in the Pacific Northwest and has always been fascinated with the epic story of the Oregon Trail. Writing *New Beginnings* allowed her to research the journey and travel parts of the actual trail. She recently traded her beloved Victorian home for a modern condo on Puget Sound, ready for new beginnings herself. In addition to working on her next book, she enjoys sketching, traveling with her husband and the frequent visits of her five grandchildren.

You can reach her at Stbeginnings @aol.com.

The employees of Thorndike Press hope you have enjoyed this Large Print book. All our Thorndike and Wheeler Large Print titles are designed for easy reading, and all our books are made to last. Other Thorndike Press Large Print books are available at your library, through selected bookstores, or directly from us.

For information about titles, please call:

(800) 223-1244

or visit our Web site at:

www.thomson.com/thorndike
www.thomson.com/wheeler

To share your comments, please write:

Publisher
Thorndike Press
295 Kennedy Memorial Drive
Waterville, ME   04901